PRAISE FOR
LOST BOY

"Christina Henry shakes the fairy dust off a legend; this Peter Pan will give you chills." Genevieve Valentine, author of *Persona*

"Multiple twists keep the reader guessing, and the fluid writing is enthralling . . . This is a fine addition to the shelves of any fan of children's classics and their modern subversions."

Publishers Weekly (starred review)

"This wild, unrelenting tale, full to the brim with the freedom and violence of young boys who never want to grow up, will appeal to fans of dark fantasy." *Booklist*

"Turns Neverland into a claustrophobic world where time is disturbingly nebulous and identity is chillingly manipulated . . . [A] deeply impactful, imaginative, and haunting story of loyalty, disillusionment, and self-discovery." RT Book Reviews (top pick)

"Henry keeps the story fresh and energetic with diabolical twists and turns to keep us guessing. Dynamic characterization and narration bring the story to life . . . Once again, Henry takes readers on an adventure of epic and horrific proportions as she reinvents a childhood classic using our own fears and desires. Her smooth prose and firm writing hooked me up instantly and held me hostage to the very end."

Smexy Books

continued . . .

"We all have a soft spot for the classics that we read when we were growing up. But . . . this retelling will poke and jab at that soft spot until you can never look at it the same way again."

"An absolutely addicting read . . . Psychological, gripping, and entertaining, painting a picture of Peter Pan before we came to know him in the film: the darker side of his history. The writing is fabulous, the plot incredibly compelling, and the characters entirely enthralling."

PRAISE FOR
ALICE

"I loved falling down the rabbit hole with this dark, gritty tale. A unique spin on a classic and one wild ride!"

"*Alice* takes the darker elements of Lewis Carroll's original, amplifies Tim Burton's cinematic reimagining of the story, and adds a layer of grotesquery from [Henry's] own alarmingly fecund imagination to produce a novel that reads like a Jacobean revenge drama crossed with a slasher movie."

"[A] psychotic journey through the bowels of magic and madness. I, for one, thoroughly enjoyed the ride."

"[A] horrifying fantasy that will have you reexamining your love for this childhood favorite."   RT Book Reviews (top pick)

PRAISE FOR
RED QUEEN

"Henry takes the best elements from Carroll's iconic world and mixes them with dark fantasy elements . . . [Her] writing is so seamless you won't be able to stop reading."

Pop Culture Uncovered

"Alice's ongoing struggle is to distinguish reality from illusion, and Henry excels in mingling the two for the reader as well as her characters. The darkness in this book is that of fairy tales, owing more to Grimm's matter-of-fact violence than to the underworld of the first book."   *Publishers Weekly* (starred review)

The
MERMAID

Christina Henry

TITAN BOOKS

The Mermaid
Print edition ISBN: 9781785655708
E-book edition ISBN: 9781785655715

Published by Titan Books
A division of Titan Publishing Group Ltd
144 Southwark Street, London SE1 0UP

First Titan edition: June 2018
10 9 8 7 6 5 4 3 2 1

This edition published by arrangement with Berkley, an imprint of Penguin, a division of Penguin Random House LLC, in 2018.

A CIP catalogue record for this title is available from the British Library.

Printed and bound in Great Britain by CPI Group Ltd.

Did you enjoy this book?

We love to hear from our readers. Please email us at readerfeedback@titanemail.com or write to us at Reader Feedback at the above address.

To receive advance information, news, competitions, and exclusive offers online, please sign up for the Titan newsletter on our website:
www.titanbooks.com

For Cora—on land and on sea

PART I

THE FISHERMAN & THE MERMAID

CHAPTER 1

Once there was a fisherman, a lonely man who lived on a cold and rocky coast and was never able to convince any woman to come away and live in that forbidding place with him. He loved the sea more than any person and so was never able to take a wife, for women see what is in men's hearts more clearly than men would wish.

But though he loved the freezing spray on his face and the sight of the rolling clouds on the horizon, he still wished for somebody to love. One evening after a long day, he pulled up his net and found a woman in it—something like a woman, anyway, with black hair and eyes as grey as a stormy sea and a gleaming fish's tail.

He was sorry that she was caught and told her so, though the storm in her eyes rolled into his heart. She stopped her thrashing and crashing at his voice, though she did not understand his words. The fisherman loosed her, and she dove back into the water the way a wild thing returns to a wild place, and he watched her go.

But her eyes had seen inside him the way that women's eyes do, and his loneliness snaked into her, and she was sorry for it, for that loneliness caught her more surely than the net.

She swam away from his boat as fast as she could, and she felt his loneliness trailing between them like a cord. She did not want his feelings to bind her, to pull her back to him, so her tail flashed silver in the water and her eyes looked straight before her and never behind.

But though she didn't look back, she felt him watching, and she remembered the shape of his boat and the rocky curve of the land not too far off and the lines around his eyes, eyes that were as dark as the deep sea under the moon. She remembered, and so she returned again to watch him.

She was called a name that meant, in her own tongue, Breaking the Surface of the Sea. When she was born, she'd come in a great hurry, much sooner than all of her six older sisters and brothers. The attendant who'd aided her mother had been astonished when she tried to swim away before the cord that bound her to her mother was cut.

Her mother and father and siblings spent most of her childhood trying to find her, for she was never where she ought to be. She was warned repeatedly of the dangers of the surface and of the men who cast nets there, and of their cruelty to the denizens of the ocean.

They should never have told her, for in the telling she wanted to know more, and wanting to know more led her farther and farther afield.

Her home was deep in the ocean, far away from the land that pushed up against the water on either side, and this was because her people feared the men with their hooks and their nets and the boats that floated on the surface of the waves as if by magic. The storytellers told of silver fins caught by cruel metal and dragged to the decks of ships, where blood ran red and spilled back into the water, calling things that swam the ocean in search of dying creatures.

Sometimes there was a storm, and that storm would batter a ship to pieces and the men would fall into the water and sink, sink, sink to the bottom—the lucky ones, that is. The unlucky ones were devoured by roaming hunters with their silver-grey bodies and black eyes and white, white teeth.

When the ships were sunk, the mermaid would go to the wreckage and explore, and pick up odd things that humans used, and wonder about them. And then one of her brothers or her parents would find her, and she would be chided for her foolishness and dragged home by her wrist, staring with longing over her shoulder all the while.

One day she was swimming near the surface—far too near the surface, her family would have said—and saw a large, large ship of a sort she had never seen before. On the prow of the ship she saw a strange thing.

It looked like her—like a mermaid, but frozen and sealed to the ship.

She swam alongside the ship for a long time, trying to see how the sailors had bound this mermaid to their craft. It was not easy, for the proximity of the ship necessitated keeping out of sight of the sailors. She would break the surface to catch a glimpse of the other mermaid and then would be forced to plunge below the water again before she was spotted.

There was a fine wind and all the sails were full, and so the ship clipped along the surface, and after a time the mermaid grew tired. But she wanted to see, she wanted to know, and so she followed and followed even when she could no longer stay alongside. Her tail started to drag, and her swimming slowed, and then suddenly the ship was far ahead of her, disappearing over the flat line of the horizon.

And the mermaid was alone, and far from home, and did not know how to find her way back again.

This ought to have made her sad, or frightened, or any number of other distressed feelings. But while she was sorry she might never see her family again, she wasn't as upset as she should have been.

Rather, she felt the freedom to go where she chose and do what she chose. Yes, there would be consequences (she was not so silly as to think there wouldn't be), but they would be her choices and her consequences and not the ones laid out for her by someone else.

Freedom was far more intoxicating than safety could ever be.

She wanted to see and know more than she ever could at the bottom of the ocean. So she swam after the ship, because the ship would go to land, and the mermaid had never seen land before.

And so she crossed the ocean and came to the place where there was land. The mermaid spent many days watching the people on shore and the ones who came out to the sea on boats. Always, always she was careful to avoid the hooks and lines and cages and nets, because she had found her freedom and she loved it, and she would not be bound to someone else's will again.

Until the day she was busy trying to loose a fish caught on a hook, and it was shaking and fighting and she was trying to help, but it was too panicked to let her. She didn't see the net come down from above, and then she was caught.

She panicked then too, just like the fish she'd been trying to aid; she thrashed her tail, pulled with all her might, but all her thrashing entangled her more securely than before until she was hauled, furious and weeping, to the surface.

His eyes were dark and full of surprise when they saw what was in his net. Surprise, and wonder, and then a little sadness that she almost missed. When he raised the knife, she was sure he would fillet her then, but he only spoke some words she did not understand and cut away that which bound her.

She swam away and wondered about the man who'd let her go.

That night, the fisherman watched the sea from his cottage, which was perched on the rocks above a small cove where he tied up his boat at night. It was cold, for it was coming on winter and it never really was warm in the North Atlantic anyhow. He buried his hands in the pockets of his coat and stared out at the churning mass of water and looked for her under the moon. But though he turned his head at the sound of every faint splash, he did not see that which his heart most longed for—the sight of her fin silhouetted against the moonlight.

He'd likely been a fool to let her go. Nobody would believe the story if he told it, and he wasn't about to make a fool of himself down at the tavern in the village. He was old enough to be past the bragging flush of youth, though not so old that he would have minded seeing the light of wonder in their eyes had he brought a mermaid home.

He could never have done it. That he knew for certain. He could not have taken that wild thing that looked on him with such wild eyes and forced her to stay with him, to make her a prisoner, to profit by her hurt.

She hadn't looked as he expected her to, the way he'd been told since he was a boy listening to tales that a mermaid should look. Those stories spoke of pale bare-breasted women with long flowing hair, human women in every way except for their tail fin.

What he'd caught in his net had been far more alien, a creature covered in silver scales all over, with webbing between its fingers and teeth much sharper than any human's. But her eyes had been a woman's, and they'd looked into his heart as a woman's eyes do and seen all the loneliness there.

He'd felt in that moment that his heart was visible outside his chest, that if she'd wanted, she could have grasped it in those long scaly fingers and taken it away with her.

Then he'd come to his senses and loosed her because he knew he should and the state of his heart was no concern of the mermaid's.

But still he watched the water in hope, for the dearest wish of all fishermen is to see a mermaid, to brush up against something magical and hope some of that magic would stay with him for always.

He watched and watched, but he did not see her.

When finally the moon was past its zenith, he put away his dreams and went inside to sleep. He knew he would never see her again and in his own practical way thought at least he'd seen her one time. That was more than most fishermen. He'd touched magic, and he should not want for more.

He did not see her, but she watched him from beneath the water near his cottage, and she knew he was looking for her. She couldn't say how she knew this except that his eyes had been a little sad when he let her go. His loneliness had burrowed into her heart, and the ache of it burned inside her.

The mermaid had heard stories, spoken-under-the-breath-in-secret-places stories, about those of her kind who had left the deep and walked upon land.

There was no special magic about this unless you considered that mermaids were magical in and of themselves; the mermaid did not consider herself anything special because she had always known her own kind.

In those stories, those secret stories, the mermaid only had to touch dry land and her fin would be transformed into legs to walk about. If she touched the water of the sea again, her fin would return.

The mermaid had never wished to walk upon land before, but suddenly she found she wanted this with all her heart. She could think only of all the things she'd never seen that were hidden past the shore: all the people and all the things for which she had no name and wanted to name so she could place them in her memory and keep them there.

It was dark, even with the moon, and there was a stretch of sandy beach hidden in the rocks, a little cove where the fisherman tied up his boat at night.

The mermaid thought she would swim to that place and

touch the dry shore and see if the stories were true. Her heart was bursting with anticipation—how wonderful, how free, how perfect it would be if she could pass between the shore and the sea. Not like a man did, of course—men swimming in the water were awkward, flopping things with their limbs splashing out in all directions.

No, she would be as lithe as a fish in water and graceful as a human on land and all the world would be open to her. All the world and its wonders, and she would see them, every one.

She swam into the cove, and when her head rose above the water she saw the jagged rocks rising on either side and the boat nestled inside. Beside the boat was a small wooden pier and a short beach that connected to a set of steps leading up to the fisherman's cottage.

There were no lights in the cottage, and the mermaid was certain the fisherman was inside and asleep and would not look out and see her there. Even if he did, she reasoned, he would only see a shadow moving against another shadow— the light of the moon did not reach this place.

The mermaid swam to the shore, until she could feel the wet sand dragging beneath her fin and she could no longer kick up and down for there wasn't enough water. She reached for the dry land just beyond the lapping waves—reached, and then paused.

What if it did not work? What if those stories, those always-whispered stories, were not true? What if her heart longed always for the land and for the man with the lonely dark eyes and she was to never, ever have what she wished for?

For some the possibility of failure would be a check, would make them turn back to the familiar. Not the mermaid. She had to know, and the only way to know was to reach out, to touch the shore.

Her fingers brushed the dry sand, and she reveled in the wonder of it, of the feel of each grain as it passed through her hands free and unencumbered by water. It made her laugh out loud, to touch this thing she'd never touched before.

And then she felt a horrible wrench deep in her gut, and a tearing in her fin, and she tried to cry out but it was caught in her throat. This was terrible, *terrible*, there was no wonder here at all—only pain and then cold, the most profound cold she had ever known. The waves lapped against her bare legs, and she could feel the chill of the ocean. She had never felt the ocean's cold before. It seemed to sink into her blood and marrow and freeze her from her muscles and bones out to the delicate skin that covered her instead of scales.

How do humans live with this cold? she thought. Every part of her felt fragile, as if she would burst into pieces if someone put a fingertip on her. The sand, so wonderful only a moment before, scraped her raw wherever it touched, and her shoulders shook with cold.

Her teeth clattered together in her mouth, and she reached up with sandy fingers to touch them because they felt different, somehow *flatter*. They were flatter, not pointed as they had been before, and more like a human's teeth.

Her scales were gone and her teeth were gone and in return she had these *things*, these legs, which felt not free and light like her fin but like heavy bonding weights pulling her into the earth.

Had she thought it would be marvelous to be a human? Had she thought she would have all the world before her? The world was not open to her. Her legs were like a net, a net that caught her and kept her from swimming free.

She almost let go then, to push back into the water and let her scales cover her body and swim back, all the way back to the deep, deep ocean where her family would be waiting for her.

Then she shook her head hard, though she trembled all over with cold and fear. She would not return in shame so they could shake their heads and say she never should have left in the first place.

She wanted to know what it was like to be a human. Humans walked on their legs. So she must stand.

But how? Nothing about her body seemed familiar. She did not know how things connected, how to push and pull all these alien parts to get what and where she wanted.

The first thing, she felt, was to get clear of the ocean. Her human form was not meant for this place. The mermaid put her arms in the sand and pulled the rest of her body out of the water—slowly, so slowly, gritting her teeth as the sand scraped against her.

Once she was out of the water she discovered the night air was nearly as cold and that it blew into the cove and swirled in eddies around her. It made the water that clung to her freeze, and her delicate human skin rose in bumps.

This is why humans put the skin of other creatures on their bodies, she thought. She'd seen them in wrapped in furs, or in sealskin boots, and thought them barbaric. But now she realized that they must have these coverings, or else they would die. She felt, at that moment, like she might die from the cold.

Cold. She was so cold.

She craned upward to see the fisherman's cottage. Inside there it would not be cold. He would cover her with a fur and dry the water away and she would be warm, warm, warm. And then he would smile because she had come to him from out of the sea so he would not be lonely anymore.

The fisherman. She must reach him. To reach him she must walk. To walk she must stand, and it didn't matter that she didn't know how.

Her legs had a bend in the middle. She could feel it, feel the place where the leg separated into two connected parts like her arms.

She pushed up to the palms of her hands and bent her legs until her knees were in the sand, and she huffed out her breath in the cold air because everything seemed so much harder than she expected. How did humans simply stand up on these stiff fins at the ends of their legs and walk?

The mermaid rolled her ankles experimentally, curled up her toes, and by slow and careful practice found herself standing (wobbling) on her new feet. She did not feel very certain about what to do next.

She'd seen humans walking on their ships and knew that each foot took turns leaving the ground while the other stayed. This seemed almost impossible as she stood there trembling all over and feeling that at any moment she might find her face in the sand.

But the fisherman was at the top of the stairs. And so she must climb.

The mermaid lifted one of her feet, and the wonder of being able to do it at all struck her then. She stared down at her legs, at the foot stuck in the sand and the other lifted in the air, and laughed out loud.

And then she did fall forward, landing on her elbows and knees, and had to start it all over again.

She struggled to stand. Once there, she shuffled one foot forward very carefully and then the other—one after another, *scritch-scratch* across the sand. All the while she clutched her body with her arms—they seemed so thin and frail, so incapable of protecting her from the frozen air that bit through her skin and into her blood.

Then she reached the stairs and looked up, and had the horrible realization that she would not be able to shuffle here. Each step was high and made of wood, and there was nothing to hold except the rock face.

The mermaid felt very tired then and wanted to do anything but climb the steps. But climb them she did, and later she had no notion of how she'd done this, except that it took a very long time.

When she reached the top, the moon had almost disappeared beneath the horizon of the sea. Her hands and legs were bloodied and covered with splinters from where she fell on the stairs, and her teeth chattered with such force that she felt they might break.

The mermaid stumbled to the door of the cottage and reached for the handle, as she had seen the fisherman do when she watched him from the water.

The door swung open, and she clung to the frame. Inside the cottage there were many things that were strange to her—things the fisherman would teach her the names for, things like a kettle and a pan and flour in a jar and tea in a wooden box and a table and a chair (soon he would need two chairs, one for each of them).

Beyond the room full of strange things there was another doorway, this one without a door in it, and she heard the sleeping-breathing noise that humans made and knew the fisherman must be there.

The doorway seemed a long way from the one she was in, and the rough wood of the floor would hurt if she tried to slide across it as she had done the sand—this she knew from climbing the stairs, where unpredictable splinters had jabbed into her tender new skin.

It took a long while for her to cross to his room. When she reached it, she saw him asleep in bed, the blankets pulled up tight past his chin. He lay on his side, and only the lids of his eyes and the black tufts of his hair were visible.

The room seemed warmer than the others, heated by his sleeping breath, and she wanted so much to be where it was warm. She knelt beside his bed, stroked her fingers into his hair, and watched as his dark eyes opened. She saw the recognition in them, and she never wondered how he knew it was her, the same mermaid he'd caught in his net.

A long time later he told her that it was her eyes, that her eyes were the same no matter what form she took, and when he saw them, he knew she'd returned to him.

He lifted the blanket, and she saw that underneath was his man's body with no coverings on it as humans usually wore. She went to him then, and his warmth covered her, and his love filled her heart and made her want to stay.

He taught her how to speak his human-speak and told her his name was Jack. Her name was not something they could say in human, so he told her many names for many days until he said the one she liked, and so she was called Amelia.

Amelia loved Jack, but she could not leave the sea altogether, and at night she practiced transforming from a mermaid to a woman, until she could pass easily between one and the other without the pain that had struck her down the first time.

So she stayed with him, and loved him, and lived as a woman on land and a mermaid in the sea for many years. At night, when there were no other fishermen about and her husband lay sleeping in their bed, she would go out to the rocks and leave her human dress there and dive into the black water, and there she would stay, at least until her heart remembered the eyes of the man she loved and she would return to him.

She loved him almost as much as she loved the sea, and so they were well matched, for he loved the sea almost as much as he loved her. He'd never thought any person could draw him more than the ocean, but the crashing waves were there in her eyes and the salt of the spray was in her skin and there, too, was something in her that the sea could never give. The ocean could never love him back, but Amelia did.

Many years passed, and they were happy and content, but there were no children. Neither of them spoke of their secret hopes or their secret sorrows, but sometimes they would sit upon their deck and watch the water churning below the rocks and he would take her hand and she would know he was thinking of the children that never became.

They lived near a village—close enough to supply them with what they could not provide themselves but not so close as to force them to be neighborly when they had no wish to be. Jack loved Amelia and the sea, and Amelia loved the sea and Jack, but they did not love the questions that too-keen neighbors asked, questions about where Amelia had come from and where were her people and when had they gotten married and oh this was so sudden, wasn't it?

Still, they grew accustomed to Amelia after a time, as folk will. They were a good people, but suspicious, and the mermaid's eyes were always too direct, too beautiful, to make them comfortable. And where there is discomfort there is sometimes jealousy, and sometimes curiosity, and the two mingled on their gossiping tongues until the villagers were accustomed to the taste.

"That wife of old Jack's, they say she goes out in the moonlight and dances with the devil and that's how she stays so young and lovely."

"That's foolishness, Martha. Where would she go to dance up there? Their house is perched on the rocks just so. A good nor'easter would push it into the sea, I expect, and there are no forest clearings for dancing to be seen," her companion replied, with more than a touch of New England asperity.

There was more than a touch of New England superstition lingering, though, enough that some folk believed the tales of moonlight and demon-dancing. Many treated Amelia just the same when she came into the village, but there were those who never would.

The years passed, as years will. Jack grew old, though Amelia did not, and after a time the people of the village began to remark on this—even the ones who were inclined not to believe the worst of her in the first place.

They had not known, Jack and Amelia, that when she crawled out of the ocean to be at his side, they would not grow old together. Mermaids, it happened, lived a very long time, though they did not reckon time in the same manner as men. Amelia watched her young, strong husband grow brittle, his face as grey and weather-beaten as the prow of a ship.

Still she loved him, and loved him more for she knew his heart, and after many, many years she found she loved him even more than the sea.

And so the sea, who can be bitter and jealous herself, took Jack away—perhaps in hopes that Amelia would love her best again.

It was an ordinary day, mostly grey but with peeks of sun, and the wind was light and fine. Jack kissed her good-bye as he always did and made his way—slowly now, so slowly—down the many steps to the cove.

Amelia watched from the door of the cottage as he rowed out of the cove. He waved to her when he saw her standing there, and she waved back. She had a feeling then that this would be the last time he would wave to her, that this was their final good-bye.

This feeling clutched her heart so strongly that she believed it was truth, and she ran from the cottage down the steps to the cove to call him back.

It was too late then, far too late, for the wind was blowing into the cove and it took her voice and threw it against the rocks instead of carrying it out to the ears of her beloved.

She watched him row farther out, farther away from her, and join all the other boats out to draw their trade from the sea.

For one wild moment, she thought of changing into a mermaid to follow him, to bring him back home. But the presence of all the other boats stopped her.

There were nets there, and hooks and lines. The one time she'd been caught in a net it had led her to Jack, but she had no desire to be caught again. What if the fisherman who caught her didn't believe that she was Amelia, that she was Jack's wife? What if he carved her up with his knife to sell at the market?

This fear made her slightly ashamed, for she'd always been brave, but it was easier to be brave when you had nothing to lose. And she did have something to lose now— her home, her life, her happiness.

After all, what if this feeling was only that—a feeling? Would she put her—their—secret at risk for nothing? And what could harm Jack on that sort of day? It was a fine day with no signs of storm.

She was only worrying because he looked so frail lately, she reasoned. But when he came home that night she would tell him in no uncertain terms that he wasn't to go so far out to sea alone any longer.

All day she tried to go about her chores as usual. She found that she was constantly at the window, looking and hoping, but the sun went on its usual journey and the fisherman did not reappear at the horizon.

As night fell, she went out to the rocks and waited. The cold air bit into her bones as it had done the first night she'd walked as a human, so long ago. Amelia didn't go back inside, to wait by the fire or to put on a coat. She stared at the ocean as if the intensity of that stare would make her Jack appear there, tired and careworn but safe—*Above all things let him be safe.*

But she could not make him appear, no matter how hard she wished it, so when night fell and all the other fishermen had tied up their boats until the morrow, she went down to the cove and took off her dress and touched the water of the ocean.

In a silver flash she was in the water and swimming faster than any human ever could. Amelia followed the line she thought Jack had taken, out to the open water where he could cast his net.

She swam and swam. It was dark and the land slowly disappeared behind her, but still she swam. She swam, surfacing to look for his boat, always sure that when she came up, she would see his dear face looking sheepish and saying he'd lost track of the time.

Finally she broke the water and saw it—his boat, the one with her name carved in the side so she knew it was his. It sat still and empty, the ocean lapping against its sides, and no sign of Jack anywhere.

Amelia swam to the boat and heaved herself over the side, her fin trailing in the water, sure that he was only asleep in the bottom. But there was no Jack, or nets, or fish that he might have caught. There was only the empty boat, oars tucked neatly inside.

She cried out then and plunged back into the water and down to the deep. Mermaids can see through the dark of the ocean.

Amelia was sure, absolutely certain, that if only she looked far enough she would find he'd fallen in the water and was trying to swim back to the surface. She knew he was trying to swim back to her. He would never leave her. Not her Jack.

She would find him soon. Very soon. She was sure of it. He was just out of sight, but his hand was reaching up for her and she would find him and she would save him and they would go home, home where they belonged, home on the cliff by the sea where they could see the ocean they both loved.

But she didn't find him, though she looked and looked. After a long time, she went back to the surface and found his boat again. She searched all over it for any clue, any sign of what might have happened to her Jack.

There was nothing, only the empty boat and the folded oars and no sign that Jack had ever been there at all.

Amelia knew then that the ocean had swallowed him, torn him away from her, and a great bitterness filled her heart. She hated the ocean, hated the vast and heartless expanse that had taken Jack from her.

She wanted only to be out of the water then, away from the lapping waves and the boat that had borne her love away from her and delivered him into the cruel depths.

Mermaids do not cry, but Amelia had spent too long as a human, and so as she swam back to shore the tears streamed over the scales on her face and mixed with the brine of the sea.

When she touched the sand of the cove, she put on her human dress again and climbed the stairs back to the empty cottage. There she sat by the cold ashes in the fire and wept bitter tears until she felt wrung dry.

Jack's boat never came back to the cove, and some of the other fishermen noticed the empty pier, and they told their neighbors that they saw Jack's strange wife standing on the rocks every day, staring out at the sea.

They assumed poor old Jack had been taken by the ocean, as was not uncommon, and some of them even spared a kind thought for his wife, who watched for him day after day. But mostly they wondered when she would give up and leave, for she was not from that part of the world, and now that Jack was gone they thought that she, too, would go.

But Amelia did not leave. She stayed there in the cottage on the rocks, year after year. The wood of the cottage became white from the wind and the salt spray, and Amelia's dresses grew as thin as her face, but she would not leave.

And she did not grow any older.

The people of the village could not help themselves talking, for winters were long and brutal where they lived, and a mystery is good for many an endless night. They wondered what kept her there on those rocks, and where she might have come from, and if, perhaps, she might have come from the sea.

This idea was met with less derision than that of Amelia dancing in the moonlight with the devil. These were an oceangoing people, and everyone knew that mermaids swam the ocean. Everyone knew that a mermaid might fall in love with a human man.

And far from making the people frightened of her, this knowledge seemed to comfort them, for it meant that in her own way Amelia belonged to them. She, too, was part of the ocean that gave and took everything from them.

Because she was one of them, they would protect her, and when she came into the village (much less often now) their eyes and their voices were softer than before. She was their Amelia, their wonder, their mermaid.

But the rumors about this strange and unusual woman who never grew old, and who might be a mermaid, traveled from village to village and town to town, as they do, until they reached the ears of a man whose business was in the selling of the strange and unusual.

His name was P. T. Barnum, and he'd been looking for a mermaid.

PART II

THE
MUSEUM

CHAPTER 2

NEW YORK CITY, APRIL 1842

The mermaid was not, to Barnum's way of thinking, anything like a mermaid ought to look at all. He'd expected something that looked a lot more like a woman, like those Italian paintings that showed them all bare-breasted and full-hipped with long flowing hair. Barnum knew quite a lot of God-fearing types who disapproved of those paintings. Disapproval, Barnum knew, meant controversy, and controversy sold tickets faster than the seven wonders of the world. Barnum didn't mind controversy as long as he could sell tickets to see a real mermaid.

This thing that Moses had brought him did not resemble those paintings in the least.

"Levi," Barnum said.

Two men stood around the table with Barnum. Both stared at the object that lay there—one with optimism on his face and the other with his brow creased in consternation.

"Yes, Taylor?" Levi said. Levi's face was a study in careful neutrality except for that creased brow. He'd been a lawyer, Levi had, and he still had a lawyer's face, a face that gave away nothing until he wanted it to.

Levi was one of the few folks allowed to call him Taylor. Nobody called Barnum "Phineas." He'd been named after his grandfather and his grandfather was Phin, but Barnum was always Barnum to everyone except to his wife and to Levi and to his family back in Bethel.

"Does that look like a mermaid to you?" As he said this, Barnum gave the third man a narrow-eyed look. That man, Moses Kimball, shifted his weight and looked hopefully at Levi.

Levi didn't think much of the mermaid. Barnum could tell, and he felt sure Moses was bound for disappointment from that quarter.

"Well, Taylor," Levi said, "I'm a lawyer, not a naturalist, but I would say that thing is the body of a monkey sewn to the tail of a fish."

And that was precisely what it did look like. It was only about three feet long, with skinny arms and a dried-up face and pendulous breasts, and covered all over with grey-black skin that looked as though it might flake off any second. The bottom half did not resemble the coy shining tail of myth but rather definitely that of a fish. It did not seem even particularly well preserved.

Barnum nodded in satisfaction. He preferred to be correct, and he'd correctly assumed that the thing was not a mermaid and that Levi didn't think much of it. "Not a mermaid, then."

Levi shook his head. "I shouldn't say so."

Moses Kimball spoke up then, and his expression indicated he felt his reputation as a museum proprietor was at stake. He had a long bushy grey beard that moved up and down as he spoke.

"The fellow I bought it from, Eades, said his father exhibited it in England to great success."

"That may be so," Barnum said, meditating on the so-called mermaid. "That may be so, but that doesn't change the fact that it's nothing more than a humbug."

Moses's face fell. Barnum sensed him trying to rally.

"I think you could exhibit it here to great success," Moses said. There was a little touch of desperation now, the need to make sure the trip from Boston was justified. "People want to believe in mermaids."

Barnum knew, better than anyone, that human tendency to want to believe, to want to see the extraordinary. He even knew that people sometimes enjoyed humbugs. All that business in the New York papers about winged men on the moon seen through a telescope! Everyone had believed it, and no one had really minded when it turned out it wasn't true.

That was because as much as folk wanted to believe, they couldn't help doubting. If they kept themselves in a state of belief mixed with a little healthy skepticism, then they could never be wrong. Nobody liked to be wrong. Most people would rather be humbugged than be flat wrong. If they were tricked, then it wasn't their fault, and they could always say they'd never really believed in the humbug anyway.

He could probably make something of this stuffed monkey Moses had brought him—it wouldn't be the first time he'd made something out of nothing—but he couldn't deny that he was disappointed.

He'd wanted something *spectacular*. This was not spectacular.

"What if we put a girl in a tank with a fish costume on her bottom half?" Barnum said to Levi. "We could place her in with the fishes and the whale skeletons. You have to believe mermaids are real if she's right there with all the other sea creatures."

Levi contemplated the idea for a moment before shaking his head in regret. "Bound to have some churchgoers complaining about indecency if you had a girl swimming bare-chested in a tank."

Barnum waved that away, warming to his idea. "We can

cover her up with seashells or some such thing. That will make the church ladies happy."

"What about *my* mermaid?" Moses asked. Disappointment had settled on his shoulders like a cloak.

Barnum knew Moses was thinking of the long journey from his Boston museum, seemingly for nothing if Barnum didn't exhibit the monkey-fish in New York.

"I'll think on it," Barnum said. "We might be able to use it in the exhibit with the girl. The body of one of her ancestors or some such."

Moses brightened a little. Barnum could tell he was pleased that his trip wouldn't be wasted.

"If you're going to use a girl in a tank," Moses said, clearly in better spirits now, "you ought to use one from somewhere far away. That way the girl's family won't go to the papers and expose you."

"Even with that I'm not so sure this would work," Levi said. "How long can a girl hold her breath underwater? And you'd be lucky to find one who can swim. Most women can't, you know. I don't think most men can, come to that."

"You're down on all my plans today, Levi," Barnum said, frowning at him.

"Dropping a girl in a big bucket of seawater isn't the same as putting a shriveled old woman in a room and calling her Washington's nanny. It's a lot harder. You'd have to find a suitable girl, to start, and I'm pretty certain the sort who would swim half-naked in a tank isn't the sort you want talking to the newspapers," Levi said. His face was calm, but his tone was irritated. "And we got found out the last time, in the end. Imagine what everyone will say if Barnum tried to pull the wool over their eyes again."

Barnum didn't like this reminder of the way the Heth exhibit had turned out. They'd sold her as Washington's nanny and it seemed in the end that she was not as old as advertised, but it really wasn't Barnum's fault. He'd been lied to in the first place. Levi ought not to be bringing it up in front of Moses, anyhow.

"Let me worry about the details," Barnum said, frowning at Levi. "First thing is to find a girl who looks like she came out of the sea."

"All you have to do is go up to northern Maine. There's supposed to be a woman up there who really is a mermaid," Moses said, laughing.

Barnum gave him a sharp look. "Whereabouts in Maine?"

"Why?" Moses asked.

"I might want to take a gander at the lady," Barnum said. "See if the stories are true."

"Come now, Barnum," Moses said. "You can't possibly believe that some widow who practically lives in Canada is a mermaid. It's just a story told by fishermen to pass the time while they drink."

"*You* can't possibly believe that people will pay a dime to see a stuffed monkey-fish," Barnum snapped. "Just tell me about the mermaid."

Barnum listened closely as Moses told him about a woman who lived up the coast in a cottage by the sea. He said the villagers who lived near there noticed she seemed to come from nowhere and that she had lived for many years with her husband and had never grown older.

"That doesn't mean she's a mermaid. That might make her immortal, though," Barnum said. "Or at least, we could say she's immortal. Can't really be immortal, of course."

Of course, he didn't say how intrigued he was by the story of the eternally young woman. After all, he'd been raised to believe that immortality occurred in the afterlife, when those who were chosen lived forever in heaven.

But the possibilities of this girl . . . She might make an even better exhibit than a mermaid would—imagine the scientists wanting to come and examine her! He'd make a fortune charging them for her hair and blood and whatever else they wanted to look at under their microscopes.

Of course, the trouble with Joice Heth had happened because he'd given his word about her autopsy. True, he hadn't had to charge the public to watch it—that had made it impossible to suppress the truth that the lady was not as old as he'd claimed she was—but he couldn't resist the chance. Barnum thought all publicity was good publicity, and even if folks thought he was a con artist, then at least they knew the name of Barnum.

"Or the lady is just a dab hand with her lotions and potions, and not an immortal at all," Levi said.

"You'd have to be able to prove she's lived as long as she says she has," Barnum mused, thinking of Heth again. He'd been just as fooled by her papers as anyone else had, really. Of course he wouldn't have exhibited the woman if he thought she was only 80 years old, not 161. "People don't believe anything like that without papers and certificates and what-all."

The trouble, too, was that a forever-young woman was a lot like saying an old black woman was older than she actually was. The public might not pay for the same humbug twice. And above all, Barnum wanted people to pay.

"But I haven't told you the best part yet!" Moses said. It was clear from his manner that he didn't think anything of this story but was enjoying the telling of it all the same. "One of the men who told me the story had heard it straight from a fisherman who claims he saw this woman shed her clothes on the beach at night and step into the ocean. Right after that she disappeared under the water. A few minutes later, he says, he saw the flash of her silver fin."

"And how much whiskey had this fisherman drunk before he saw a girl turn into a fish?" Levi said.

Barnum wished Levi would stop interrupting and let the man finish his story.

"It wasn't so much what he said, but what the villagers did after," Moses said. "He came into town raving about what he'd seen under the moonlight. You'd expect that folk would be curious about a story like that, wouldn't you? Even if it was only to scoff at?"

"Yes," Barnum said. He had a feeling growing in his belly, a feeling that told him there was more to this than some tale that came out of a bottle. He'd learned over the years to trust that feeling.

It meant that something great was going to happen—or he could make something great out of nothing, even if it didn't seem so at first. This woman, whoever and whatever she was, was going to make people remember him.

"The fisherman told my friend that not one person expressed interest in his story," Moses said. "Not *one*. They all pretended not to hear a thing he said. They changed the subject or gave him a blank stare. And he found the next day that he couldn't sell any of his catch in the village no matter how hard he tried. Soon, he went down the coast to friendlier waters.

"There he heard that some of the people of that village had told tales of the woman years before, that she danced with the devil to keep her face young and other such nonsense. Those stories had been passed from town to town as they do in those parts. But then the woman's husband died—gone missing at sea—and the stories just stopped."

"Until this fellow, this friend of a friend, came talking about a mermaid," Barnum said.

Maybe he *would* get his mermaid after all. A mermaid was a much more spectacular exhibit than an immortal woman. A mermaid wouldn't require papers to prove her magic to the gaping crowds. It would be visible for all to see—no need for tricks. At least, no need for tricks that the human eye could see. Of course Barnum didn't actually believe this nonsense about the mermaid being real. But if there was a story about her, it would make things easier. It meant that if anyone went looking into the woman's background, they would find mermaid rumors. It's easier to sell a half-truth than a complete lie.

"What's the name of this town, again?" Barnum asked.

Moses told him, and Barnum said, "You're right; that is almost in Canada."

"You're not going to go all the way up there to find out if this woman is a mermaid," Levi asked.

"No," Barnum said. "You are."

Moses looked from Levi to Barnum and clearly made a decision that concerned discretion and valor. He bundled his dusty mermaid into the bulky carrying case he'd used to bring her from Boston. Then he extracted a promise from Barnum to use the mermaid in whatever exhibit was finally established in the American Museum.

"What kind of terms do you want?" Barnum asked.

Moses glanced at the thundercloud on Levi's brow and hastily said, "We can talk about it later, Barnum."

Levi kept his temper until Moses trundled out the door with his case.

"I'm not going to some godforsaken town up north just because a drunk fisherman says he saw a mermaid once," Levi said. "I won't do it, Taylor."

The trouble was, from Barnum's point of view, that Levi wasn't Barnum's employee, so to speak. He paid Levi for certain jobs, and by the job. If Levi didn't want to go look for this mermaid girl, then there wasn't anything Barnum could do to force him.

Levi had helped Barnum with the Joice Heth humbug, and Barnum wanted his help attracting folk to the museum. Levi could be quite convincing—the boy should have taken up acting; he was that good at it—and it was his performance that had given so much credibility to the exhibit of the old woman. Barnum knew that if Levi went up north to find this widow, he would be able to convince her to return to New York with him. Levi just had a way about him.

But Barnum would have to convince Levi to help him first.

"Now, Levi," Barnum began.

"Don't think you can 'now, Levi' me, Taylor," Levi said. "I hate boats. I hate the ocean. I hate the smell of fish. I'm not going to Maine."

"Levi, if we pass this girl off as a mermaid, we'll make more money than we even dreamed of with Joice Heth."

"*You'll* make money, you mean," Levi said.

That stung, at least for a moment, until Barnum privately acknowledged that he ought to have given Levi a larger share last time. It was Levi whose face everyone saw, Levi who did all the talking to the paying guests.

"You'll get your fair share," Barnum said. "I give you my word."

"Why don't *you* go if you want the girl so badly?" Levi asked.

"One of the museum exhibits can't just get up and walk out," Barnum said, gesturing around them.

Barnum's office was, in fact, in the third viewing saloon of the museum, right between the waxworks and the mirrors. The museum was closed now, the comforting murmur of the crowd disappeared. Levi had often asked Barnum how he could work with everyone gawping at him like that, but there was nothing Barnum loved better than the sight of the paying public.

"You could leave if you wanted to," Levi said. "There are plenty of other things to look at here besides you."

"I can't leave Charity and the girls," Barnum said, lying through his teeth. He thought it might be the only argument that would convince the other man, who, despite his bachelor status, had a healthy respect for the sanctity of the family.

Levi gave him a look that said his gambit was weak.

"Have a heart, Levi," Barnum said. "We're living inside the museum, for heaven's sake. I can hardly leave Charity alone here while I go off to another state for weeks looking for a mermaid."

Barnum and his family were, in fact, living in a former billiard hall on the first floor, as Levi very well knew. But it was only temporary, Barnum promised himself. Temporary until he made his fortune. Then he'd live in a fine house, like all the other fine people in New York, and they would have to greet him like their equal for he would be just as good as they.

"I have not eaten a warm dinner . . ." Barnum began.

". . . since you bought this place." Levi sighed the sigh of those who've heard it all before.

He ought to have used a less-worn theme, Barnum reflected. He'd repeated this statement frequently since the opening of the museum to communicate his devotion to its success. But Levi didn't have the same investment he did. It didn't say *Lyman's American Museum* outside above the balcony where the band played. It said *Barnum's*.

Barnum rapidly sorted and discarded several statements. He couldn't think of anything, which was unusual for him. So he lit a cigar, pushed away from his desk, and said, "Hell, Levi."

Levi gave Barnum an unreadable look.

"She's not a mermaid, you know," Levi said.

"I'll believe in mermaids if it will sell tickets," Barnum said.

"It will likely take you just as much money to sell the illusion as you'd make," Levi said. "Never mind if someone decides she's indecent. That's a whole other set of problems."

"Why are you borrowing trouble? We don't have the woman here yet and you're already thinking like a lawyer, looking for traps that aren't there."

"I am a lawyer," Levi said dryly. "Even if I've been a part-time performing monkey for you."

"I don't pay the performing monkeys," Barnum said. "Help me out, Levi. We can both profit by this."

"And what about this woman?" Levi asked.

"She can profit by it, too, if she plays her part," Barnum said easily.

He had the other man now. He knew it. Levi never relented a little bit unless he was going to relent the whole way.

"I don't want her used," Levi said. "If she wants to leave, then she'll be allowed to leave?"

The shadow of Joice Heth hung over both of them, and for a moment Barnum thought he heard the old woman's voice speaking, an ancient croaking drawn up from her wizened body, asking him to release her.

"Let me go to die and go to glory as a free woman."

Barnum looked up. It wasn't Joice's voice he'd heard, but Levi's.

"That's what she said, Barnum," Levi said.

Levi never called him Barnum unless he was upset. He'd been halfway to agreeing until the Heth business came up. Now Barnum was going to have to soothe the other man down so he'd go to Maine and collect this woman they were arguing about. Except they weren't really arguing about the mermaid. They were arguing about the past. Barnum wasn't interested in revisiting the past. The past was the past, and only the future could bring profit.

"Levi—"

"I was the one who was with her all day, Barnum. Not you. You didn't hear her."

Barnum nodded. He *had* heard her, heard those very words, but he acknowledged that Levi had taken the worst of it. Barnum's part had been to drum up business—put advertisements in the papers, sell tickets. Levi had accompanied the woman to every town and every stage, been the public face of the business, as it were. "If you go now and do this for me, I promise that I'll give the woman a fair contract."

Levi narrowed his eyes. "She'll be paid? And permitted to leave if she chooses?"

Barnum privately thought that if the woman was really a mermaid—not likely, as Levi had said, but there was always hope—she wouldn't be going anywhere. There wasn't a chance in heaven or hell that Barnum would let something like that go once he had it. But he was careful not to let this show on his face as he answered his old friend.

"Of course, Levi. Anything you want."

Levi didn't like the ocean. At least, he thought he might like a tropical ocean—those oceans described in travelogues and seen in pictures of faraway islands with golden sand and palm trees.

As a child he'd imagined living on an island like Robinson Crusoe, complete with a parrot and a native servant. Of course, Robinson Crusoe had to contend with cannibals, and Levi didn't think he was up to dealing with those kinds of problems. He had enough trouble with Barnum and his schemes.

The churning, cold green of the North Atlantic was not at all to his taste—nor, he reflected as his insides swooned about queasily, was it preferred by his stomach.

Barnum had insisted that a boat was more efficient for his purposes—if there really was a mermaid in Maine, then he wanted Levi to get her and bring her back to New York posthaste, and the patchwork of dirt roads leading through northern Maine did not lend itself to quickness.

However, there wasn't a passenger boat from Boston to this obscure little town. Levi had taken a steamer to Rhode Island and then a train to Boston and now a horrible fish-smelling craft heading north to draw its trade from the seas. There was ice and crashing waves, and Levi wondered why on earth anyone would fish so early in the season, but Barnum had managed to find one crew of madmen, and the captain of these madmen had consented to take a passenger.

The fishermen on board laughed at his city shoes and inadequate coat and the way he turned up his nose at the hardtack for breakfast. Levi wanted badly to reach a place that had a feather bed that didn't rock from side to side and all the whiskey he could drink.

But Barnum wanted a mermaid, so Levi was going to get him a mermaid.

Once upon a time, Levi thought he could have fame and fortune, that his life would be better, more glamorous, more exciting if he helped Barnum sell his humbugs to the public. Barnum was an old friend, and he'd convinced Levi that playing the showman was a lot like playing the lawyer, only more fun. He'd get to convince folks of a different kind of truth—an actor's truth, a storyteller's truth—rather than dig out the truth in a courtroom. And Levi had been dissatisfied with his quiet life and thought it would be a lark to go along with Barnum for a while.

The shine had long since come off the work for Levi, but he didn't much fancy going back to lawyering either. So he stayed and hoped that maybe he could find some of that magic again, the magic he had felt when he first started. And even if he couldn't, then maybe he could stop Barnum from hurting someone else the way they had hurt Joice Heth. If Levi did that, even without the fame and fortune, it would be worth staying.

He didn't believe in the mermaid story, of course, and he didn't really think Barnum did, either. But Barnum was smart enough to know that if there were rumors about this woman, it would lend veracity to any tale they told once she was on exhibit. If a poking New York reporter decided to make this miserable journey to the north, then he would find the same stories that had drawn Levi there, and nobody would be able to *prove* the girl wasn't a mermaid.

That was the trick, really—making sure nobody could prove what Barnum said wasn't true. They were free to raise objections and make conjectures, but without proof . . . well, without proof every person who claimed the mermaid was false would just be giving Barnum free advertising.

Levi knew Barnum hadn't liked the way people turned on him about the Heth woman, despite all of his bluster otherwise. For himself, Levi had never been able to feel entirely comfortable about the business. It had started off fun and quickly soured when he realized that Joice Heth didn't want to be displayed like a dancing bear for the rest of her days. He'd tried his best to keep the old woman content, and surely he and Barnum had done a better job of it than her owner in the South.

But the truth was that Barnum had paid to put that woman on display, and paying for her made Barnum—whatever he might say—her owner, too. Levi didn't know how he felt about slavery in the South, but he knew he didn't feel so good about it when it was standing next to him.

Whatever the truth of this widow on the rocks (as Levi had come to think of her), he wouldn't force her to return to New York if she didn't want to go. He'd had enough of forcing people to do things they didn't want to do just because Barnum said so.

And Levi would see that Barnum gave the girl fair pay for her work. It was her body people would be gaping at in the tank, after all. Barnum forgot about things like that sometimes. He saw every person passing as a potential coin in his pocket.

It never occurred to Levi, while contemplating his sea-borne misery and righteously demanding her compensation from Barnum in his mind, that the woman might not want to leave her home. He'd told Barnum that he would leave her in Maine if she truly didn't want to come, but down deep he didn't think she would refuse.

Of course there was no place more wonderful than New York City in all the world (Europe could keep their London and Paris), and any person would be thrilled to leave their country life to go there—especially if they had a free ticket and a job waiting. That was how Barnum had lured him away from Pennsylvania in the first place.

Levi was pretty certain that the woman wouldn't turn down the chance to get away from the middle of nowhere. Everyone wanted to be someone, and how could you be someone when you lived in a cottage on the rocks by the sea?

But when Levi finally made it to the mermaid's village, he discovered that the people there were carved from stone. Their faces looked like leather, and their accents made sounds he didn't understand. They didn't know anything about this woman he spoke of, and they weren't interested in knowing. They narrowed their eyes in suspicion, and his money wasn't good anywhere.

It was clear, overwhelmingly clear, that they had no use for him and did not want him and would do everything in their damned Yankee souls to drive him away before he reached his object.

The result of this was that Levi found himself holding his suitcase outside a tavern, sadly whiskeyless and unable to even find a patch of straw for the night, much less a feather bed.

He cursed Barnum's scheming (under his breath, for there were sharp-eared ladies going about their afternoon shopping and his father would have boxed his ears if he'd heard him say such things before the fairer sex) and vowed that if he had to sleep on the sidewalk that night, he would never so much as carry a letter to the post for Barnum again.

Despite the complete lack of helpfulness from the townspeople, Levi wasn't ready to go back to Barnum and explain why he'd returned to New York empty-handed. He knew the woman lived on the coast, not in the town, so all he had to do was make his way toward the sound of the crashing sea. Surely she would be easy enough to find then. How many seaside cottages could there be in this wretched state?

Several hours later, Levi admitted that first, there were quite a few seaside homes in this wretched state (an almost incomprehensible number, to his mind—who on earth wanted the sea encroaching on them all day and night?) and second, the coastline was longer than it appeared on a map.

As nightfall approached, he wandered, weary and foot-sore, along a kind of track in the snow (*why was there still snow in April? It wasn't natural*) that ran along next to the enormous boulders that seemed to block off huge portions of the coast. At least they blocked off huge portions of the coast to sane persons—those who did not think it right, proper, or fun to clamber over rocks in order to reach the churning green ocean below. Levi did not like the ocean, and what he'd seen of it on this trip had done little to increase its appeal.

He had to admit that he was more than ready to give up this search. Nearly every home he'd encountered had been peopled by a flinty-eyed fisherman or his wife who, naturally, had no idea which of their neighbors might be a mermaid.

The best thing to do would be to hire a wagon to take him to the nearest town that was not filled with hostiles and give it up as a bad business. Perhaps he could convince Barnum that the dried-up monkey mummy of Kimball's would do just as well.

He dropped his case in the snow on the track beside him. In addition to everything else, there was more snow up here than Levi had ever seen in his life, and he'd been trudging through it for hours. The sun was going down, he was nowhere near civilization, and he'd had enough.

And then he saw her.

She stood on the cliff staring out to sea, her unbelievably long witch-hair not blowing in the wind from the ocean but seeming to embrace it, to twine around the very air and move with it in an impossible dance. The cold did not appear to disturb her, for she wore only a rough wool dress and boots and no coat or even a shawl to cover her shoulders. She was young, much younger than any of her neighbors near or far, and even from this distance—perhaps a quarter mile—Levi could tell her skin would gleam like a pearl in candlelight.

He saw then the rough little cottage tucked onto the rocks behind her and the slight curve beneath it that would lead to a cove beneath.

This was the woman. He was sure of it.

As he picked up his case and hurried toward the still figure, he hoped that at the very least the woman would be hospitable, for if he didn't get out of the cold, he felt certain his toes would freeze together.

His feet crunched in the snow, and he must have sounded like a lumbering bear to her, but she did not turn or indicate that she heard him at all until he called out.

"Hello!" he said.

He stopped when he was a few feet from her, not wanting to startle her. Her back was very straight, and the wind carried her scent to him, the salt of the sea mixed with the oil he could see gleaming in the coils of her hair.

She turned then, but very slowly, almost as if she were under a spell and wanted to stay there. Her eyes were closed, the lashes thick and dark against her white skin.

Then the lids rose, and he thought, *Of course she's a mermaid. What else would she be?*

Those eyes were not of the shore, he thought. They were as grey as the storm that boiled below them, the constant swirl and crash that was the sea. But more than that, they were alien. The expression in them was not of a fellow human but of one who was apart from humanity and looked at him as something strange and curious.

He felt himself shrinking beneath that gaze and wondered suddenly if this was how Joice Heth had felt—the discomfort of being dissected by a look, the desire to shrivel up and disappear under eyes that wouldn't stop watching.

"Yes?" the woman said.

Levi shook away the fancy that struck him. Of course she

wasn't a mermaid. Her gaze wasn't any more or less forthright than the rest of the folk around here. He just hadn't seen grey eyes very often, and certainly not ones just that shade of storm-tossed ocean.

"I was hoping you could help me," Levi began, then stopped. Now that he was here, what was he to say to this woman?

"Yes?" she asked again. Her tone was disinterested. It said it wasn't any matter to her if they stood upon the rocks in the cold wind forever.

Her witchy hair blew all around her face now that her back was to the wind. Levi was sure that if he approached her, the tendrils would grab him and pull him into the water and he would drown.

She was making him fanciful, and Levi knew better than to be fanciful. But there was something about her, something strange and compelling, and he understood why rumors flew so thick about her.

He understood, too, in the part of him that was Barnum's spiritual kin, that those eyes and that hair and that so-direct look would draw crowds into the museum like no other.

She might not really be a mermaid, but by God, Levi and Barnum could sell her as one.

* * *

Could I trouble you for a cup of tea?"

That was what the man asked, in that way people did when they thought it would be no trouble at all. Amelia had tea, of course, but she didn't know that she particularly wanted to share it with a stranger. And this stranger stared at her with too-avid eyes, eyes that told her he'd heard the rumors about her and come to see if they were true.

It had been a decade, give or take a few years, since Jack's death. For a long time afterward, Amelia found she was unable to change, to even approach the sea. It had become something hateful to her—the mistress who'd stolen her husband away.

Amelia had stood upon the rocks and cursed it and wished all of her grief and anger on the vast unfeeling waves. She wished for a sudden shifting of the earth so that all the water would drain away from her sight, or that a vast fireball would descend from the sky and scorch all of the ocean into a desert.

In short she wished for ridiculous, impossible things but none more ridiculous or impossible as when she bent over in heartbreak and wept long tears over the rocks and promised anything, anything, *anything* at all if only the ocean would return her love to her.

And though she cursed and wept and pleaded and bargained, the ocean never listened or acknowledged the troubles of one small land-or-sea dweller. The ocean has a rhythm, but it has no heart.

After a long time had passed, Amelia stopped looking for his boat or wishing the great ocean would be destroyed because of the whim of her broken heart. Somewhere far away lived her family and her people, and perhaps she might like to return to them someday, and she would not be able to if the ocean was gone forever.

More than that, though, she realized her grief had ebbed. While it would always be an ache in her chest, the hard knot of it had loosed, her sadness slowly unraveling.

She'd felt some panic then—panic that the loss of sadness would be the loss of Jack. When she tried to remember his face, she could not. All she could see was the boat moving slowly away from shore, away from her.

Amelia ran into their bedroom then and found one of his sweaters, burying her face in it. His smell clung to the wool, just faintly, and when she breathed it in there he was again— the lines around his eyes, the flash of his teeth when he laughed, the clomp of his boots on the floor.

All at once she understood that to spurn the sea was to spurn Jack, too, for the sea had delivered them to each other.

That very night, Amelia had returned to the cove where first she changed from mermaid to woman. She was filled with the same anxiety and excitement she'd felt the first time. Would she still be able to change, or would the enchantment that allowed her to pass freely between sea and shore have expired when she rejected the ocean?

Amelia was so consumed by this that she didn't notice the man alone on his boat, the stranger who saw her shed her clothes and dive into the water. She was so delighted that her fin still formed from her human legs that she swam to the surface and broke through, arcing her body into the night air so every last scale of her secret was revealed to the moonlight.

It was only later, when the women of the town closed around her like schooling fish that she discovered *she* had been discovered—and more importantly, that the people of the town had known for some time. Their careful denunciation of mermaid stories had kept Amelia safe for many long years.

And yet somehow despite this a man was standing on her cliff asking for a cup of tea.

A man with her story in his eyes. A man she would not have noticed if he was jumbled into a crowd. He was of average height, with brown hair and brown eyes and a clean-shaven face. He carried a suitcase, and something else— exhaustion. The man appeared weary to his bones.

Amelia reflected that as he had likely walked all this way from town, he probably was exhausted. Cold, too—she noticed the fine trembling of his hands and the way he tried to disguise the puffs of breath that told her he was in distress.

"You can come in," she said abruptly.

She moved past him and toward the cottage. He seemed taken aback by the sudden movement. Amelia heard him scrambling behind her, as if he were afraid she might change her mind and leave him there.

Amelia wasn't the least curious about his purpose—that she'd discerned the moment she saw him—but she was curious about his drive. What could have pushed him all this way? Was he a reporter from a newspaper? And why was his accent so different from the others who lived nearby?

She was suddenly conscious of the fact that she'd never left this very small area since she'd come to land. That she'd swum thousands of miles of ocean to get here hardly seemed noteworthy.

Jack had grown up here, been more than content to stay here, and so Amelia had, too. The foreign sound of the man's voice was an abrupt reminder that there was more to the world than northern Maine. It was also a reminder that she'd once followed a ship with the intention of seeing all the world and all its wonders, and she never had seen more than this corner of it.

Amelia entered the cottage, poured water from the basin into the kettle, then stoked the fire hot. All the time she was aware of the man's eyes on her, watching her.

But it would not be her who asked why he had come. She was under no obligation to make things easier for him. He could state his purpose, or gape at her, or leave. Whatever he chose was nothing to her.

Finally he cleared his throat and said, "You don't have a stove."

She straightened and gave him a long look. "Mister, I can see I don't have a stove."

He cleared his throat again—that was a habit that would grate on her in no time if he didn't quit it—and said, "It's just been a long time since I've seen anyone cook over a fire."

"A stove is still a fire," she pointed out. "Only one enclosed in iron."

She might have added that it seemed foolish for Jack to buy a stove when a fireplace worked just as well. She supposed if she cared about such things he would have gotten one, but she didn't. She didn't care about stoves or parasols or whatever such things Mr. Parsons tried to tempt her with at the general store. Amelia had only ever desired two things— her freedom and Jack's love.

"Ma'am," he began.

"It's customary to introduce oneself when meeting someone new," she said.

The man flushed from the collar of his shirt all the way up to his hairline. She went about taking down the tea chest and the sugar—Amelia loved sugar in her tea, the more the better—and the teapot and cups. While she did all this, the man appeared to pull himself together.

"I'm sorry, ma'am," he said. "I've gone about this all wrong. My name's Levi, Levi Lyman, and I've come here from New York City with a proposition for you."

She nodded in acknowledgment. "My name is Amelia

Douglas. Perhaps you already knew that, or perhaps not. Perhaps you came all this way because you've been listening to stories carried by a foolish fisherman."

The red in his cheeks deepened. "I confess, Mrs. Douglas, that it was a rumor that brought me here to you."

Amelia pulled the whistling kettle from the fire and poured the water into the teapot. "And what, exactly, did this rumor say? That I go out at night to dance with Satan and keep myself young forever? That I am a witch who came from nowhere and the children of the village must keep away lest I eat them?"

As she repeated the words she'd heard whispered behind her back, she felt something long unacknowledged—they hurt. It hurt to have her neighbors think so poorly of her, and even if their opinion had changed, the old unease lingered below the surface, reminding her always, *always*, that she was not the same as them.

She could walk like them, and dress like them, and speak like them, and even take one of their names, but she was not one of them. She came from the sea, and humans would always sense the strangeness in her even if they didn't know why she made them shift uneasily, or why they didn't want to spend too long looking directly into her eyes.

"I did hear such tales of you," Levi Lyman admitted.

Amelia passed him a cup of tea and indicated the sugar. Her placid face indicated nothing of what roiled inside her.

"I'm surprised you've the courage to come and take tea with a witch."

He said, "I haven't. I've come to take tea with a mermaid."

She put several spoonfuls of sugar in her cup and stirred. "You seem to have traveled a long way for nothing. I am only a fisherman's widow, and I haven't seen any mermaids frolicking in the Atlantic from my cliff."

"Naturally you would not if you were the mermaid in question," Mr. Lyman said.

Amelia felt a prickling of warning. This man would not be laughed away or sent off with a flea in his ear. Somewhere, deep beneath his too-casual manner, there was determination. Even worse, there was a kind of belief. Belief was more dangerous than all the tale-telling in all the pubs of the world.

Humans, Amelia knew, would do anything for belief. They would proselytize from the highest mountain for belief. They would collect like-minded people and form mobs for belief. They would kill one another for belief. She must break that belief before it had a chance to fully flower.

"Mr. Lyman," she said, quite calm. "Mermaids do not exist. Nor do unicorns or dragons or sea monsters or witches. They are stories told to children, or by the inebriated—who are often the same as children, as you may know. I'm sorry you've come all this way following a silly story, but it is just that—a story."

Her tone made it clear that she thought him very much a fool for believing it.

"Mrs. Douglas," he said. "You may or may not be an honest-to-goodness mermaid, but it doesn't matter. P. T. Barnum can make you a mermaid, and make everyone in the world believe that it's true."

Amelia frowned. "Who's P. T. Barnum?"

"P. T. Barnum is a purveyor of wonders, a seller of miracles, a showman of the first order. Mr. Barnum's museum in New York City is filled with treasures, many never before seen by the viewing public."

"Ah, I see. Mr. Barnum is what we call a snake-oil salesman," Amelia said, her lips curving. After all of this the man was nothing but a representative for some huckster!

Levi Lyman plowed on, seemingly oblivious to both her interruption and her contempt. "Mr. Barnum has sent me to ask you, Mrs. Douglas, to come to New York City and perform in the museum as his mermaid."

"Perform," Amelia said, her voice flat. "You mean put myself on a stage in a costume like a dance-hall girl."

Amelia did not despise dance-hall girls, for she was well aware that it was a life many women were forced into against their will. But she also knew that most folk thought of such performers with contempt, disgust, and superiority. Amelia knew how to pretend, how to behave in the accepted manner of the humans around her, and the humans around her expected her to be a "good Christian woman." A good Christian woman would never lower herself to *perform*, and her scathing tone communicated this.

Mr. Lyman's face shifted. "You would not be performing, precisely. Rather you would be . . . an exhibit."

Amelia raised an eyebrow. "Mr. Barnum wishes me to exhibit myself? He presumes much."

Her intonation of "exhibit" absolutely dripped with scandalized outrage.

Mr. Lyman seemed to have lost his thread. She could see him grasping about for it, trying to reembroider the words that had come out wrong. "Well, you see, what Mr. Barnum would like is for you to, er, swim about in a tank . . ."

"Wearing, I suppose, a costume that no decent woman should wear in public."

Amelia was rather enjoying herself now. She observed the shifting calculations in his eyes, the increasing desperation to climb out of the hole he'd inadvertently dug. Soon enough he wouldn't know why he'd come here in the first place. Then, Amelia thought, she could be rid of him. And perhaps once she was rid of him it might be time to consider a change. She did not want to spend the remainder of her life on land dodging people like Mr. Lyman, people who wanted to find a real miracle and make it pay dividends.

Mr. Lyman put down his cup of tea. "I apologize, Mrs. Douglas. At no time did I mean to imply that your morals were not of the highest standards."

He stopped, started to speak, stopped again. And sighed.

When he sighed, he seemed to be blowing out all his troubles, his foolishness, his frustration, his belief. He looked up at her with eyes that now burned with shame and sadness.

That sadness was fatal to Amelia. It pierced her, made her sorry for him, and she drew herself up, hoping to pull armor around her body to protect her from what he would say next. It would be, she knew, the truth, and she was powerless against the truth.

"Mr. Barnum has a friend, a man called Moses Kimball who runs a museum in Boston," Levi Lyman said. He wouldn't look at her now but rather kept his gaze fixed on the fire. "Moses came to Mr. Barnum with a curiosity to exhibit in the American Museum—that's Mr. Barnum's museum. It was a mermaid skeleton."

Amelia barely swallowed her gasp. Could it be? Could the remains of one of her people have been swept to shore by the tides? Her momentary panic was quashed as he continued.

"Of course it was nothing but a humbug. Any fool could tell it was just a dried-up monkey sewn to a fish tail. But it got Mr. Barnum thinking. And if you knew Mr. Barnum, you'd know he thinks no small thoughts. Moses wanted Barnum to put the monkey-thing on display, but Barnum didn't think anyone would believe it, especially after . . ."

He trailed off, tugged at his collar. "Well, anyhow, he

didn't think it would be enough to convince the paying public that mermaids were real. So he struck on this notion of having a girl dress up as a mermaid, swim around a tank, and wave at the little ones. I told him it wouldn't work, that we would be caught if the girl was a fake, but you don't know Barnum. Once an idea gets in his head you can't knock it loose with a stick and a net. And then old Moses told him a story. A friend had told him this story, he said, a friend who heard it from a fisherman. And that fisherman said—"

"That he saw a mermaid swimming in the moonlight," Amelia said, her voice soft. "Yes, I know that story."

"Of course it's ridiculous. I know that. Pretty sure Barnum does, too, although with him you never know. He might believe, or hope for it to be true, or not really condone any such thing but know others might. The one thing Barnum does believe in is money and the getting of it."

Amelia scowled at this. Money was fairly meaningless to her except inasmuch as it was needed for things like sugar and vegetables and cloth to make the occasional dress. Mr. Lyman saw her expression and hurried to correct any poor impression brought on by the mention of dollars and cents.

"He wants to make money, sure, but mostly what he wants is to amaze folks. He wants to take them out of their little lives and show them something wonderful. I could tell—I could see it in his eyes when he was talking—that the idea of the mermaid was just what he wanted. What could be more magical, more wondrous, than a woman who could change her tail into legs, who rose out of the sea like Venus?"

Amelia's memory of the first time she changed was not so wondrous. She did not share the remembrance of cold and the shock of falling instead of standing on her fresh new legs. But for a moment she'd felt the enchantment of his words, seen the shining eyes of the children as they gazed upon that wonder—the mermaid.

Then she remembered how Jack had feared for her, and how carefully they had hidden her secret. She recalled, too, that she would be the one everyone stared at. She wouldn't be one of the paying customers of this wonder but the main attraction.

"It sounds delightful when you put it that way, Mr. Lyman. But I fail to see how it has anything to do with me, especially if you don't believe the tales."

"It's because the stories were told about you, specifically," he said. "If Mr. Barnum were to hire any girl from anywhere and present her as a mermaid, we'd be found out in a minute. Some reporter would sniff out that 'Christiana, the wonder of the Seven Seas' was actually Bertha Cummings from some backwater in Connecticut. The show would be over. But if *you're* the mermaid and a nosy reporter tries to track down your origins, what will he find?"

"The same story that brought you to my door," Amelia said. The logic was sound, but she would give no such concession to him. She did not want him to go away feeling any encouragement.

"Well, Mr. Lyman, I'm sorry you've come all the way from New York for this, but I've no wish to leave my home. You'll have to find Bertha from the backwater, I'm afraid."

Her tone was final. There was no space in it for pleading, arguing, or bribing. She wished him to go.

He stood, his face stiff. "I'm very sorry to have troubled you."

She nodded. She could be magnanimous now that he was leaving. He picked up his suitcase and stopped by the front door. Night had fallen while they had their tea. Amelia noted his uncertainty as clearly as if he'd spoken it—*how to get back to town?*

He must not stay at the cottage. The only thing that protected Amelia from the cruelty of wagging tongues was her status as a virtuous widow. The vaguest of improprieties would destroy her.

"If you go west from here," she said, pointing behind the cottage and away from the sea, "you'll find a dirt road. This time of evening all the fishermen go down to the village for their evening ale. Some of them have carts and I'm sure would be happy to take you for a coin or two."

He looked doubtful. "It's very dark. I doubt I could find my own nose."

"The moon is rising," she said, and opened the door.

Sure enough, the white moon was breaking over the edge of the sea. Soon all the land would be lit by its cold eye. Amelia felt the pull of the ocean, the longing to disappear under the waves and then crash through into the air, into the moonlight.

She led Levi Lyman around the cottage and pointed to the track that led to the road. It was just faintly visible now, but it would become clearer as he walked and the moon rose higher.

"Good-bye, Mr. Lyman," she said firmly. He was leaving whether he liked it or not.

"Good-bye, Mrs. Douglas," he said, and lifted his hat to her.

She turned and left him there, not looking back to see what he chose to do. It was entirely possible, she admitted, that he might curl up there in the snow and she would find him in the morning, blank-eyed and frozen.

Amelia paused just before she reentered the cottage and listened. His footsteps crunched in the snow, moving away. *Good,* she thought. That was good. He was leaving.

She shut the cottage door behind her, trying to shut out the confusing tangle of thoughts stirred up by the stranger.

New York. He came from New York. It was a city, a city with hundreds and hundreds of people. You could get lost in a place like that and nobody would know who you were. You could say you were anybody you liked and no one would know different and you wouldn't be trailing around stories about dancing with the devil or swimming in the moonlight.

And oh, to have something new to see, someone new to talk to! Hadn't she promised herself that she would see all the wonders on land? There were wonders to be had in New York, she was sure.

(But what about the sea? How will you return to the sea?)

Amelia didn't know anything about New York except that it was large. But it must have ports, she reasoned. She'd heard the shopkeepers talk about ships traveling from New York to Boston. A place with ships meant she could find the ocean anytime she wished.

(But what about Jack? If you go away, if you're not here waiting, how will Jack find you when he comes back?)

That thought, the speaking of her secret heart, made her gasp in pain she'd thought long-forgotten.

He's not coming back. He's not coming back.

"He's not coming back," she said, and the words chased the dust out of the empty corners and settled there.

"He's not coming back," she said again, and the words crawled into her cold bed and hid beneath her pillow.

"He's not coming back," she said.

The third time was the breaking of the storm, the breaking of the spell that had kept her on the rocks staring out to sea, believing that if she only looked hard enough he would appear.

This was the secret she kept beneath her tongue, the wish she never spoke, for to speak it would make its magic disappear.

But now she'd spoken it, and the curse would drown her wish in unshed tears. He wasn't coming back. He was never, never, never coming back to her.

She'd fallen to her hands and knees, gasping for air, her fingers curled into the rough wood of the floor.

Amelia rose and opened the door and went out into the night. Only the ocean could soothe her now, the terrible ocean that kept her heart beating even as it tried to crush her beneath the weight of sorrow.

CHAPTER 3

The next day Levi Lyman left the village forever.

It was much easier to hire a carriage to leave the place—everyone had been so helpful, so eager to hurry him away.

The night before he'd managed to find a stone-faced local on the road driving a small cart hitched to an ancient horse. The horse clopped along slower than a baby's crawl and the cart wheels struck every rock and hole in their path, but Levi didn't care. His feet were sore, and he was tired of feeling his case bang against his leg.

The man told Levi (in what seemed to be as few words as possible) that he could find a meal at the Green Goose and that the proprietor also had beds for the night. This was the very place that had refused Levi's custom earlier in the day, so he doubted the owner would provide for him.

However, upon entering with said stone-faced local and enduring several withering glances from others, he discovered that, miraculously, his money was good again. This might have been because he mentioned that he was leaving in the morning. The proprietor seemed much cheerier after that.

The next morning he discovered another local man out front with a wagon pulled by two strong-looking horses. This individual, though not interested in conversation of any sort (Levi tried several times and was rebuffed with the all-purpose "ayuh" on each occasion), was perfectly willing to accept a half dollar in exchange for a ride to the next, larger town. At this larger town Levi would be able to procure a coach ticket to Boston (and why Barnum hadn't done this in the first place instead of sending him on that miserable sea voyage was beyond him).

Levi did not think on his failure—though he knew Barnum would grumble at the wasted expense—but only of reaching a larger place, where the beds were comfortable and the townspeople less forbidding.

He was a friendly person by nature—it was one of the reasons Barnum sent Levi out to "do the talking," as he called it. The chill that emanated from the Mermaid's Village (as Levi referred to it) could freeze the most pleasant nature.

As for the woman herself—well, it was a shame she hadn't been interested in his offer. She was beautiful, sure, but beauty could be found anywhere. What she really had was an otherworldliness, an alien quality that couldn't be duplicated.

It was her eyes, he thought. Not just the color, but the something deep down that said she'd seen things seen by no man. Yes, Levi could well believe that people thought her a mermaid. It was too bad she didn't want to play one for Mr. Barnum. Well, they would sort something out. Levi reckoned he could sell Moses Kimball's monkey-mummy if they only set it up right.

The journey to the next town took half a day. By the time Levi checked into an inn—staffed by a cheery innkeeper who was more than happy to provide a bath and whiskey— the whole encounter had taken on the quality of a dream.

Still, when he slept that night, he dreamed of a mermaid with black hair and grey eyes following him down the coast. The next morning he paid for his coach ticket to Boston and resigned himself to delivering bad news to Barnum. The showman, he knew, would not be best pleased.

Amelia stood on the street corner, staring up at the words written on the side of the massive building.

BARNUM'S AMERICAN MUSEUM, it said.

Amelia wasn't a strong reader—Jack could read a little, and had taught her what he knew—but there hadn't been much call for it at home. Here there seemed to be words everywhere—on the corner signs and in huge letters on the buildings and lining the pages of newspapers hawked by small boys in the street.

The words only added to the cacophony—everywhere there was color and noise and people, oh so many people. They brushed up against Amelia when she walked or tried to lure her into their shops with their wares or cut abruptly in front of her, making her stagger to a halt and cause a pileup of irritated folk behind her.

They talked fast and moved fast and part of her thrilled at the newness of it all, while the other part of her wished for the solace of her cliff—the rocks and the wind and the unchanging ocean. It was, she reflected, not too late to turn back.

He's never coming home, she reminded herself. *You can stand there forever waiting for a ghost or you can see the world. That was why you followed the ship in the first place, so long ago.*

And the world was not in her cottage. She had to go out and find it. And she had.

Some of the buildings seemed as tall as the cliff she stood upon day after day, and they were all pressed up against one another with hardly any space between. Even in the village at home, where the buildings were clustered more closely together, there was breathing room. In New York, it looked like breathing room hadn't been a consideration.

After Levi Lyman left, she carefully chose a few articles of clothing—the best she had, which wasn't saying much—and cleaned the cottage. She took the bedding from the mattress and placed it inside her trunk with some cedar blocks. She didn't think about what she was doing or why, but soon it was done.

She rigged an oilskin pouch to be carried on her back and placed all the things that might be necessary to her inside it. It was as watertight as she could make it once she sewed the edges together. There would be no need for human things until she came ashore in a human place. Humans, she had noticed, did not appreciate the naked form. Even showing one's ankles was frowned upon.

Though she pared down to just exactly what she would need—clothing and money—the bag was still a little bulky because of the necessity of including shoes. Amelia hated shoes and never wore them unless she had to, but she didn't think she would be able to get away without them in a city.

There was no need to pack human food. Amelia had never done this in front of Jack, but she was perfectly content eating raw fish from the ocean. Her mermaid teeth were made for this, after all.

Once everything in the cottage was prepared, Amelia went down the stairs to the cove, shed what she wore and left it on the beach, hooked the oilskin pouch over her shoulders, and dove into the water.

She thought that the people of the village might believe she'd returned to the ocean forever, as a mermaid should. She hoped this would comfort them when they found the cottage empty and her clothes on the sand.

The pouch was awkward and it dragged against the water, but there was nothing for it. She couldn't arrive in New York without the expected human things. She must try, at least for a while, to blend in with the real humans.

The journey took longer than she expected, for the pouch slowed her down and she was not accustomed to swimming such long distances any more.

This weakness frustrated her. Once she had swum the length of the ocean and down into its farthest depths. Now she was soft from life on land. Her nightly swims were not nearly enough preparation for such a long trip.

Jack had maps in the cottage of all the Eastern Seaboard, and Amelia knew how to follow the curves of the land and how to listen to the sailors' talk when she came upon a ship, and in this way she was able to find her way to New York and not foolishly come ashore in Boston.

But her life in Maine had not been any kind of preparation for the city in which she now stood, staring up at the band that played from a balcony over the entrance to the museum. It was by far the worst group of musicians she had ever heard.

Admittedly her experience of music was limited to the occasional Independence Day parade (Jack liked these), but she was certain every member of this band would be better off in a different profession. One almost wanted to flee inside the museum just to escape the din.

The building itself was enormous, taking up all the space in view so you couldn't see anything but it unless you turned around. The upper floors were decorated with large, brightly colored paintings of animals—animals more exotic to Amelia than any creature in the ocean. She wondered if there were live animals inside. Flags of all sorts fluttered in a long line that wrapped around the building.

Amelia watched the people going inside the museum, noting that they paid a fee. Her money was hidden inside a pocket in her dress that she'd sewn for just that purpose— she didn't like having a string pouch hanging from her wrist as many ladies did.

The oilskin bag had been abandoned once she came ashore. Amelia had waited until the cover of night and found a secluded spot (which took some doing—every port was bustling, even at night) to dry her hair and clothing. At dawn she'd dressed and ventured into the maze of New York City, her heart beating faster than she thought it ever could. She was finally seeing something of the world, and it seemed a large part of the world was crammed onto this tiny island.

Amelia shivered a little as she stood there. She hadn't thought to pack a cloak, and anyway there wouldn't have been space in the bag with the shoes. The breeze was cold, though not as biting as it was at home.

She was aware of the faint smell of the sea clinging to her and thought this must be why so many of the passing ladies looked at her askance. The streets reeked of horse manure and rooting pigs, so Amelia was surprised any ocean scent could cut through the stink. Still, it wasn't as if she could do anything about it. Her fellow museumgoers would have to accustom themselves or move away—it was all the same to her.

Amelia moved forward then, following the continuous stream of people into the massive building. As she paid her twenty-five cents, she noticed the ticket agent's eyes rake over her hair and hands.

Ah, that's the mystery solved. Now she knew why so many people had given her funny looks out in the street. She had no bonnet or gloves, and her hair was pulled into a single plait down her back instead of the customary (and unattractive, she thought) bun at the base of the neck.

Humans cared about such foolish things. What would happen if everyone saw her uncovered hands and hair? Would the stars fall from the sky? Would the earth crack in two? She hadn't space in her oilskin bag for silly things like bonnets (even if she owned one, which she didn't), nor the jewelry, parasols, or fans that adorned other women.

This attitude contributed to the general opinion of her as a witch, Jack had told her once. Women who did what they liked instead of what other people wished were often accused of witchcraft, because only a witch would be so defiant, or so it was thought.

"*Let them think of me as a witch if it makes them happy,*" Amelia said. "*I won't wear a bonnet just to please them.*"

"*And a very bewitching witch you are,*" Jack said, and his eyes sparked as he reached for her.

She realized then that she stood in the gaslit hall of the museum, perfectly still. Her throat was stuffed full of unshed tears. She swallowed them down and shook her head to clear it, for folk were passing her with curious glances. Amelia didn't want to attract so much attention.

She moved forward, ignoring the insistent hawking of vendors selling illustrated guides to the museum.

"Only ten cents! Every visitor should own one!" they called in shrill voices.

The guide was of no use to Amelia. Her funds were limited, and she reckoned she wouldn't be able to make out all the words in any case.

Amelia followed the flow of the crowd into another room. At first she didn't understand what the appeal of this room was supposed to be. The walls were paneled in wood, broken up by dozens of windows. Patrons were peering into these little windows (each one only slightly larger than a face) and exclaiming in delight.

She lined up to take her turn at a window next to a man wearing a very tall hat and checked trousers. How Jack would have laughed at those trousers! Amelia felt a pang; she was here to think about something other than Jack, yet somehow every strange thing brought him to mind.

The man in the checked trousers (whose coat trailed a strong scent of pipe tobacco) glanced into the window, consulted his duly purchased illustrated guide, nodded to himself, and gave way for Amelia. She put her face to the glass.

Inside was a tiny scene, like a child's doll house. A little man poled a thin boat with curved ends through a river. This river connected to other rivers, with more sailors and boats, and graceful bridges arced over the water with little groups of people gathered on them. The people were pointing at buildings that lined the edges of the rivers. Amelia was strongly reminded of the clumps of tourists that surrounded her at that very moment.

A woman next to Amelia harrumphed loudly, indicating her impatience, and Amelia moved to the next window. There she saw a palace rendered in miniature, a white building with a courtyard before it.

Without the guide or anyone to explain what the scenes meant, Amelia quickly grew tired of them. However charmingly assembled, they were nothing more than blank toys to her, devoid of knowledge or context. She moved with the crowd into the next room.

There she was immediately confronted by an assortment of stuffed birds. Though most visitors gasped at the loveliness of various plumages, Amelia had to look away. It hurt her heart to see the remains of these beautiful wild things, now reduced to nothing but an outer skin without a song.

It made her think of something Mr. Lyman had said about the mermaid skeleton—nothing but "a dried-up monkey sewn to a fish tail." P. T. Barnum wanted to exhibit it—and her alongside—with these other dead things.

She wondered then why she had come. There had been a vague notion of doing as Barnum wished—becoming a mermaid on display so that she could gain enough pay to travel the world as humans did. While she could swim anywhere she liked, she recognized the difficulty of coming ashore—her trip to New York City had proven that. Amelia would need luggage, clothing, the things that people were expected to have. It would be easier if she could travel by boat or train, and even a fisherman's widow knew you needed money for that.

But this—this room full of dead animals—did she want to be a part of this? Did she want these throngs of people consulting their illustrated guide before staring at her through the glass like those little doll scenes? How was she to escape her rocks and her cottage and her grief and live as a human without money?

The only things she knew how to be were Jack's wife and a mermaid, and no one would pay her to be Jack's wife. She'd been living off the money Jack had earned before he died for many years now. It had lasted long because she could eat fish from the sea and didn't need much that wasn't already in the cottage. But if Amelia wanted to travel like a human, she would need more. And she wanted to see everything there was to see. So she'd come to the place where a man called Barnum wanted to put her in a tank to swim for these gaping hordes.

It seemed suddenly to be the height of foolishness to have left her cottage, her home. Was viewing any wonder of the world worth the potential cost to her—to be an exhibit stared at by strangers, to possibly be captured by those who might hurt her? What had she been thinking?

She hadn't been thinking, she admitted to herself. Her sadness had threatened to swallow her whole and so she had run from it, run to this place, the only place she'd thought to go because a man had come to her door looking for a mermaid.

Amelia stumbled backward, away from the stuffed birds that stared with their glossy blank eyes. She bumped into an older gentleman (another tall hat, Amelia noted, thinking of the wool cap Jack wore when he went out to sea) who snapped at her to watch herself. She fled toward a corner of the room, away from the press of people, only to be confronted by another stuffed creature.

It was grey and huge, though not as big as some of the animals in the ocean. It had a long tentacle between its eyes, something like the arms of an octopus except without suckers on the underside. The eyes of this animal, too, were made of glass, as dead as a shark's black gaze. The eyelashes, though, were long, giving the animal an oddly tender look.

A nearby group pointed at the creature, calling it an "elephant," and marveled that "Barnum had it all the way from darkest Africa." Amelia wished that she had some magic beyond that of changing her tail to legs. She would lay her hands upon this poor stuffed thing and return it to life again. It would charge through the gawking crowds and into the street, startling all the horses and carriages and scatter the rooting pigs in the streets. It would make silly women faint. Perhaps it would make its way to the ocean, where it would swim back to its home in darkest Africa, wherever that might be.

Just then a din such that Amelia had never heard started up at the opposite side of the saloon. It was music, but a kind of music she could not recognize, loud and blaring and strangely sour.

"It's the Highland Mammoth Boys!" a woman exclaimed after consulting her program. A rush of people streamed toward the source of the noise.

Amelia covered her ears, shrinking into a notch between the elephant and the wall. The noise seeped through her fingers, making her teeth vibrate. The elephant emitted a strong scent of mothballs, and her eyes watered.

Why had she come? All she wanted now was to escape this place of strange noises and preserved death. The curiosity that once led her to the love of her life had led her to a place that seemed a lot like the hell the too-good women of her village had spoken of with both relish and frequency. She squeezed her eyes shut, childishly wishing it would all go away, and that when she opened them again, she would be back home in her own little cottage with Jack beside her.

He won't be there. He's not coming back. He's never coming back.

But no matter how many times she thought it, her heart refused to believe it was true, and running away from their home had not made her heart believe. He could be there even now, looking around the empty cottage with sad eyes, wondering where she had gone.

The music grew louder, and now it was accompanied by the sound of heavy feet clattering rhythmically on the floor and the cheers and claps of the crowd gathered around. Amelia pressed her hands tighter to her ears, tighter, and the world began to bubble and sway beneath her clamped eyelids. Her skin was suddenly cold and damp. Her knees curled into her chest as she tried to make herself smaller and smaller: small as a mouse, small as a mote of dust, small as the wishes in her secret heart.

Then she felt gentle hands at her wrist—big hands, masculine hands—pulling them away from her ears. The shock had her eyes flying open—*Jack*—but of course it wasn't Jack.

"It *is* you," Levi Lyman said, and his face had some of the same wonder she'd seen when the museum visitors looked at the elephant. "How is it you've come to be here?"

She felt a spurt of guilt—guilt for having sent him away without a second thought—followed quickly by panic. She'd been caught, caught here in this place, and now Levi Lyman would take her away to Barnum and they would put her in a cage. Everyone would come and see her and point and laugh and then men with knives would come and carve pieces from her flesh to study and she would never see the world or the ocean or her little cottage ever again . . .

Amelia yanked her wrists from his hands and tried to stand, tried to run, but she was as weak as the first time she'd stood upon the shore. The noise made her dizzy, and when she gasped, she breathed in death and all the blood in her body rushed into her face and then emptied and then there was blackness and a voice calling far away, "Mrs. Douglas? Mrs. Douglas?" Someone gathered her up, gentle as a bridegroom, and then all was dark and blessedly silent.

Amelia opened her eyes again to find herself the subject of some scrutiny. A dark-eyed little cherub with a head full of ringlets, perhaps eight or nine years old, stared at her with the fixed gaze of one determined to have answers.

The very instant Amelia met this stare, the girl said, "Is it true you're a mermaid?"

"Yes," Amelia said, without thinking. The child's personality demanded the truth, and it hadn't occurred to Amelia not to give it to her.

"I *knew* it," she breathed.

Then the girl turned abruptly and ran from the room, shouting, "Mama! Mama! She *is* a real mermaid, I told you so!"

Amelia realized she was on a rough velvet sofa, covered in a heavy wool blanket that made her sweat. She pushed herself up to a sitting position—slowly, very slowly—and marveled at how weak she felt. Almost immediately she wished she'd stayed prone, for the room tilted sideways and she had to lean back with her eyes closed again.

Where was she now? The last thing she remembered was Levi Lyman staring at her in amazement. Was that little girl his child? He hadn't mentioned a family; but then, Amelia reflected, they hadn't exactly gotten to know each other at their last encounter. She'd been too busy being clever with herself.

Amelia heard a rustle of skirts and peeked from beneath half-open lids at this new intruder. A pretty woman, a little careworn but dressed in the fashion of the respectable middle class, had entered the room. She held a toddler in one arm, a little girl who pulled on her mother's bun-tucked braids with fat fingers. The woman's stomach bulged—evidence of yet another child on its way. The woman's hand was pulled by the insistent curly-haired moppet. The girl pointed at Amelia.

"See, Mama, there she is," the girl said. "Look at her eyes and you'll see that she really is a mermaid. Uncle Levi told me she was, and she even said it was true."

"All right, Caroline, that's enough," the woman said, her face flushing a little when she noticed Amelia was awake and watching them. "Go along now to your room while I see to this lady."

"But I want to talk to the mermaid!" Caroline said. "I want to know how she changes into a fish and what her home is like under the sea and if she likes being a fish better than a girl or the other way around. If Helen can stay, I want to stay."

Caroline's mother glanced at Amelia, then at her daughter, and seemed to decide it was better to let the girl stay than have an argument before a stranger.

"Very well, but you must be quiet," the woman said.

She came toward Amelia then, with the slow, awkward progress of every woman carrying a baby. She gave a small polite smile and said, "How are you feeling now? I'm Mrs. Barnum, but you may call me Charity if you like. My husband is the owner of the museum."

Charity Barnum settled on a chair positioned near the corner of the sofa. Her older daughter curled on the floor with her head on her mother's knee. The younger child wriggled in her mother's arms, clearly dissatisfied with the lack of lap space available with her mother's pregnant belly in the way.

"You gave Mr. Lyman quite a scare," Mrs. Barnum continued when Amelia did not respond to her first question. "It was all I could do to keep him from carrying you off to the nearest doctor."

Amelia heard the words but couldn't make sense of them. From the moment Charity Barnum entered the room, Amelia was hypnotized by the roundness of her belly. Of course Amelia had seen pregnant women before—and babies and children, too—but always from a distance. She hadn't any friends in the village and had never been so close to a human mother.

There were, again, pregnant females among her own people, but that was so long ago she could hardly remember them. Anyway, that was before Jack, before the years of quiet wanting and heartbreak, before she sealed that unfulfilled desire closed so it couldn't hurt her.

Now this woman was before her, this sad-eyed woman who seemed drawn despite her plumpness, a woman with two children already expecting a third—a third!—and for the first time Amelia felt the green poison of jealousy in her veins. That one person should have so much and she nothing at all . . . it was almost too much to bear.

Amelia wondered, if she'd had a child—a chubby little doll like the small one now toddling around the room— would that have assuaged her grief after the sea took Jack? If some part of him lived on, would she have stood on those rocks day after day searching for him?

If she had not been there, waiting for him on a cliff by the sea, she certainly wouldn't be here now, wondering if she should take a job as Mr. Barnum's mermaid. There would have been no rumors about her, no accidental revelations of her real self to drunk fishermen.

Mrs. Barnum gave a little cough. Amelia realized she'd been staring and woolgathering and let the silence go on too long.

Oh, this was why she always had so much trouble around humans! There were endless rules to follow, and she didn't know or care about most of them. It never bothered Jack if she took too long to respond to his question or if she was silent for many minutes. At home she'd never had to interact with anyone in a parlor, for she'd never been invited to tea or anything else. She knew how to be properly human just long enough to complete a transaction at the general store.

"I'm feeling much better now, thank you," Amelia said. This, she was certain, was the correct thing to say even if she didn't feel better at all. One of the rules she did know was that truth wasn't particularly valued in polite company.

"I imagine you're hungry," Charity said, watching Amelia with an uncertain look on her face.

Amelia wondered if she'd not put enough conviction into her statement about feeling better. It didn't seem as though Charity believed her.

"I've asked the cook to bring you some beef tea," the other woman continued.

Amelia stopped herself from wrinkling her nose at the mention of "beef tea," but only just. She didn't know what it was except that it didn't sound very appetizing. What she really wanted was some regular tea with lots of sugar in it, but she didn't know how to ask for it.

Amelia vaguely remembered some restriction on making such a request when you were a guest, and Charity Barnum had seemed so pleased to offer the "beef tea." Amelia didn't want to hurt her hostess's feelings; Mrs. Barnum had the look of someone whose feelings were trampled upon with regularity.

The mermaid cast about for something to say, as one was supposed to do. Her interactions in the village had been limited primarily to the purchasing of goods and conversations about the weather. She didn't even know the state of the weather from this room as there were no windows.

Luckily Mrs. Barnum rescued her by taking up the conversation again.

"Mr. Lyman told me you are from Maine. Where are you staying while you visit New York?"

Amelia stared at her blankly. "Staying?"

She felt the first grip of panic then. *Stay. Of course.* She needed a room to sleep in, a boardinghouse or some such thing. That was what humans did. She knew this very well but had not thought of the necessity of arrangements.

She had not thought of anything (she could now admit this when faced with all the things she'd done wrong) except escaping her cottage and her rocks by the sea and the emptiness of her life there. It wasn't even that the place had been haunted by Jack. At least a ghost would have filled up the blank space.

Amelia had run from nothing, run with the same impulsiveness that had her chasing that ship so long ago. There was no plan other than a vague idea of taking up the offer Mr. Lyman presented. Of course she should have had some place to stay. She could hardly return to the harbor night after night.

Mrs. Barnum gazed at Amelia in expectation.

"I'm staying with friends," Amelia said.

Mrs. Barnum's expression told Amelia she didn't believe this story in the slightest but was too polite to say so. The older child huffed loudly.

"This is all very boring. When are you going to ask her about being a mermaid?"

Charity Barnum's eyes widened. "Caroline! You know better than to speak in such a way. Apologize to Mrs. Douglas."

Caroline's chin jutted mutinously from her small face.

Mrs. Barnum turned to Amelia. "I'm terribly sorry. We're having some difficulty finding a nanny at the moment—you know how hard it is to find good help—and she's accustomed to staying with me all day. I'm afraid that like many mothers I am a little more indulgent than I should be."

A blush rose in Mrs. Barnum's cheeks as she spoke, and her eyes darted around the room. Amelia followed her gaze, took in the sparse furnishings, and realized they hadn't the funds to pay for a nanny. Why this should be a source of embarrassment Amelia did not know—she and Jack had much less than this woman—but she was aware of the human custom that said discussing money was distasteful.

She'd never thought so much about the differences between herself and humans. Jack had never made her feel as strange as fifteen minutes in this woman's parlor had done.

Charity Barnum watched her anxiously, waiting for Amelia's polite reassurance that she was not offended by Caroline's behavior. Again, Amelia knew that it did not matter so much if she was actually offended or not, just that she told her hostess it was fine.

Before she had an opportunity to say a word, the child spoke again.

"*Mrs.* Douglas? How can you be a mermaid if you're a missus?" Her tone said that such things were not possible, and obviously this woman was a fake, because mermaids couldn't be something so mundane as a "missus."

"Because a fisherman trapped me in his net when I was swimming in the ocean," Amelia said, speaking directly to the girl.

All the scorn disappeared from Caroline's face. She approached Amelia with wide eyes, caught in the net of the mermaid's story. "And when he caught you he kept you, and that's how you became a missus?"

Amelia shook her head. "No, Jack would never do such a thing, for wild things should be free and I was very wild."

Wild and young, Amelia thought. She didn't look any older, but she was, and it was hard to think of that young and hopeful girl, the one who had walked so confidently into Jack's cottage and expected him to love her.

"And so he let you go?" Caroline asked.

"Yes," Amelia said.

"But you fell in love with him anyway," the little girl said, and took Amelia's cold hand.

"His eyes were so lonely," Amelia said, and her voice sounded like it came from someplace far away, not inside her body.

Caroline squeezed her hand. "And his loneliness made you sad."

"And made me realize I was lonely, too," Amelia said.

"So you fell in love and you were never lonely anymore."

Amelia's face was wet then, though she didn't know when she'd started crying.

Caroline climbed into her lap and put her little arms around Amelia's neck and rested her head against the mermaid's heart.

"And then he died, didn't he?" the little girl whispered. "And now you're alone again."

Amelia couldn't speak. Her voice had gone away, back to a place where Jack was pressing his face against hers, back to the time when she could breathe him in.

Caroline leaned back to look into Amelia's eyes. "Don't worry. You can be our mermaid and live with us and you'll never be lonely again."

"Caroline," Charity said, but soft and full of weeping.

CHAPTER 4

Levi stood outside the door, his back pressed against the wall. In his hands he held a tray with a dish of beef broth, rapidly cooling, and a small hunk of bread. He'd waylaid the cook on her way to the parlor and convinced her to give over the tray.

He'd wanted an excuse to see her, though Charity treated him like a member of the family and would not have objected if he joined them without any specific reason. But his heart thrummed in anticipation as he took the tray from the cook; he didn't think the mermaid would be able to hear it beating for her, but he couldn't be sure.

The sight of her in the museum had seemed an impossible thing: the illusory manifestation of his deepest heart's desire rather than an actual happening. Until she was there, he hadn't realized just how much he'd longed to see her. He had convinced himself that the visit to the woman on the rocks was nothing more than a minor adventure. If he dreamed every night of flashing fins and grey eyes rising from the water then at least those shadows were banished by the time he stood at his shaving mirror every morning.

Even if he'd accustomed himself to the idea that she was really in New York, he couldn't understand *why*. Why, after she'd sent him away without a backward glance? Could she have changed her mind about Barnum's proposal?

Could she have come to see you? a very small voice in the back of his mind asked.

Of course not, the sensible part of him replied.

But that little voice murmured behind his ear all the same as he lifted her fainting body and felt how thin she was, so thin. At the same time there was something strong and powerful under her skin and she smelled of the sea, of salt and storms and the merciless wind and monsters that rose from the dark.

He knew then, without any other proof, that she was a mermaid, a real mermaid, and far from wanting her in Barnum's tank, he wanted her to return to the ocean or to her cottage on the rocks or just go anywhere but there, for Barnum would take all of her magic and twist it out of her until the enchantment was gone, and Levi was afraid for her, so afraid.

He didn't know where to take her then. He couldn't run

through the streets of New York bearing a strange woman until he reached the harbor. What would he do when he got there—toss her into the water and leave? Would the ocean heal her?

A doctor, too, was out of the question. What might happen if the doctor examined her? Was her secret written somewhere on her body, waiting to be discovered? Levi saw that she had legs instead of a fin, of course, but knew nothing of how a change might be triggered. If a well-meaning assistant laid a cold compress across her forehead, would the mere presence of water make her change? What did he know of mermaids?

Nothing, except that he knew he held one in his arms and the safest thing had been to bring her to the Barnums' apartment in the museum. But he couldn't escape the feeling that he was depositing her inside a cage and there was nothing to be done about it.

Now she was there in Charity Barnum's threadbare parlor, and he stood outside holding the tray, listening to the grief in her voice. As he listened, the dream inside him died a little, for anyone who loved her dead husband so much had surely not come all that way just to see Levi Lyman again.

Hope would not leave him entirely, for hope is a clinging, tenacious thing, almost impossible to dislodge. She might not have traveled all that way for him, but that didn't mean he couldn't convince her of his value.

First, though, he had to keep her safe from Barnum. This couldn't be like Joice Heth again. Levi wouldn't let it be like that again.

Levi straightened and went into the room with his face carefully neutral. He was a showman, after all. In that he and Barnum were two pod-peas.

Amelia and Caroline were snuggled on the sofa like puzzle pieces finally united. Charity gazed at Levi as he entered, and he saw so many things in her eyes—bewilderment, disbelief, mild embarrassment. She had the red-nosed wet look of someone who would like to cry but is determinedly squashing that impulse.

The atmosphere seemed thick with unsaid words, and it was Levi's impression that most of those words were Charity's. He let a smile turn up his mouth in hopes that it would make the others smile, too.

He was a performer, playing his part. It was his performance that had sold Joice Heth to the world. For the first time that thought heartened him. Barnum would never be able to sell a mermaid to the public without Levi. That meant Levi would always be with Amelia, making sure Barnum treated her well.

And he'd always be with Amelia. That was a reward in itself.

"How are you feeling now? The cook sent this for you," he said, presenting the tray with a flourish.

Caroline wriggled away from Amelia so the mermaid could take the tray. Amelia set it in her lap and wrinkled her nose at the dish.

Levi laughed at her expression, and all the ladies looked at him in surprise, even little Helen. His laugh cut through the miasma of unspoken things, made it dissipate. Caroline laughed, too—the laughter of a child who doesn't know why she's doing it, only that the grown-ups are and she wants to be a part of it, too.

"I don't like beef tea, either," Levi confided to Amelia. "Caroline, do you think you could go to the kitchen and have a pot of regular tea made up?"

He cut his eyes to Charity, who nodded.

"And bring lots of sugar," he added, winking at Amelia.

She gave him a startled look, though he didn't know if it was because she was surprised he remembered or just because he'd winked at her.

"And can we have some bread and butter also?" Caroline asked, abandoning her new friend for the delights of ordering tea just like a grown-up.

When Caroline left, Levi asked again, "And how are you feeling now, Mrs. Douglas?"

She stared at him with those eyes, those very straightforward eyes, and said, "That is not what you wish to know, Mr. Lyman. You wish to know why I am here after I was so rude about your offer."

Charity shifted, her petticoats rustling. She was clearly uncomfortable with this degree of frankness.

Levi, though, was already accustomed to the mermaid's ways. It felt natural to meet her honesty with his own.

"Yes, I wondered that."

Amelia took a deep breath, and Levi felt she stood on some great precipice. He wished he could tell her that he was there beside her and that he wouldn't let her fall.

"I wish to accept Mr. Barnum's offer of employment. And I have some terms of my own as well," she said.

Of course this was why she came. She wanted something, and Barnum could give it to her. Levi remembered the simple cottage in Maine, the handmade furnishings, the threadbare dress she wore. She needed money. Well, he would make certain that she got it. This would not be like Joice Heth again.

Perhaps if he repeated it to himself enough times it would be true—*not like Joice Heth, not like Joice Heth*. Barnum wasn't going to take Amelia and make her perform even if she didn't want to. He wasn't going to cheat her of money for his own benefit. Levi would be there to make sure of it. Though the person who needed to hear that this would not be like Joice Heth was Barnum. Barnum's memory could be dangerously short.

"Should I speak directly to Mr. Barnum, or do you represent him?" the mermaid asked.

Levi did not think it was a good idea to bring Barnum in at this stage. He might scare Amelia off. Not that Barnum wasn't any good at negotiating deals—he was, exceptionally so—but Levi didn't think Barnum's hard tactics would work in this case.

"Mr. Barnum intended for me to represent him all along," Levi said easily. "And I'm certain we can come to terms that suit everyone. There's just one small matter we need to resolve before any performance."

Amelia understood him immediately. "I have to show you that I really am a mermaid."

Charity gave a little gasp, and Levi and Amelia both turned toward her. Levi had half forgotten Barnum's wife was in the room. The world had narrowed to just him and Amelia.

Charity's face reddened. "Surely you don't believe such nonsense, Levi! It's one thing for this woman to tell stories to Caroline, but you should know better. You're a grown man." She turned to Amelia. "And you, Mrs. Douglas—if I had any idea that you were planning to deceive my husband in such a way, I would not have had you in my parlor."

"It's not deception, Mrs. Barnum," Amelia said. "And I can prove it."

Levi knew it had cost Charity something to say those words, especially when she was usually withdrawn in company. He also knew that anything she said was less about Amelia than it was about Barnum. Charity endured more than anyone, scraping by while Barnum pursued fame, fortune, and the general fanfare of his name. Barnum also wasn't averse to mocking Charity when with others. It was likely the best thing for her that Barnum wasn't often in the family apartment.

"It's not a humbug, Charity," Levi said, but gently. He didn't want to dismiss her as he'd seen Barnum do so often.

"Of course it is! It's just another one of Taylor's ridiculous schemes, and this woman is a part of it. There are no such things as mermaids," Charity snapped.

Amelia only shook her head and said, "I'm sorry you think so."

Levi stood. "Perhaps we should discuss this elsewhere. You shouldn't get so excited in your condition, Charity."

"Sit down, Levi Lyman," Charity said. "I know better than you what I can and can't do in my condition. It's not appropriate for you to take this woman somewhere else after placing her in my care. Besides, if she's here to speak to Taylor, then there is no better place than his own parlor."

Levi could have pointed out that these statements clearly contradicted her earlier feelings, but he sensed that Charity was in uncharted waters. She knew very well that Barnum was a regular old confidence man and that he recruited folks to perpetuate his legends.

But Amelia was something else, something different. Even in the conviction of disbelief Charity could sense that, Levi was certain. He'd felt it himself when first in Amelia's presence.

It was her eyes. Those eyes were not human, and they never would be, no matter how long she lived among them. She hadn't caught the habit of looking away periodically when talking or demurely casting her eyes downward.

Levi wondered what her husband had been like. Her directness must not have troubled him, else she would have at least tried for his sake. She seemed to have loved him that much.

And so Amelia and Levi agreed to their terms of employment under Charity's disapproving eye. Amelia wanted a certain salary; Levi convinced her to ask for less but take a percentage of the ticket sales. Barnum was sure to make money hand over fist off this woman, and any salary he paid her would be much less than she could take in sales. They agreed to a trial period of six months, after which either party could leave or a new contract could be negotiated.

At this point Levi was glad of Charity's presence. He wanted a witness in case Barnum decided to ignore the six-month provision and try to force Amelia to stay. There was no fear that Charity would side with Barnum in that case—she was scrupulously honest and didn't mind contradicting him if the truth required it.

Amelia didn't know all the terms and phrases used in contracts, but she clearly knew what she wanted and was determined to get it. She told Levi she wanted enough money to travel the world. He forbore from telling her that women didn't generally travel about on their own—there was no point in discouraging her, it might make her leave—but he knew she'd need a great deal more than she had now. He couldn't guarantee her enough money to see everything she wanted to see, but he promised to make a good start of it. It made Levi feel better knowing that she wasn't about to let Barnum take advantage of her, and that he could guide her in that effort.

And he'd be there to make sure of that in any case. He wouldn't let her sign a contract that wouldn't benefit her.

Levi said he would have it all written up, and then she and Barnum could sign it so it would be official. He saw a flicker in Amelia's eyes and wondered if she already had second thoughts.

He slapped his hands on his thighs and stood. "Now to tell Taylor," he said, and frowned a little. "We'll have to make an arrangement for your, er, demonstration as well. At a date and time of your choosing."

Amelia nodded at this, though Charity scowled.

Caroline, who had returned partway through the proceedings proudly bearing a tea tray, spoke through a mouthful of bread and butter.

"Are you going to show how you turn into a mermaid? Oh, I want to see that!"

"And you will," Levi said. "Soon everyone in New York City will see the marvelous wonder of Barnum's mermaid."

Amelia's hands clenched suddenly, as if she didn't like the idea of being "Barnum's" mermaid.

"It's not too late," Levi said softly.

She looked up at him, her gaze hardening. "I won't change my mind."

He reached out a hand to her. She stared at it for so long he wondered if she would take it. Finally, she placed her fingers in his. Levi was struck by the sudden desire to hold tight, to never let her go. Only the certain knowledge that she would hate anyone who tried to catch her let him release her once she was standing.

"Where is Mr. Barnum?" she asked.

Levi grinned. "In the museum, of course. He's an exhibit."

"Just like me," Amelia murmured.

No, Levi thought. *There's no one in the world like you, and as soon as Barnum sees you he'll know it, too.*

Barnum didn't seem to belong in his own parlor. That was the first thing Amelia thought when she saw him.

Levi had gone to fetch Barnum from the museum—"It won't do to have this conversation out in the open with everyone watching," he'd said—and Amelia had waited in the apartment with a silent Charity and a chattering Caroline. The toddler, Helen, began to fuss just as Levi returned with Barnum, and Charity seized the opportunity to depart, bestowing a cold nod on Amelia as she left.

Amelia was sorry the other woman thought her a trickster, but there was nothing to be done about it. When Amelia was in a tank in the museum and Charity finally saw her there, she would have to believe. In the meantime, there wasn't any purpose in trying to change Charity's mind.

Barnum wasn't especially tall or especially handsome—he had dark curly hair and a squashed potato nose and a dent in his chin and dressed like most of the other men she'd seen in New York. He would have been perfectly ordinary except for his manner, which seemed to suck up all the air in the room. There was more of his personality than could fit inside his body, and she could see how he could trample you with that personality. Amelia was fairly certain he'd already done it to Charity, and she wasn't about to let him do it to her.

"Mrs. Douglas, Mrs. Douglas," Barnum said, grasping her hand and shaking it up and down with more force than was strictly necessary. "So my friend Levi here managed to convince you to come and see us, did he? You'll be our mermaid in the museum?"

"Yes," Amelia said.

She could tell by his expression that he expected her to say more. To his credit, he didn't linger or indicate that she was at fault but rolled on with his own conversation.

"Now Levi tells me that the two of you have come to some agreements about terms. He's a lawyer so he's going to lay all of this out for us in a contract and then we'll both sign it and it will be all legal and binding."

She didn't really care for the way he said "binding"; it made her think he was imagining something more permanent than she intended.

"Why don't we have Mr. Lyman review the terms for us now?" she said coolly. "There is one term, in particular, that should be clear before we go on."

"I'm certain that any financial arrangement—" Barnum began, but Amelia interrupted him. She felt a flash of satisfaction when she saw irritation cross his face.

"It's not about finances. It's about my magic," she said. "As part of the terms I need to demonstrate to you that I am, in fact, a mermaid. You can likely tell me where is the best place for this demonstration, but I will tell you that I need both privacy and the cover of darkness. As well as salt water, of course. There is no change without salt water."

This time she had managed to silence him. A number of feelings marched in succession—surprise, disbelief, and finally indulgence.

Ah. He's going to go along with me because he thinks I'm touched in the head.

"Yes, of course," he said smoothly. "Whatever you like, my dear."

He won't be "my dear"-ing me later, Amelia thought. *He won't be able to believe his eyes.*

It was the first time she'd ever truly acknowledged to herself that she was something unique among humans, that her ability made her special. Just thinking it made her realize something she'd not thought about properly before.

Barnum needed her. Oh, he could certainly fake up a mermaid with a girl and a costume, but it wouldn't be like her. It wouldn't be a real mermaid.

He needed her, though he might not know how much yet.

She gave a little smile and nodded to Levi. "Let's discuss our terms, then, Mr. Barnum."

The boy had done it. He'd *done* it.

Barnum had thought when Levi returned from Maine empty-handed that he'd be stuck showing that old mummy Moses brought him. Lord knew it would have been a slog to sell that shriveled thing—though he could have done it, he was sure; he could sell anything to anybody, and anyone who knew him could tell the truth of that.

But this girl! Never mind her claim that she was a real mermaid—a thing Barnum could hardly countenance— she *looked* like a real mermaid. All that black hair flowing everywhere and her eyes . . . Barnum had never seen eyes like that.

He knew now why there were so many rumors about her. And of course, the woman seemed to believe it herself. She was addled, no doubt, but her belief would help sell the mermaid notion to the public.

He'd have to keep her contact with newspapermen at a minimum, at least at first. The girl was a little *too* honest. Those remarks about the "dead things" in the museum wouldn't do. Levi could do all the talking for the time being. He was good at that.

Barnum would think up a spectacular costume for her. It would be tricky, because as Levi said there were always the church ladies to consider, and church ladies would not approve of a bare-chested nymph frolicking in the water.

Barnum remembered those grim-faced women at the Congregational Church in Bethel, and Sundays spent on hard wooden pews being told that man was by nature depraved, that God had selected a chosen few to enter heaven and that everyone else was destined for hell no matter what they did in life.

He'd decided pretty young that if it didn't matter what he did, he might as well have fun. As a showman, he downright relied on humankind's essentially depraved nature.

Barnum hoped that the girl—Amelia, her name was—wouldn't object to the type of costume he wanted. Which reminded him that he would have to get her to eat more. She was as thin as a washboard. Men liked to see a nice, round, healthy-looking woman—round in all the right places, that is. He'd speak to Charity about it, make sure his wife knew the girl was to eat and to have Cook make plenty of fattening foods.

Charity hadn't liked the notion of the woman staying with them in their apartment, but Barnum had stood firm. It was his apartment and his museum, and he wouldn't have his mermaid walking to and from a boardinghouse like some common serving maid.

At least he wouldn't have her doing that until she'd made her debut to the world. The first glimpse anyone would have of that girl would be onstage in the museum.

After that, any public appearances (including walking to and from appropriate lodgings) would be in the interests of publicity.

Barnum frowned, thinking of the plain wool dress and ugly shoes Amelia wore. He'd have to buy her a new wardrobe. She needed both fashionable day wear and some exotic and glamorous things, something that would befit a mermaid.

While he was at it, he'd have to come up with a better name for her. "Amelia Douglas from the Middle of Nowhere, Maine" didn't have a ring to it. Everyone knew mermaids were from warm places, anyhow, not some ice-encrusted northern town.

The Caribbean Mermaid? The Bermuda Mermaid? No. He'd think of something, though. His mermaid was going to be a wonder such that the world had never seen.

There were other problems to consider. He'd need a tank big enough to show the girl—though she was skinny, she wasn't the size of a goldfish, and she would need room to swim around. That would cost a fair bit; he'd have to find someone to make a tank especially for him.

Then there was the trick of showing the mermaid's "change." There would have to be some illusion involved there. No one, not even the most gullible audience members, would buy that the girl was a mermaid if they didn't see her walking on two legs first.

He knew a bit about magician's illusions. There had been a magician in Barnum's Grand Scientific and Musical Theater traveling show. He had seen Joe Pentland practicing his tricks plenty of times, and Barnum knew about things like holes in the floor to pass new objects into a hat or the sleight of hand that disguised the disappearance and reappearance of a coin.

Once Barnum had actually stood in as an assistant when the original man ran off right before a show. His mind tried to slide away from what happened next—how was he to know that squirrel would bite? Pentland had pulled that creature out of his hat dozens of times without incident.

Despite the regrettable outcome—Barnum shrieked in

pain, smashed the table, and generally caused such a commotion that the audience asked for its money back—he knew enough about curtains and panels to rig up something that would convince everyone the mermaid was real.

And he'd even be able to satisfy Moses and use that old mummy. There could be a separate exhibit with a "scientific" history of mermaids with the monkey-fish at the center of it all.

But first he had to get the public excited about all that. He sat at his desk in the museum, listening to the building settle. The only other sound was that of his pen scratching on paper as he laid out his plan. If he did this right, there would be money falling from the sky.

His mermaid was going to make his fortune. He could feel it.

Amelia had never before slept in a place where she couldn't hear the ocean. The small guest room where Charity placed her had only one small window, and that provided hardly any air. Amelia had struggled simply to open it in the first place. Nobody seemed to have done so before, and open windows were treated with suspicion by Charity, who appeared content to sit in stifling rooms all day.

Amelia could not smell the ocean from the window, not even the merest breath of salt. There were people out and moving about despite the hour, a continuous clop of horses' hooves or bootheels on cobblestones.

The ever-present stink of pigs and animal waste drifted into the room, and Amelia closed the small window in frustration. People *chose* to live in this place, a place where all they could see were buildings and animals and more people and more people and more people, everywhere you went.

Barnum told her proudly that more than three hundred thousand people lived in the city, and more came every day. Amelia marveled that so many would choose to abandon the ocean or the forest or the wide-open fields and choose to live stacked on top of one another in a place where pigs had free rein in the streets. She wondered that she herself had made this choice. New York was supposed to be a marvel, but it mostly just felt like there was no space anywhere.

As for Barnum himself . . . she'd seen the way he looked at her as they'd talked. Like a possession. Like one of the dead things the throngs gawped at in the museum.

She'd noticed, too, the way Levi Lyman tried to stand between Barnum and herself, the way he gave her looks that told her it was better if she didn't speak as much and left it to him, and how he'd so firmly stated the terms of their agreement in a way that would brook no argument from Barnum. It was clear from his manner that he'd designated himself her protector. She didn't need protecting, but it was touching all the same.

Amelia let him do it, because she wanted a good look at Barnum. She might not be able to read words very well, but she could read faces, and her mind worked just fine, thank you very kindly. She had a fairly shrewd idea of what Barnum intended—to use her to wring out every coin he could get and to give her as few of them as possible.

Well, she wasn't going to allow him to do that. She was doing this for her own reasons, and she would be damned before she let P. T. Barnum cheat her. She hadn't crossed the ocean to be taken in by a confidence man.

Besides, she thought with a little smirk, he still thought she was a fake. His face clearly told her he believed her to be soft in the head. She would enjoy the expression on his face when he saw her change. She would enjoy serving crow to him on a platter.

Amelia rolled onto her back and stared at the cracks in the ceiling, just visible in the gloom. She breathed in through her nose and out through her mouth, trying to duplicate the sound of the sea.

If she closed her eyes, she could almost pretend she was back in the cottage, Jack asleep beside her, listening to the ebb and flow of the water crashing into the rocks below.

CHAPTER 5

Amelia wrinkled her nose at the crush of people aboard the steamer. Was there nowhere she could go where she was not surrounded by hordes?

Despite living in Barnum's apartment for three weeks and taking regular excursions into the streets of New York City (accompanied always by Levi Lyman, who she suspected was following instructions from Barnum to not leave her alone), she was still not accustomed to the feeling of constantly having bodies all around her. Perfumed, sweating bodies, bodies that smelled like wet wool or pipe smoke or starched petticoats. There was never anywhere to get a breath of fresh air; it seemed to her very often that there wasn't enough air to go around.

At least she could breathe in the sea from the ship deck,

though that was nearly drowned out by the belching smoke coming from the belly of the contraption.

On either side of her stood Levi and Barnum, flanking her like the two burly constables she'd seen dragging an intoxicated man along Ann Street.

Neither Levi nor Barnum had touched her other than to offer an arm to assist boarding, but she had the distinct feeling neither of them would hesitate to grab her if it seemed she might slip away.

Though Levi's reasons are different from Barnum's, she admitted. Amelia had not failed to notice the looks Levi gave when he thought she wasn't looking. He had stardust in his eyes, and Amelia was sorry for it.

He had not expressed this feeling in any way, which was a relief. There could be no good outcome from such a thing, not when her heart was still full of Jack. And she could use an ally against Barnum, who would press for every advantage.

Beside her, Barnum scowled as he stared over the railing. He'd been strongly vocal against what he called "this tomfoolery."

Privately Levi told her that Barnum probably objected to the expense of going to Rhode Island. He loved to make money, but he despised spending it on things he couldn't see immediately profited. But Amelia had been adamant that she needed a secluded beach and nightfall for a mermaid demonstration, and it was faster to take the ship to Providence than it was to cross to New Jersey and take a train to the coast. There was nothing like privacy on the island of Manhattan. She wasn't about to change on a crowded beach in daylight. This first time she wanted only Levi and Barnum to see her; she wasn't ready for the world yet.

All of this necessitated staying in a hotel overnight. Amelia already knew that Barnum was terribly tightfisted with his personal expenses. Almost all the money that came into the museum was put by for the museum—either to pay off the loan Barnum had taken out for its purchase or to invest in new acquisitions to exhibit. Charity spent an inordinate amount of time carefully mending her and the children's clothing. Amelia, accustomed to thrift, saw no shame in this, but Charity clearly felt it was something to hide. People of her station did not mend their own clothes.

Amelia had been unable to hide her embarrassment when Barnum presented her with a new trunk of dresses in Charity's presence. The look on Charity's face as Amelia opened the box . . . the mermaid had never seen such hurt, or such longing.

Amelia immediately tried to refuse the garments. She did not want to start her relationship with Barnum owing him anything, and anyway he ought to save such gestures for his wife.

He was quite insistent that she needed to dress presentably, that she owned nothing adequate to need, and "Charity is too fat to wear any of these," he'd said, and laughed.

His wife's cheeks had reddened, but she hadn't spoken a word. Amelia wished she would show some spirit, but she knew Charity would not thank her for saying so.

Amelia rather liked Charity, though the woman continued to view her with suspicious reserve. The mermaid knew Barnum's wife thought her a trickster, someone out to take advantage of Barnum. There was really nothing more ridiculous than the thought of Barnum getting taken; if there was any taking to do, Amelia knew very well that he would be the one to do it.

She did not like the way he treated his wife and children at all, however. He wasn't often with them, showed scant affection to his daughters, and actively mocked Charity when others were in earshot.

It hardened Amelia's initial impression of a man out to get what he could only for himself, with no concern for anyone but the paying public.

Even without Charity's humiliation Amelia would have gladly sent away the trunk of clothing. Inside it were things Amelia had never worn before but was now expected to— dresses that required corsets and petticoats (sometimes five or six at a time), bonnets with such deep brims that Amelia often couldn't see someone standing at her shoulder, capes, black lace mitts that did not warm the hands but were supposed to be flirtatious and fashionable.

Women generally carried a parasol whenever they were outdoors; Amelia felt so foolish holding it up against the sun that it often wound up banging uselessly against her hip.

The first time she saw herself in a mirror with all the requisite geegaws and her hair parted in the middle and pulled into a bun, she'd been unable to stop herself from crying.

Charity, who'd helped her into all the clothing and expected Amelia to be as thrilled as she would be had asked, "Whatever is the matter?"

Amelia, forgetting that truth was not preferred by polite people, blurted, "I look like a human."

When Charity cautiously asked what she expected to look like, Amelia dried her face and exclaimed (in a patently false voice) that she'd never had such lovely things before.

She hated it all, every string and ruffle and bit of lace. The greatest relief of her day was unwinding the many required layers, removing her corset, and loosening her hair.

She took to lying on her bed, fully naked atop the coverlet, convinced that her garments would slowly kill her if her skin was not allowed to breathe.

The awkwardness of the skirts was exacerbated in large crowds like the ones on the ferry. Women's dresses were always bumping into other women's dresses and brushing against men's trouser legs. Amelia imagined a whole universe of polite "excuse me"s occurring at ankle level.

Levi also frowned at the water as Barnum did. The two of

them were a matched pair with Amelia in the center. Amelia suspected, though, that Levi's distress was related to the forthcoming revelation. She knew Levi believed the truth—that she was a mermaid. It wasn't anything explicit he'd said to her or even a change in his manner; rather, it manifested in the way he spoke to Barnum about her.

This was apparent when she'd repeated to Barnum the week before that she would not appear onstage without a demonstration.

"Demonstration of what?" he'd asked.

"Of my abilities," Amelia said patiently. "You should know precisely what I am before you show me to all and sundry."

It was vital that Barnum know this wasn't a "humbug," as he called it. She needed salt water and not fresh in the tank or she wouldn't change. The only way to convince him to take on the extra trouble and expense of salt water was to show him that she needed it.

She also knew that her true form, her water form, did not resemble in the least the advertisements Barnum was designing. These woodcuts depicted beautiful bare-breasted women with fish tails.

Amelia's people did not look like these. She did not look like a woman when she was in the water. She looked like what she was—a mermaid, a creature of the sea.

So she'd insisted, and quite firmly, that there would be no performance until Barnum witnessed her change.

"That's enough of this foolishness," Barnum said.

The tips of his ears turned red—a sign that he was about to display a rare bit of temper. But Levi cut him off before he could get started.

"It's not foolishness, Taylor. You'll want to see this," Levi said.

Barnum looked from Amelia to Levi. "You buy all this nonsense, Levi? I thought you said you never went near the water when you were in Maine."

"I didn't need to," Levi said.

He wasn't loud or angry or blustering. He just looked at Barnum with steady dark eyes until the other man relented.

"This had better be worth it," he grumbled.

Barnum still didn't believe, even though he'd bought the tickets and reserved the hotel rooms. He had to acknowledge there was no mermaid program without her, and with Levi on her side, he'd been close to a mutiny. Amelia knew Barnum wouldn't risk the whole show, so he'd decided to err on the side of keeping her content.

He'd have preferred, she knew, to be in the museum thinking up schemes and illusions. Barnum had proposed a ridiculous notion that involved Amelia changing into a costumed fish tail in the water of the tank.

"The audience has to see you change from girl to fish, you see? We can use curtains and lighting to do the trick. I was thinking if we showed only your silhouette—"

"You won't need tricks," Amelia interrupted. "You only need salt water, and I'll prove it to you."

Barnum gave her a dubious look and went on describing his plan to fool the public. She sighed and let him go on talking. He would see soon enough.

She was, she admitted to herself, a little nervous. It was a strange feeling, a queasy shaking in the hollow of her stomach. It took Amelia a long time to figure out just what it was, for she couldn't recall ever feeling that way before.

This was the first time she'd ever purposely shown someone her water form—the time Jack caught her in his net she hadn't *meant* to be seen.

And she certainly hadn't meant for that fisherman to see her, either—the drunk who'd spread tales of her all up and down the coast of Maine.

Amelia wondered what the villagers would think if they heard she was displaying herself in a tank in New York City. They'd protected her from interlopers like Barnum and Levi, had let her live and grieve in her own way, and she was grateful to them.

But this was her choice now—her choice to be something other than Jack's wife, or one small town's mermaid mascot.

What will you be to Barnum, though? What will you be once he sees who you really are?

* * *

The hotel was nowhere near the beach, of course. Beachfront property was expensive, and Barnum never paid an extra penny unless it was to a purpose. Besides, they didn't want to bump into hotel guests while about their business. The mermaid was a secret until someone paid for a ticket to see her.

Levi knew that if circumstances were different—say, if they were touring the country to display the mermaid—Barnum would book them in the finest room in town, with all the attendant fanfare. As it was, Barnum grumbled about the cost of two rooms and the fact that Amelia needed her own.

Amelia gave the showman such a look at this that Barnum actually blushed. It was no small thing to embarrass Barnum; Levi thought he'd been born shameless.

Barnum arranged for a coach to take them to the waterfront several hours after dark. The coachman asked no questions, although he did look askance at two men and one woman leaving a boardinghouse in the middle of the night.

Amelia's face was veiled. Barnum and Levi wore their hats low over their faces. Levi was unlikely to be recognized, but Barnum might be. You never knew who had been to the museum and spotted him at his desk in the exhibition hall.

Amelia was completely silent during the ride. Levi wondered what she was thinking, then wondered if he would ever have the right to know the answer, if that was a privilege she would ever give him.

The horse and carriage stopped on a little rise, and the three of them climbed out. Amelia waved away Levi's hand when he offered to help her down. Barnum told the driver to return in an hour, and the three of them waited until the coach was out of sight before descending to the beach.

There was a path that led through tall scrubby grass down to the sand below. The moon rose full and high, and the stretch of beach they were on seemed dangerously exposed, to Levi's way of thinking. Farther down the beach, perhaps a half mile or more, a large hotel was perched on the rise. But there was no one nearby, no movement on the water or the sand, and Levi thought it would be safe. He hoped it would be safe.

Barnum grumbled about the rocks, the footing, the scratchiness of the grass, but Amelia moved forward with surety toward the ocean. Levi realized he hadn't seen her this way since Maine; in New York she was just a fraction more hesitant in everything she did. It was as if she constantly weighed and measured every action and potential response for correctness. The result was that she was always sober and distant; he couldn't recall ever seeing her smile.

Levi had made a game of trying to make her happy— taking her to all his favorite places in the city, bringing her sweets he thought she would enjoy, reading humorous stories aloud in Charity's parlor.

Amelia's response was always the same—grave

appreciation. It did seem sincere, but there was no joy in it. She reached the beach long before they did. Levi was a little way behind her on the path, and Barnum farther back, not bothering to disguise his curses.

She shed the bonnet and veil first, dropping them in the sand like trash, and unbound her hair as she walked. She'd changed into the same plain dress she wore on her arrival in New York, and now he knew why—the dress was off her body in a flash, a feat she'd never have managed with a gown made for corset and petticoats.

Beneath it she wore nothing at all. He gasped when he saw how thin she was, even thinner than when she arrived, despite Barnum's edict that she fatten up.

Amelia stopped when she reached the edge of the water. Levi paused at the bottom of the path, staring. Her pale skin seemed luminescent in the moonlight. Barnum stumbled to Levi's side, muttering under his breath and shaking sand from his pant cuffs.

Amelia glanced over her shoulder, just long enough to be sure they were watching, and Levi sucked in a hard breath. She was smiling.

There was so much pure joy on her face it was like he'd been shown happiness for the first time. Then her feet touched the water and it happened.

The moonlight was as clear and strong as sunlight on that beach and there was no mistaking what happened, but it was still hard to accept. His brain didn't understand even though he *knew* she was a mermaid.

Grey scales climbed her white skin, and as they did, her legs seemed to fuse and then disappear and she fell forward into the water.

Her tail flipped up into the night air. She quickly wriggled out of the shallows and disappeared.

It had all happened so quickly that part of him still didn't believe it. One moment she was there and human; the next moment she was something else and gone.

Barnum was still, as still as death, and when Levi glanced at him, Barnum's eyes were straining out of his skull. Levi had never seen someone's jaw actually drop open in surprise, but Barnum's practically touched his collarbone.

"Levi?" he asked. He didn't sound like himself. His voice sounded like it came from far away, like it had to climb out of his chest.

"Yes, Taylor?"

"Did we just see that girl turn into a mermaid?"

Levi grinned. "Yes, Taylor, we did."

Barnum paused. "Did you see the scales?"

"Yes, Taylor."

There was another short silence. "You don't think that was some sort of humbug, do you?"

"I don't see how it could be," said Levi.

"I don't see how it could be, either," Barnum said. Then,

with just a touch of anxiety, "Where do you think she's got off to?"

Levi had watched the water intently since she disappeared. "I imagine she's gone swimming. She hasn't been able to since she arrived at the museum."

Barnum grunted. "Soon she'll be able to swim all she wants. Once I have that tank built."

"I don't think it's quite the same, Taylor," Levi said. "A tank isn't the size of the ocean."

"I hope she hasn't decided to swim away on us," Barnum said.

He sounded more like himself again—businesslike, his eyes on the main chance.

"It would be a lot of trouble to track her down when I've finally managed to catch a real mermaid."

"You didn't catch her, Barnum," Levi said, and his voice was sharper than he intended. "She came to you willingly, and if she wants to leave, she will. She doesn't owe you anything."

Barnum made a placating gesture with his hand. "All right, all right, no need to get worked up. The girl is as free as the proverbial bird. Although I did spend a load of money on those clothes."

"She didn't ask you for them," Levi said.

"Fair enough, fair enough," Barnum said.

Levi didn't think Barnum would let it go that easily. He

was sure to tot up every expense against what Amelia earned. It was up to Levi to ensure he didn't get away with it.

Just then there was a splash, and Amelia's head broke through the water perhaps fifteen or twenty feet from shore. She floated there, her head and shoulders just above the gentle waves, staring at them.

Levi crossed the beach, wanting to see her better, wanting to know everything there was to know about her. He stopped when his boots touched the damp sand. He wasn't afraid of getting wet, but he didn't want to startle her. She was suddenly more animal than human, like a deer he'd stumbled upon while walking in a forest. She would be still until he moved and then she would dart away, leaving nothing more than a flash of her tail to remember her by.

He couldn't discern every detail, but it was apparent even from this distance that there wasn't much of the human left about her. Those shiny fish scales covered her everywhere, not just her legs. Her jaw was longer, the shape of her face a little different, the nose flatter, the nostrils wider. She was altogether a different mermaid than the ones painted by dreamy-eyed artists.

This wasn't half woman, half fish. This was an alien creature, and she didn't belong to Barnum or anyone else.

Then she shifted and swam slowly toward the place where he stood. Her head stayed above the water, her eyes fixed on his. Those eyes—they were Amelia's eyes, grey and straightforward and demanding, demanding that he accept what he saw and not some fantasy.

He kept his gaze on hers and nodded. He understood what she wanted. He saw what she was and not what he wanted to see.

As she reached the shallows, all the details of her body came into sharper relief—the webbing of her hands, the pointed claws, and (just for an instant) her sharp, sharp teeth.

He thought sailors must drink a great deal of rum at sea to believe mermaids were beguiling sea nymphs. This creature looked as though she'd rather slash your throat than seduce you.

Amelia swam toward him—or slithered really, pulling herself along the shallows. She reached for the sand that was just past the licking of the waves, just near where he stood so still and waited for her.

Levi saw the scales disappear, the smooth, pale human skin reappear from the point where her fingers touched the sand and then all along her body. It was almost as if her body turned itself inside out; underneath the mermaid the human mask waited.

She stood, shivering, and he ran to fetch her dress. He averted his eyes as he handed it to her, which seemed to amuse her. Amelia gave a little snort of laughter as she pulled the dress over her head.

Wonderful, he thought gloomily. *All those days I tried to make her laugh and the only time I succeed is when I try to respect her sense of modesty.*

He took his coat off and put it around her shoulders, for she was still shaking with cold.

"Thank you," she said, and then glanced past his shoulder. "Well, Mr. Barnum?"

Levi had forgotten Barnum completely. He followed Amelia's gaze and found the other man giving him a speculative look. Levi wondered what it meant.

"Well, Mrs. Douglas," Barnum said. "That was spectacular. Indeed, one of the most spectacular events I've ever witnessed."

Amelia nodded her head. "I won't change without seawater. Do you understand now? Whatever tank you have must have seawater in it, not fresh. And I will need sand or soil to touch when I get out, or I won't change back."

"Why?" Levi asked.

Amelia shrugged. "It is the nature of the magic."

Later, when Amelia was in her room and Levi was in his bed staring at a small brown spider moving slowly across the ceiling, Barnum said, "If that girl is magical . . . what does that mean? Does it mean there are really such things as fairies and witches and ghosts? And if there are, does that mean God made them, or the devil?"

Levi had never heard Barnum talk like this. Taylor didn't usually worry about problems of a philosophical nature.

"If she's here on earth, then surely God made her," Levi said.

He was convinced of no such thing, but he didn't want Barnum to contemplate the possibility that Amelia was an evil creature. No good could come of traveling down that road.

"The Bible says God created all the animals and people, too."

"Very true," Barnum said. "But which one is she? Does she have a human soul, or is she a dumb animal?"

"She's no animal," Levi snapped.

"No need to get angry," Barnum said mildly.

"You can tell just by speaking to her that she has a soul," Levi said. If Barnum had heard her weeping for her dead husband he'd never think otherwise.

"Doesn't mean she hasn't been sent by the devil to tempt man," Barnum said.

Levi took a deep breath. He had to get Barnum's head away from this line of inquiry. If Barnum decided Amelia was an animal, he might also decide their contract was null and void, or that he would be within his rights to chain or cage her. Levi couldn't let that happen.

"The only thing she's going to tempt is money out of purses," Levi said. "A real mermaid, onstage in Barnum's American Museum. You'll be turning people away."

"Too right we will!" Barnum said.

He sounded cheered by the thought. Levi knew then that

Barnum would fall asleep counting coins in his head, imagining the *clink-clink-clink* as everyone in New York paid to see the mermaid.

As for Levi, he drifted off into a restless sleep and dreamed not of money but of Amelia.

He stood on the shore of a sea he'd never seen before, the water stretching out blue and clear into the far horizon. His boots were covered by water, and the water rose and rose to his ankles and shins and knees, but still he stood and waited. The water was at his waist, and then his chest, and then finally she was there.

She emerged from the depths, grasped him in her arms, and pulled him down, down, down. He couldn't breathe, and it was no longer clear and blue and beautiful but cold and dark. All he could see was the steady gleam of her eyes and her sharp, sharp teeth.

He woke covered in sweat, gasping for air, imagining he could still feel the seawater filling up his lungs. After a few moments he settled down again but couldn't shake the dream enough to sleep.

He could tell by Barnum's breathing that the other man was also awake, but neither of them spoke to the other for the rest of the night, though they both knew of whom they were thinking.

CHAPTER 6

AUGUST 8, 1842

The crowd gathered outside the New York Concert Hall murmured and swelled and shifted the way large groups of people do, almost as if they were one giant being instead of many smaller ones. Every minute brought another addition, until the gathering was so large there was surely no way for everyone outside to fit inside the hall.

There was an occasional bark of masculine laughter and the answering trill of a feminine voice, but mostly everyone seemed to be in a state of tense excitement. The doors were to open precisely at noon, and as the appointed time approached, there was much rustling of coats and consulting of pocket watches.

The exterior of the hall boasted an eight-foot-high

transparency of a beautiful, bare-breasted woman with the caption *SEE THE FEEJEE MERMAID* hung over it.

For weeks everyone in New York who could read a newspaper had heard about Dr. Griffin, late of London's Lyceum of Natural History, and the mermaid he'd discovered while on an expedition in Fiji.

By late July, everyone in the city was positively inflamed with mermaid fever. That, of course, was exactly as Barnum intended.

Once they returned from Rhode Island, Barnum got to work. He wrote several letters about Dr. Griffin and his mermaid and arranged to have them sent from all over the country to assorted New York newspapers. His name, of course, was not associated with the letters or the mermaid. It was vitally important that no one think this a humbug like Joice Heth.

These letters seemed to trouble Amelia. "But he didn't catch me, and I don't know where Fiji is."

"Don't tell any reporters that," Barnum said. "As far as the paying public is concerned, you're an exotic creature from a tropical island."

Amelia frowned. "That's a lie."

Barnum waved a hand at Levi in frustration. "You explain."

Levi thought it unfair that Barnum left it up to him to

elucidate the difference between a lie and showmanship. Before he could collect his thoughts on the subject, Amelia asked, "And who is Dr. Griffin?"

"That would be, er, me," Levi said.

She stared at him. She didn't say that this was also a lie. Her look told him that it was and she knew very well that he knew this and she wanted to know why Barnum was spreading such an absurd tale.

"It's not a good idea for us to present you as an, uh, associate of Barnum's. At least not at first."

"Why?"

The shadow of Joice Heth filled the space between Barnum and Levi. Levi wasn't sure what to say, but then Barnum spoke.

"Because almost everyone thinks I'm a liar," Barnum said. "There was another woman who . . . performed for me, and I'm not saying she wasn't a humbug, but I was just as humbugged as everyone else and I certainly wouldn't have said what I did if I hadn't been fooled in the first place."

Amelia's brow creased in consternation at this outburst, and she looked to Levi for clarification.

For his part, Levi had never realized Barnum was so sensitive about the topic. Barnum tended to be dismissive of any allegations in that case. Levi had thought Barnum just didn't care what folk thought of him. He certainly behaved that way most of the time.

Amelia was still looking at him expectantly, so Levi said he would explain another time.

"I still don't understand why we have to tell so many lies."

"They aren't lies. Not really," Levi said. "Think of it as you're telling a story. In this story, I'm a naturalist from London and you're a mermaid from Fiji. It makes everything more interesting if we tell people I caught you in a net in a faraway place and brought you here."

"I'm not a fish, Mr. Lyman," she said with the first spark of temper. "I'm not an animal. And your story isn't true, so why should anyone believe it?"

"Because we're going to make them believe it," Barnum said impatiently. "Take the girl to a play so she'll understand."

Levi was happy to do this, as it meant he would have plenty of opportunities to hold Amelia's arm and fetch her a lemonade and hopefully have a conversation with her that didn't end with him feeling like a fool.

But Charity nixed any idea of Levi and Amelia going out alone. The fact that Amelia was a widow and not a maiden did not feature in Charity's eyes.

Though Charity still viewed Amelia with suspicion, she had also developed a contradictory feeling of propriety regarding the mermaid.

In Charity's view, Amelia was a guest in her home and therefore in her care. "Therefore, Levi Lyman, you won't be going about with this young woman unescorted."

They were in the Barnums' parlor when this edict was handed down. Amelia had allowed Caroline to teach her cribbage, which the little girl most definitely did not know how to play. The cards were in a jumble on the table, and Caroline seemed to score according to some arcane rules of her own.

Amelia had looked up at the sharp tone in Charity's voice and said, in her calm and unhurried way, "I'm not a young woman."

"What do you mean? You're not yet middle-aged. One can tell just by looking at you," Charity said.

"One can*not* tell just by looking at me," Amelia said mildly. "I don't age the same way you do."

"How old are you?" Levi asked.

Amelia shrugged. "I'm not certain. I don't keep time the same way you do, but I think I lived with Jack thirty or forty years, and without him ten or more years after that."

Levi did some quick calculations in his head. That meant if she was, say, nineteen or twenty when she married Jack Douglas, she could be well over seventy now.

Charity made a small hiss of disbelief. "That's impossible."

"So, I am told, is being a mermaid," Amelia said.

Charity sputtered some more at this, for Barnum had told her that "without a doubt, this lady is a mermaid," but she would not believe it without the proof of her own eyes. She'd been fooled by Barnum's tricks before.

"Well, you don't look a day over twenty, which is how I'm going to treat you," Charity declared. "And young unmarried women do not go about in the evening with young men unless they are escorted."

Levi had seen plenty of unescorted young women going about with both young and old men, but these were not respectable women and that was not a topic for a lady's parlor.

With Charity's edict firmly in place, it was determined that she and Barnum would attend a show at the theater with Levi and Amelia.

Amelia spent the evening being inscrutable, as always, and Levi had no chance to draw her out. He had no inclination to show his hand in front of Barnum, either, especially since Barnum kept peering at Levi like he was one of the exhibits in the museum.

After the play, Amelia turned to Levi and said, "I understand now, about the stories and the show."

She never spoke again of the "lie" of Fiji, though he could tell she would never be comfortable with it.

Of course Amelia had known she would be exhibited. She simply hadn't thought of what Barnum called "the show." The idea wasn't that she would be already floating in a tank and folk would file past her, though that was what Amelia had imagined. She'd been picturing those little miniature scenes in the first saloon in the museum, and the way everyone took turns looking in at them. Barnum thought that wasn't nearly interesting enough.

"It's not interesting enough to have a real mermaid onstage?" Amelia asked faintly.

"Got to build anticipation," Barnum said. "Get the audience excited to see you. Whet their appetite. Levi, what do you think of dancing girls?"

Levi appeared nonplussed by dancing girls. After a moment, he said, "Dancing girls won't go down smooth with the respectable ladies."

"I'm not talking about obscene dancing girls," Barnum said. "I'm talking about girls dressed up in costume who will sing a song about Fiji. Amelia here can dance and sing with them and then the other girls can fall away and leave her alone onstage and then—"

"No," Amelia said.

Barnum looked startled, his squashed-potato nose reddening at her curt reply. "No what?"

"No dancing," Amelia said. "If you want to have dancing girls onstage, that's your lookout, but I won't be one of them."

Barnum narrowed his eyes at her. Amelia stared right back. She wasn't afraid of him. She'd crossed the ocean by herself, and she wasn't about to be bullied by Barnum. He ought to have known that from the start.

He opened his mouth, no doubt to remonstrate with her,

but Levi held up his hand. "I don't know about having dancing girls when we move Amelia to the museum, but they certainly won't be appropriate when she's at the Concert Hall. It's supposed to be a scientific presentation, and I'm supposed to be a naturalist from London. If we make it too much of a performance, folks might not believe the evidence of their eyes when Amelia changes."

"They've got to believe," Barnum said. "When they see her there will be no doubt that she's real."

"But if you razzle-dazzle them," Levi said patiently, "they might think her change is just more razzle-dazzle."

"You may be right at that," Barnum said, chewing on the end of an unlit cigar. "Well, we'll leave off the dancing girls. For now."

This last was pointedly directed at Amelia.

"No matter if or when you decide to use them, I won't be one of them," she said.

"You agreed to perform for me," Barnum said.

"I agreed to be a mermaid, not to dance. My contract doesn't say anything about dancing."

Barnum threw Levi a dark look, as if this oversight were somehow his fault.

"I've got to go and check on the progress of the blasted *tank*," Barnum said, glaring at Amelia now.

"You can't have a mermaid without water," she said.

Barnum mumbled something indistinct and left the

room, trailing his foul mood behind him.

"Don't worry about him," Levi said.

"I'm not," Amelia said.

"I only meant don't let him bother you," Levi said.

"He doesn't," Amelia said. "Mr. Barnum is accustomed to having his own way. That doesn't mean I'm required to give it to him."

She paused, thinking it was the appropriate thing to show gratitude for his intervention with Barnum.

"I do appreciate your help, Mr. Lyman. It never occurred to me to argue that dancers would make the show less credible."

His eyes flickered at the "Mr. Lyman," as they always did, but she just couldn't bring herself to call him Levi. It seemed too much like an invitation for him to pour all the stars out of his eyes and into her hands.

"Barnum's trouble is that he's got lots of ideas but he's never bothered to think them through to the end," he said. "And it's no trouble to help you, Mrs. Douglas. No trouble at all."

He wanted to say more—it was there in the lines of his face, something yearning, something longing, something leaning toward her and hoping.

"If you'll excuse me, Mr. Lyman," Amelia said, and made her unhurried way to her own room.

She wasn't cowardly, but she did not want to hear the

longing thing in his heart. Only grief could come of that, for she would have to refuse whatever overtures he made and then there would be hurt feelings. There were already too many feelings cluttering up the space—Charity's suspicion, Barnum's dominance, and Amelia's own conflicted emotions on what she was about to do.

She felt she could think better, more clearly, if only she were allowed to return to the sea now and again. After the demonstration in Rhode Island, Barnum had been adamant that Amelia go nowhere near the harbor.

"I won't have some damned sailor seeing you without paying for a ticket," he said.

The harbor was not private. Amelia understood that. It was the reason why she had not wanted to show Barnum and Levi her true form there. But she had arrived in New York via the harbor; she knew how to be careful and understood better than Barnum the sheer numbers of people and boats there.

Amelia wanted—needed—the freedom of the ocean. It would not kill her if she stayed long in her human form. She knew that. But she felt as though it might. It wasn't just that she couldn't swim. She couldn't see or hear or smell the water at all, and the sheer numbers of people everywhere suffocated her.

Additionally, the polite requirement that she sit in the parlor with Charity and the children when Amelia was not engaged in "Fiji business" was oppressive. Amelia did not wish to do needlework and make polite conversation about the weather. She didn't see how Charity could even know anything about the weather when she rarely set foot outside the museum.

Since Amelia knew nothing of the wealthy classes of New York and their doings (apparently a favorite topic in well-bred parlors across the city), there was little for them to speak about other than the wind and the rain.

In the privacy of her room, she would dream of the water, or of Jack, and wonder how much money she might have after six months. Enough, she hoped, to see all the things in all the world, just as she had promised herself. She only hoped whatever she earned was worth the cost.

The tank was one thing. Barnum's glassmaker knew well enough how to make it, although the question of transporting it to the Concert Hall was a conundrum. It was decided that the panes of glass would be brought to the hall and assembled there.

The seawater was a different problem altogether. How to collect it, how to carry it, and how to keep it from fouling if it was in the tank for several days—all these problems needed to be solved, and they needed to be solved with as little expense as possible.

They wanted the moon, but they didn't realize it cost the earth.

In retrospect, Barnum agreed with Levi about the dancing girls. Not only would they detract from the scientific nature of the presentation, but they'd expect to be paid. Every person he paid resulted in less money in his pocket, and sadly the mermaid had been canny enough to ask for a cut of the ticket sales.

He suspected Levi's hand in that, but the boy admitted nothing, and the mermaid just looked at Barnum with that grave stare no matter what he said.

That look, he thought. It made him want to twist away, to hide his eyes so she couldn't see inside him.

He had a strange idea that if she looked at him for too long, she would know all of his secrets, everything that had ever made him ashamed, every humbug he perpetuated, every sin he committed.

The girl had missed her calling. She should have been a preacher's wife. That look would have compelled even the most wayward sinner into church every Sunday.

And on the long list of problems to be solved . . . she wasn't eating enough. Levi said the girl liked sweets, and Barnum himself had seen the girl putting more lumps of sugar in her tea than strictly necessary. But she didn't seem interested in any of the bakery treats that appeared with regularity around the breakfast table.

Charity gobbled up all the goodies in the mermaid's stead. She was full to bursting with his child and seemed determined to make herself even bigger, if possible. He didn't think all that was good for the baby, especially not if it was a boy. Boys needed red meat, and lots of it.

He surely did hope for a boy this time. Daughters were fine; Caroline was about the age when she was starting to become interesting, though little Helen was still a chubby squeaking ball of ruffles and curls.

But a boy! A boy could carry on the Barnum name. A son could learn everything there was to know about the American Museum and that would carry on, too. Barnum could pass the museum on to his children and they to their children and so Barnum would live on and on, his name etched forever in the annals of New York history.

However, none of that would happen if Charity had another girl. He'd have to make it clear she wasn't to eat the fancy cakes and breads any longer. Red meat, that would make Barnum's boy.

Still, he could give orders to Charity, but the mermaid was another matter. He told her many, many times to eat more, but it was clear that she wouldn't force down a single bite just to please him.

Couching it in terms of the exhibition didn't help, either.

"It's just that folks like to see a nice healthy girl," Barnum said over the breakfast table one morning.

The girl had ignored the bacon and taken only a mouthful of eggs and dry toast.

"I am perfectly healthy," Amelia said.

"Yes, but you need to be . . ." He gestured with his hands, making the shape of a curvy figure in the air. "Rounder."

"Why?" she asked, giving him that disconcerting stare that made him want to squirm in his seat.

Charity and Caroline were looking on in curiosity, too, and that made him bluster.

"Well, because, as I said, folks like to see a healthy girl."

"And as I said, I am healthy even if I am not round, so I am certain the folks will be pleased." She gave him a half smile (a mocking half smile, he thought) and returned to her toast.

Barnum thought he caught a glimpse of satisfaction in Charity's eyes before she, too, dropped her gaze to her plate and continued eating.

The hell of it was that damned mermaid always seemed to get the better of him. And everyone was on her side—Levi, Caroline, even his own wife. Didn't they see *he* was the one being wronged by the girl at every turn? He was the one bearing the brunt of the expense. He was the one who had to solve all the problems. Who was going to figure out how to get seawater into the tank if not him?

And he was the one who had to try to make a show out of a girl who didn't seem to want to be one. Barnum sat back in his chair, thinking. He always did his best thinking at night in the museum, when the building was silent but he could still imagine the murmur of voices or squeals of delight as the throngs moved through.

It comforted him to think of them—all the people who had paid to come into his museum, and all the people who would pay in the future.

Barnum could hardly remember a time when his primary thought wasn't of making money. His own grandfather, a great old humbug artist if there ever was one, had promised him when he was young a tract of land near their hometown of Bethel called "Ivy Island." This, he was assured, would be the makings of his fortune.

This prize of real estate was to come into young Taylor's possession when he was of age. Throughout his life his entire family referred to him as the richest child in Bethel, and his parents extracted frequent promises that he would not forget them once he became wealthy.

He'd spent many a long hour dreaming of the day this wonderful present would come into his possession. He imagined there was treasure to be found, gold and silver to be mined in mountain-sized quantities.

Later he considered the matter more practically. There might be forests of trees to be sold for lumber or arable farmland to be turned into parcels for rent. Yes, young Taylor built marvelous plans for his inheritance.

Then, when he was ten years old, his grandfather took him to see Ivy Island. It was a wreck, covered in brambles and swamp, and there were snakes everywhere. The land was hardly worth the paper the deed was printed on.

It was then that Barnum realized how thoroughly he'd been humbugged. His family had laughed at him his whole life. Of course they'd known Ivy Island was completely worthless, but they'd all enjoyed watching him dream of the day it would come into his hands.

He learned two lessons that day. First, it was better to be the humbugger than the humbugged. Barnum enjoyed a good joke just as much as anyone else, but he didn't enjoy being the butt of one.

The second was that no one was going to give his fortune to him. He'd have to earn it himself, and he had tried. He'd run a shop, sold lottery tickets, invested in bear grease, and spent two years as a traveling showman. He'd even started his own newspaper and was prosecuted three times (and once convicted of libel) for the privilege.

Early on, he'd made lots of money but had been a little too open-handed with the spending of it—once it was in his pocket, it dashed right out again. Lately he'd been the victim of both the Panic and the credit system implemented by that swindler Proler, purveyor of bootblack and bear grease who'd taken Barnum's money and fleeced him in return.

But the museum . . . the museum, he felt, was his chance

to make his mark and his fortune for good. The mermaid was the key to that. She was his stairway to the cream and the velvet and the life he'd always wanted.

Nobody's fortune would be made if the girl contradicted him at every turn. Still, he supposed he would have to work within the limits of her personality—and there were limits. The girl simply couldn't be convinced to put on a show in the sense that he wanted—something with flair.

Then there was the staging of the change itself. He was convinced that she must walk onstage, not simply appear already in the tank when the curtain rose. It was necessary for everyone to see what she was before to believe what came after.

But she couldn't simply shed her clothes onstage as she had on the beach under the moonlight. Every newspaper in the city would come down on him—or rather, Dr. Griffin—for indecency. Women in the audience would probably faint. The whole show would be tainted. No, that wouldn't work at all.

He sat and wondered and listened to the ghostly whispers of the museum and finally came up with a plan. It was simple and elegant and wouldn't require much of the girl. It was perfect, and he was certain she'd go along with it.

Amelia waited just offstage. The theater was empty, but the restless excitement of the crowd outside could be heard despite the closed doors.

The tank, filled with seawater, sat in the center of the stage. It had a height of twenty feet and was approximately twenty-five feet across. Every human who saw it remarked on its size, but to Amelia it looked like a very small container compared to the ocean.

Behind the tank was a ladder that led up to a small platform that jutted over the water. A white screen hung just in front of the ladder, ending at the top of the glass. When Amelia climbed the ladder steps, her silhouette would be visible through the screen. The theater would use a limelight like the one Barnum had on the roof of his museum to attract visitors.

Amelia had seen these lights outside the museum at night. They were astoundingly bright, especially in a city lit only intermittently by gas. It seemed to her that there was often more light at night out in the country. In the city, the buildings huddled close and blocked out the stars.

When the limelight shone on the white screen, everyone in the audience would be able to see that Amelia was alone on the platform. There would be no trick with a second girl in a costume diving into the water just as Amelia reached the top of the water or some such thing. She would be in the light until she reached the screen, and then the light would shine through it.

Once there, she would remove her dress and dive into the water.

"Everyone will see a naked woman, but only for a moment," Barnum had said when they discussed the show structure.

He rubbed his nose. "There's just no avoiding this. I think if it's very quick, then most folks will forget about it once they see you as a mermaid."

He looked at her expectantly. Amelia realized he meant to preserve her modesty and that he was actually concerned that she might not want to be seen.

Amelia didn't understand the human obsession with nudity as something sinful. It was particularly puzzling in light of most of the works of art she'd seen—almost all of these featured men and women in various states of undress, though Levi had told her they were "Greek and Roman and that was all right for them," whatever that meant.

In any case, she could appreciate that Barnum was attempting to be kind for a change.

"I don't mind," she assured him. "Until I became human, nobody ever told me there was something wrong with my body."

He appeared discomfited by this frankness, and Amelia realized she'd said the wrong thing again. Perhaps she was supposed to blush modestly and say she was troubled even if she wasn't?

Amelia had carefully observed Charity Barnum over these weeks to see what was generally expected of women.

All she'd found was that women spent a great deal of time saying they were pleased when they were not, smiling when they were not happy, and pretending their anger and frustration did not exist.

Jack had never expected this of her. He never wanted her to pretend to have feelings she did not have or to say something just to please him.

Having never troubled to do such things for her husband, she found the habit of being herself difficult to break.

Soon the doors to the hall would open and all the people outside would pour in. Barnum was among them, pretending to be an ordinary citizen curious about the Feejee Mermaid. His presence in the audience would ensure that no suspicion of association with the museum would come up prior to the show.

After the show ran for a week or so, Barnum would make a public offer to "Dr. Griffin" to house the mermaid at the American Museum for the benefit of the paying New York public. He was already arranging for a larger tank to be built in one of the saloons.

In this room would also be the awful mummy that Barnum's friend Moses Kimball had brought from Boston. When Amelia saw it, she had gasped and turned her head away. It might not actually be a mermaid, but it still looked like a thing that had died in horrible pain. It did not even appear as well-preserved as the other dead things in the museum, like the elephant.

She did not think anyone could possibly believe that she and that dried "monkey-fish" were from the same family, but then humans showed an extraordinary willingness to believe absurdities that only made Amelia shake her head.

Amelia heard Levi's steps behind her as he entered the wing of the stage. He looked, she thought, like a dandy. His waistcoat was striped, his hat was tall, his pants were checked, and he was nothing at all like the sober-faced and sober-dressed Levi Lyman she knew.

He'd grown out a very large and bushy beard over these last few weeks, not at all fashionable but deemed necessary. Levi had explained to her about Joice Heth, somewhat shamefacedly. Since he had been the public face of that hoax, it was important that no one suspect Dr. Griffin and Levi Lyman were the same person.

Dr. Griffin was said to be from the London Lyceum of Natural History. Levi had explained that London was across the sea in a country called England, and he had shown her pictures of the castle there from a large volume in the Barnums' personal library.

She immediately decided that London was one of the first places she would see when she left Barnum's employ. Amelia had never seen a castle. She'd asked if the castle was as big as the Park Hotel (the largest building in the neighborhood of the American Museum besides the museum itself), and Levi had laughed.

"You could put a whole bunch of Park Hotels inside a castle, especially that one," he'd said, pointing to the picture.

He had also explained that he needed a different accent since he was supposed to be from a different country.

"Do I sound British?" he asked her, sounding very unlike himself.

"I wouldn't know," she said, wondering why he asked such foolish questions sometimes. Then, because he looked disappointed, she added, "I imagine most people in the audience won't know, either."

That did not appear to comfort him. He said, in his regular voice, "I'll go onstage first. I'll tell the story of my expedition to the exotic waters of Fiji and how I encountered you while on a boat and convinced you to return to New York with me."

They had changed this portion of the story at Amelia's request, who objected to even the made-up implication that "Dr. Griffin" had caught her while out fishing.

Barnum and Levi thought this was because it implied she was an animal. The truth was that she couldn't bear for any part of this lie to resemble her real life with Jack.

Jack was the truth; he'd caught her in a net but she chose to come back to him. This tale was not the truth, and Amelia felt that if they were going to lie, then they should lie about all of it.

"Then when I say, 'Please observe, for the first time in the civilized world, the Feejee Mermaid,' you're to come onstage from this side and I'll exit to the other side and then . . ."

"I know, Levi," she said.

They'd practiced and practiced all of this numerous times. First they'd practiced on the theater stage in the American Museum—without the tank full of water, of course, but with the light and the ladder and the screen at the top. These rehearsals had essentially involved all the aspects of the show except the part where Amelia dove into the water.

In the last two days they had practiced in the Concert Hall itself, under the cover of strictest secrecy. Everyone was removed from the building, and guards were posted outside to ensure that no one tried to sneak in. Nothing could be worse in Barnum's eyes than a member of the public catching a glimpse of her without buying a ticket first.

It had been necessary to have at least one session in the tank to ensure that Amelia *could* change when she was not actually in the sea. Barnum had not been willing to take Amelia's word for it—"though a naked girl in a tank will probably cause just as much of a ruckus as a mermaid might," he said.

The change had occurred just as smoothly as it did in the ocean. Amelia didn't like the seawater in the tank—it tasted old and stale, and it lacked the swirling little animals that humans couldn't see without microscopes but that she saw with clear eyes. But it was seawater, and when she emerged from the tank and pushed her hand into the jar of sand placed on the platform, she'd turned right back into a human woman.

Levi checked his watch. He'd been compulsively doing so all morning, often enough to make Amelia glad that she didn't carry one. It seemed once you had a watch, you became inordinately fond of examining it.

"It's nearly noon," he said.

"Yes," she said. She could tell by way the sunlight no longer slanted through the windows in the hall that it was almost exactly overhead.

Levi paced in a straight line, then a circle, then checked his watch and paced back to her in a straight line again. She watched all this with a bemused stare. Walking about like that wouldn't make the time go any faster, though she decided he wouldn't thank her for saying so.

"How can you be so calm?" he asked.

"What else should I be?" she said.

He opened his mouth, seemed to think better of it, and turned away. Then he came back and spoke with such force that she took a half step away from him.

"How can you be so mild when everyone is going to see what you are? After today there won't be any more secrets. Doesn't that bother you at all?"

"It's very late in the day for regrets, Levi Lyman," she said, feeling a little temper at his tone. "And you are wrong, very wrong, to think I will have no more secrets. Yes, everyone will know I am a mermaid—or at least they'll know of the existence of someone called 'the Feejee Mermaid.' They won't know Amelia Douglas, or even the creature I was before I met Jack. Do not mistake the revelation of my body for the revelation of my heart. My heart keeps its own secrets, and they don't belong to you or anyone else just because you've seen me with a fish tail.

"Besides, this is what *you* wanted, isn't it? When you came to my cottage so many months ago you wanted me to exhibit myself. And here I am, doing just that."

He looked stricken for a moment, then looked away and murmured, "I don't know what I want anymore."

"Well, I do," she said firmly. "And as I'm the one who will be onstage, it's my wants that matter."

They might have gone on like that for some time, but the clock struck twelve, the doors opened, and Levi was left to swallow the bile of second thoughts.

The crowd seemed to swell like an ocean wave as it entered, the noise pushed before it as people stomped down the aisles and filled up the seats closest to the stage.

Amelia let their mingled breath and murmurs break over her. They were only a different kind of sea, one she'd never been in before. She only needed to swim in it, and swimming was more natural to her than walking.

Levi stood stiffly beside her, the words said and unsaid pooled in regret at his feet. She could feel them there, waiting to climb back into his mouth.

Then it was time for him to walk onstage and he was gone, and she hadn't wished him luck as she'd meant to. She meant to do the proper human thing, to behave the right way, but they were not as easy with each other as she'd thought they would be.

All the world narrowed then to just his figure onstage and the words he said in a voice that was not his. She didn't listen to them, not really, not the shapes, only the noise. She was waiting for her cue, for the words that meant she couldn't hide anymore in the wings.

"Please observe, for the first time in the civilized world, the Feejee Mermaid!" He swept his arm toward her, but he didn't meet her eyes.

The limelight appeared just past the curtain that hid her from view. She was supposed to step into it, like a net that would catch her and pull her across the stage.

The crowd drew one long collective breath, leaving no air for her.

Amelia stepped into the light.

Her feet were bare, her hair unbound, and the dress she wore little better than a shift. She didn't glance at the audience, who'd broken out into excited whispers at her appearance, but she felt the sheer weight of their numbers pressing on her nonetheless.

It had never occurred to her before that eyes could be terrible things. Eyes that turned toward her, every one. Eyes that tried to pierce her, divine her, know her. Eyes that judged and, almost worse, eyes that hoped. Eyes that said they would wait and see before they decided. Eyes that wanted every bit of her, especially the secret longings of her secret heart.

All of them were there, and she could not meet them as she usually did. The ladder seemed a long way away, a mountain to climb on a far-off horizon.

Three more steps, two, and then she turned to climb the ladder and now she saw all the faces, all the hungry faces, so she tipped her gaze up and she climbed, climbed, climbed until she reached the little platform at the top.

Then the screen hid her from the faces, and she dropped her dress to one side and dove into the water.

The change rolled over her skin and she arched up but not far enough to break the surface. She wanted to stay in the water, feel the comfort of it pressing all around her.

There came a tremendous swell of noise from the crowd, but it was muffled inside the tank. She looked through the glass and saw that many people were standing and pointing.

One woman in the front row had her hands clasped

before her and tears running down her face. Her mouth moved rhythmically, like she was saying a prayer, and Amelia didn't know if the woman was thanking her God or cursing the devil for the mermaid's existence.

A general commotion broke out near the back. Amelia couldn't tell exactly what it was—the rear of the theater was dark—but suddenly several people ran into the aisles and toward the stage.

Amelia realized with alarm that they intended to climb up to get a better look at her. Then they were on the stage, pressing in and shouting, pushing up against the glass and banging it with their fists and their eyes were bulging and their mouths were open.

For the first time in her long, long life, she felt ashamed, ashamed because her body made them gape and shout and press up against the tank with their fingers grasping.

She saw Levi pushing people out of the way and his mouth making the words *Get back, get back*, but nobody listened, nobody wanted to know or hear.

They only wanted to see her, see her, see her, and she didn't want to see them anymore but there was nowhere to look where there were not faces, ravening faces now, their hunger not sated by the sight of her but rather whetted instead and they only wanted more and more and more and she should have known this would happen and Barnum should have known this would happen and Levi tried to tell her this would happen and she didn't want to see them anymore so she curled into her fin and covered her face and wished she'd never left home.

CHAPTER 7

PANDEMONIUM AT CONCERT HALL!
Many people injured in quest to see Feejee Mermaid.'
'UNBELIEVABLE BUT TRUE—We have seen the
Mermaid!' 'MERMAID IN NEW YORK—One
woman killed—All the details.'"

Barnum read each successive headline aloud with increasing
relish. The fact that he was enjoying this and nobody else
seemed to didn't appear to register at all.

"You are a success," he said. Levi could practically see the
coins falling in Barnum's eyes. "We can charge anything for
people to see you—anything at all. The whole Eastern
Seaboard is going to flock to New York to see you."

"A woman was killed," Amelia said dully.

Levi thought she looked like a piece of tarnished silver. The shine was off her, and her grey eyes were muted.

"Yes, that was unfortunate," Barnum said. He didn't sound like he thought it was unfortunate at all. "But the show was a sensation. People won't be able to get enough of you! All the tickets for tomorrow's presentation have already sold out."

"I'm not doing any more presentations," Amelia said.

Levi thought it would come to this. When they'd finally managed to clear the crowd out of the hall (with the help of several city constables), he and Barnum had been unable to rouse her from her isolation in the tank no matter how hard they knocked and yelled.

Finally Levi had stripped down to his underclothing and climbed into the tank. Barnum certainly wouldn't do it. The water was salty and slightly stale, and up close he found himself fascinated by the silver pattern of scales all over her.

He touched her shoulder, and it was as if she was roused suddenly from a deep sleep. Her right arm slashed out, those very dangerous claws barely missing his stomach. Levi was certain that if she'd touched him, his guts would have spilled out on the floor of the tank.

It was then, strangely, that he truly understood that she was not of the land but of the sea. The woman was temporary. The mermaid was who she really was.

After a moment the reflexive defense lowered, her eyes

focused, and he knew she saw him. She looked around, bewildered, and Levi wished he dared touch one of the floating tendrils of her hair. He wished he dared take her in his arms and tell her it was all going to be fine.

But he was not of the sea. He didn't even like the ocean. He was a mundane creature who needed to breathe the air, and so he pointed upward so she would understand his intentions and kicked awkwardly up to the surface, trailing all his wishes behind him and hoping she couldn't see them there in the water.

Now Barnum gloated over the evening headlines and Amelia sat there, a piece of glass that might shatter at any moment. Levi thought then that he could hate Barnum. Oh yes, he could hate him very easily. The least Barnum could do was notice the feelings of those around him.

Well, what did I expect? Levi thought. He never noticed when Charity was miserable, and he'd never noticed when Joice Heth was, either.

"There won't be any more performances," Amelia repeated. "I won't do it. That woman died. She was knocked to the ground and people stepped on her. The last thing she felt on this earth was boots stomping over her spine and no one stopped, no one paused, no one tried to help her up. They just kept right on rampaging toward me. So I won't do it, Barnum. I won't have it happen again. I won't be the cause of someone's death."

"Now, Amelia"—Levi knew Barnum was alarmed if he was calling her by her first name—"there won't be another incident like that."

"How can you know?" she said, her tone scathing. "You can't divine the future, else you'd be charging a nickel for the service."

The insult rolled right over Barnum, the way most things did. "We'll take every precaution for audience safety. We didn't expect the response to be quite so enthusiastic."

Levi couldn't let that pass. "Enthusiastic? The crowd turned into a pack of animals. How can you plan for that?"

"We'll hire guards," Barnum said. "I can't have people running at my mermaid like that. It will be an extra expense, but—"

"She's not your mermaid," Levi said.

"She's certainly not *your* mermaid," Barnum said with a nasty edge in his voice.

"Barnum. This is not about money," Levi said. "If you want to talk about expense, let's talk about the funeral expenses that woman's family has to pay."

Barnum's eyes narrowed. "Actually, I must disagree with you there, Levi. It is about money. This young woman signed a contract with me, a legally binding contract, and I've already invested a significant amount based on the promise of that contract. If she leaves now, she'll owe me for those expenses."

His eyes gleamed. He thought he had Amelia trapped.

Amelia stood. There was no dramatic flounce, no angry set to her shoulders, and when she spoke, her voice was completely even.

"If I want to leave, you can't stop me, Barnum. The ocean is vast and you are small, no matter how many buildings have your name on them."

She left the room. Levi watched her go, paralyzed by uncertainty. Perhaps it would be better for her, for everyone, if she did go.

If she left, then the longing he felt would fade away instead of eating him alive.

Barnum said, "Don't just sit there gaping like a fish. Go after her."

"You go after her if you want her so bad," Levi said. "You're the one who says she signed a contract and owes you money. That's nothing to me."

Barnum gave him a sly smile. "I'm not the one who's been playing Lancelot ever since the girl arrived."

"What do you mean by that?" Levi said.

Barnum shrugged. "Only that there's more than one reason for the girl to stay, and you would likely do a better job of convincing her than I. You did a better job in the first place—convinced her to swim all the way here from the great white north."

"I didn't," Levi said. "She came of her own accord, and she's leaving of her own free will, too."

"Still, you wouldn't like her to disappear into the ocean and never return, would you? How can all your dreams come true then?"

Levi flushed. He truly thought he'd done a better job of disguising his feelings. If Barnum had noticed (especially since Barnum noticed nothing that was not related to dollars and cents), then everyone had, including Amelia.

He burned at the thought that she knew he longed for her and had politely ignored it.

Then he realized he didn't want her to go. Barnum was right, and Levi hated that Barnum was right. It didn't matter if Amelia knew how he felt—he couldn't let her disappear into the ocean forever without at least trying to make her stay.

All of a sudden he was up and out and after her, but not so fast that he didn't catch Barnum's self-satisfied smile.

Amelia didn't bother taking anything. She walked out of the dining room and out of the hallway and out of the front door and into the night wearing only the dress and shoes she'd arrived in.

Barnum did not own her. Barnum could not dictate to her. Barnum could not keep her from diving into the harbor and swimming away, swimming as far as Fiji if she wanted.

No ship could find her if she did not want to be found.

That poor woman. She kept thinking it over and over, kept remembering the horror of finding the bloodied broken thing that used to be a person in one of the side aisles. How had nobody else noticed her? How could they have not seen?

That woman would always be with her now, trailing behind her like a ghost.

Amelia still did not understand all the streets and directions, but if she wandered long enough, she was sure to find the water. It was an island, after all.

And once she found the water, she would leave this horrible place and never return. Why had she stayed? Once she saw the stuffed dead things in the museum she should have known. She'd wanted to leave then but convinced herself it would be all right, that she'd started on a certain course and must see it through.

Now she knew better. Now she knew that death lay in wait everywhere, not just in the ocean that had stolen away her love.

Amelia was thinking only of escaping Barnum, so it took some time before she was aware of the trail of murmurs she left behind her. She gradually became aware of people staring as she passed, many of them not bothering to disguise their interest.

"That's her, isn't it?"

"The mermaid."

"I'm sure it's her."

"Where is she going?"

"Where's Dr. Griffin?"

"That's the mermaid."

"The mermaid."

"The mermaid."

Amelia trained her eyes forward, pretending she didn't hear. She thought that if she didn't acknowledge the words, then they wouldn't be true and the people would leave her alone, let her pass.

It was a foolish thought, one born of hope rather than reason. Only a few hours before, they had stormed the stage to get closer to her. Out here, in the street, she didn't even have the protection of glass around her.

A man suddenly yelled out, "Yes, that's her! That's the mermaid!" and then they surged toward her, pressing against her, stroking her hair, reaching for her arm, her hand, a bit of her skirt.

All of them shouted—shouted questions, offered her money and jewels, tried to grab her and drag her to the nearest newspaper office to sell her story.

She tried to speak, to push through, but they choked her with their questions and their breath and their insistence on knowing, knowing, knowing everything about her. She threw out her hands, wished for the claws of her water form. If she had them she would slash her way free, never mind the blood, why were they stopping her, why were they standing in her way?

She had no strength as a human, at least none to compare to that which she had in the water. She could not move the demanding shouting faces, and the more she tried to turn away, the more they wanted.

Even in the tank she was able to curl into her fin. If she tried to curl into herself here, she would be trampled. Trampled like that woman in the theater.

But maybe that would be better. Maybe if she simply lay down in the street, they would batter her until she was dead and then she could stop pretending she'd cared about anything since Jack died.

That thought made her stop struggling, though everyone around her continued to push, continued to scream, continued to touch and grasp and grab at her.

Was it true? Did she want to die rather than go on without Jack? She took out this idea, turned it over, examined it.

All those days and hours she stood on the cliff . . . was she waiting for a sign, something to tell her it was all right to let go? Perhaps she'd hoped for a bolt of lightning, or an arrow carelessly loosed to plunge into her heart.

She didn't know how such things might affect her, though—her body seemed immune to the diseases that killed humans, and old age might never take her. If she'd stayed with her people, perhaps it would have been different.

Amelia recalled old ones among them, and of course there were folk who died. Was it the change that kept her young?

If so, she might never die. There might be no power on the earth to end her life.

All of the days and all the years stretched out before her, every one of them cursed without Jack.

Then there was a different kind of shout, and she remembered where she was and the people all around her.

Someone called her name. "Amelia! Amelia!"

She spun on her heel, and behind her was Levi, shoving his way through the crowd.

"Dr. Griffin!" several people shouted.

Some of them moved toward Levi, loosening their grip on Amelia just enough that she was able to break through the crowd.

A man, determined to have what he wanted from her, followed her out and clutched a fistful of her hair near the scalp. She supposed she should have screamed, but she was too astonished to do so.

Amelia reached behind her and grabbed the man's hand with both of hers, digging in with her too-short human fingernails. He yelped in pain and released her, but now the crowd, temporarily distracted by the appearance of "Dr. Griffin," recalled that she was there and washed toward her again.

She threw a glance at Levi, saw him struggling to reach her, but she couldn't wait for him. They were coming for her again, those hordes, those hungry faces, and she had to escape.

Amelia met Levi's eyes, tried to tell him with just her gaze that she was sorry. Then she ran, and ran, and ran until the crowd lost the will to keep up with her (for many of them ran after her), but she kept running even after they fell away, because running felt like swimming, and the faster she ran, the freer she was, fast and free and far away from everything that hurt.

Levi found her hours later, sitting on the edge of a tiny dock with a small dinghy tethered to it. She sat like a child, knees curled into her chest and arms wrapped around her knees, her hair pulled all around her shoulders like a blanket.

He'd despaired of finding her at all, but he kept looking anyway, promising himself one more hour—just one more— and then he would give up and go home.

When he did find her, it was like a repeated memory, the same sensation of illusion he'd had when he found her huddled in the museum. She looked up when she heard his footsteps on the dock. Her shoulders hunched, her body ready to spring away from any strange intruder. She didn't speak when she saw him, but her shoulders relaxed. He had the sense, though, that she was still reserving the right to dart away if she chose.

He lowered himself to the dock beside her (with a momentary pang for his suit trousers—Dr. Griffin dressed much more elegantly than Levi Lyman). He cross his ankles and leaned back on his hands, affecting a casualness he did not feel. Then he waited. He had found her, and it was enough. Whatever happened after that was her choice.

Below them the water lapped gently against the pilings, and in the distance was the occasional splash of a sea creature slapping against the surface. It should have smelled fresher here, away from the manure and sewage and pigs, but mostly it smelled of fish and the rotting vegetation that built up against the pilings.

Amelia, it seemed, was content to sit there indefinitely. She might be mute until she finally shed her clothes and returned to the water or until Levi gave up waiting and returned to Barnum. Levi, who was not a particularly patient human, was not willing to wait that long.

"Why didn't you go?" he asked, when it seemed she might never speak.

"I thought I wanted to die," she said. "Out there, with all those people surrounding me."

"Because you felt overwhelmed?" he asked, trying to understand. He didn't see what this had to do with her not leaving.

"No, because I didn't want to live without Jack. I never thought about it before—just how long my life might be." She paused. "Then I thought I should just lie down in the street and let them trample me like they did that poor woman in the theater. That would be correct, wouldn't it? That would be the right punishment for me."

"Punishment?" He'd never heard her speak this way before. "Why should you be punished?"

"That's what all you Christians say, isn't it? That when you sin, you should be punished?"

"But what have you done that's a sin?" Levi asked. "I can't see how this is your fault."

"I was the cause of her death," Amelia said, her voice breaking. "They were all running to see *me* and she got in the way."

Levi felt that anything he said would be inadequate. He didn't know the words to make that expression on her face go away, that crumpled, bruised look. Amelia didn't crumple, usually, and she never seemed to bruise. But this . . . she felt responsible. He didn't know what to do to take that away.

"You couldn't know what would happen," Levi said finally. He could taste the bland uselessness of these words.

"You knew," she said, suddenly fierce. "You tried to tell me."

"I didn't know it would be like that," he said. "I was . . ."

He trailed off. Telling her he was worried about her seemed too close to a confession, too close to telling her how he felt. It wouldn't help, that confession, and it might even make her flee. She seemed balanced on a knife-edge—the burden of his feelings might cause her to fall.

"I thought it might be too much for you to be seen by so many. I knew that it couldn't be undone," he said.

"And I told you that it was my choice," Amelia said. "But I was too foolish to understand what I was choosing."

Levi felt helpless against her grief. He had no right to touch her, to comfort her. He could not find the words to console her. It was as if she were still under glass on the stage, separated from him and the rest of the world.

He had no power to make her stay, and neither did Barnum—that was abundantly clear. Barnum's powers of persuasion were useless in her case. She'd always viewed Barnum askance, recognizing the slick oil that was at least half of his personality.

Amelia didn't need Barnum in the same way he needed her. That gave her power over him. But Levi wanted her to stay. He didn't have the ability to wipe clean her grieving heart, but he wanted her to stay.

"Stay," he said. The word emerged without his conscious thought, a thing he'd never meant to say out loud. And then again—"Stay."

She looked at him then, and she was Amelia, cool and direct and demanding. "Why?"

So many reasons I cannot say. The words lodged inside his throat, and he fell back on platitudes.

"Because we'll make it safer. It will be better next time."

She looked doubtful. "How can you be assured of that?

One thing I have learned in all my years among humans is that their behavior is not predictable."

"Yes, it is," Levi said. "If it weren't, we couldn't build societies. We expect each other to behave a certain way, and so we do."

"Then how do mobs happen?" Amelia asked. "How do people suddenly decide to join together and rampage?"

He recognized that this was a sincere question, not a rhetorical one. She didn't understand people, even after so many years of living among them. Well, to be fair, there couldn't have been many mob scenes in that isolated village of hers.

"We expect certain behaviors of each other," he said slowly, thinking about his answer as he spoke. "I think, when something happens like at the Concert Hall, one person behaves out of the normal fashion. Then another person thinks it must be acceptable, and so they copy that behavior. And so it goes on and on like a chain of fire until everyone's caught it."

"And how do you think we can keep the fire from starting again?" Amelia said.

"We take certain precautions, like Barnum said," Levi said. He saw the angry flicker in her eyes when he mentioned Barnum. "We hire guards. We make it clear that there will be acceptable standards. I find that when the rules are clear, most people will follow them. They don't want to be censured by their fellow man. And . . ."

He hesitated, because he knew she wouldn't like this, and it might be the wrong thing to say. It might be the thing that drove her away.

"And?" she asked.

"I'm sorry to say this, because I know you like your freedom, but I don't think you should go about on your own anymore. If you're alone, you might be mobbed again."

She gave a little shudder, and he knew she felt the crowd pressing all around her again.

"No," Amelia said. "I don't like it. But I have to agree that it is not wise for me to walk without an escort. Charity prefers that I have one, in any case. She seems to think it's improper otherwise."

"Does that mean you'll stay?" Levi asked.

It was pathetic, the way he couldn't keep the hope out of his voice. It made him wince.

She stood then, a smooth, fluid motion that left him feeling awkward as he scrambled up beside her.

She stepped out of her shoes, pulled off her dress, and dove into the water.

He watched for a sign of her, for her tail arcing into the air, but there was nothing.

Still, he felt that she hadn't left forever. He believed (perhaps foolishly) that she would have said good-bye. She wouldn't have said it to Barnum, but she would have told him. He'd earned at least that courtesy.

No, she was only pretending she was still free to act as she had done before—to swim without eyes on her, to be a mermaid in the sea instead of in a tank.

He waited. He must have nodded off, for suddenly she was there again, pulling herself onto the dock and calmly dressing as if he weren't there.

Then she faced him, and he offered his arm. She linked her own with his, and he breathed in her saltwater perfume and believed that in that moment he was the most fortunate man in New York.

CHAPTER 8

Amelia thought to steal back into her guest room and present herself at breakfast as though nothing had happened. Whatever argument she might have with Barnum—and there was still an argument there, for he was certainly confused about who owned her other than herself—she was reluctant to involve Charity in it.

Amelia found the door to the apartment unlocked (*almost as if Barnum expected me to come back*) and said good night to Levi there. She sensed a reluctance in him to leave, but Barnum had arranged for Dr. Griffin to stay at the Park Hotel. There were sure to be reporters there waiting despite the hour. Levi had told her on the walk home that the sensation of the mermaid would guarantee that.

"You shouldn't have to answer their questions if you don't wish to," Amelia said.

"That is what Barnum pays me to do," Levi said. "To talk to reporters, even if it is the middle of the night."

"How did you come to meet him?" she asked.

"Oh, we are friends of old. I was working as a lawyer and Barnum hired me to help him with another exhibit. I could talk on most subjects, and that seemed handy to Barnum," Levi said easily.

There was a glibness to his response that told her it wasn't the entire story, but Levi didn't seem inclined to continue. He must be speaking of the Joice Heth exhibit, which he had told her of previously. This was a topic of the utmost sensitivity for both Barnum and Levi. It occurred to her then that Levi, too, was irritated with Barnum and his present behavior.

Levi had confided in her that Barnum had promised him that Amelia would not be treated like Joice—that is, a possession to be used as Barnum saw fit. Amelia had no intention of allowing herself to be treated thus, but it was a comfort to know that Levi was on her side. She should tell him so, she thought. He should know that she appreciated what he did for her.

Then she remembered the way he'd asked her to stay and thought better of it. If she wasn't careful, if she didn't maintain the proper distance, he might believe she would welcome his attentions.

There was an empty room at the hotel for Amelia as well, but she wanted the comfort of the familiar this one last time. If it was not home, then she at least knew what was expected of her here.

Amelia slipped inside the apartment. Inside all was dark. She knew that if Barnum was still awake, he would likely be inside the museum. She had often heard him returning in the wee hours of the morning when she was unable to sleep.

She had nearly reached the door of her room when there was a footstep behind her and a tiny mewling noise. Charity stood there, in a white muslin nightgown and cap, with newborn Frances on her shoulder.

When the child was born, Amelia had been nearly overwhelmed by longing. She was so tiny, so pink, so blind and helpless, and yet this small thing could scream the house down, send everyone running to do her bidding. The first time Charity allowed Amelia to hold Frances, the mermaid had been afraid she might break this fragile thing if she gripped too hard.

But Charity had laughed and shown her how to be cautious of the baby's head, and then smiled fondly on the two of them as Amelia had leaned in and breathed the delicate scent that came off the baby's skin. Human babies actually smelled new, she discovered, new and sweet. Mermaid babies did not have this, or rather Amelia did not remember it being so. Then again, she could not recall ever holding a new mermaid.

"Are you staying, then?" Charity asked.

Amelia couldn't tell from the tone of her voice whether Charity welcomed the idea. She'd been horrified by the news of the mob at the Concert Hall, but despite the fact that a good portion of people had seen Amelia change from a human to a creature of the sea, Charity still seemed to think it was a trick of some sort. She herself had not attended due to the need to stay with the baby.

Barnum had refused to take Caroline if her mother was not present, and Caroline's resulting tantrum had been in full flow when Amelia and Levi left for the Concert Hall.

Amelia said, "I will stay, for now."

Charity approached her, so that they stood only a few feet away from each other in the dark. Amelia could not read the expression on Charity's face. The shadows kept shifting, playing tricks.

"Are you really a mermaid?" Charity asked.

"I've told you I am," Amelia said.

She felt a little stab of impatience; would the woman believe nothing without the proof of her own eyes? Charity was a regular churchgoer, and Amelia felt there was nothing more absurd than believing in a God who never spoke or appeared to you but disbelieving a mermaid that sat in your parlor.

"Everyone said—Taylor, and Levi, and all the papers." One of her hands fluttered against Frances's back.

"Yes," Amelia said.

"Why . . ." Charity said, and trailed off.

Amelia thought she would never dare say whatever she was about to in the light of day. Charity felt protected by the darkness and their solitude and, most importantly, the absence of Barnum.

"Why would you come here if you could swim in the sea and be free?" Charity asked.

"I fell in love," Amelia said.

"Yes," Charity said. "But after he died, you could have returned to your own people. You could have had the life you had before."

"I don't think I could have," Amelia said. "I left because I wanted something I didn't have, and once I loved Jack and lost him, I wasn't the same as I was before. Love does that. It changes you in ways that can't be undone."

"Yes, it traps you," Charity said. "It puts you in a cage that you can't escape."

Amelia moved a little closer. She wanted to see Charity's eyes, even if they were just a gleam in the darkness.

"You must have loved him once."

"Of course I did. And he romanced me, you know, despite the fact that his mother did not approve. He was younger than I, and handsome, and determined to have me. He was a clerk in a shop, and I was a tailoress in Bethel, his hometown. He said that my face haunted his dreams the first night we met."

Amelia had trouble imagining Barnum as a young lover. She could hardly imagine him caring about anything so ephemeral and unlikely to profit him as love.

"What happened to him, that's what you're wondering," Charity said with a little laugh. "Marriage was an adventure for him, until it wasn't. His mother didn't think I was good enough for him, thought Taylor could do better than a mere tailoress. We married in New York City without her knowledge. He'd told her he was coming here on business and came home with a wife. I think part of the reason he loved me was the excitement of keeping the secret. Once you're married, there are no more secrets, only staid respectability. I don't think Taylor has ever really wanted respectability, else he wouldn't be in the business he is in. And I keep disappointing him with girl children instead of boys."

"Why is a girl less valuable than a boy?" Amelia asked. She'd heard this before and did not understand it. Did not women bear the next generation? Was not that power more profound than anything a man could do?

"Men like to have sons to carry on their name," Charity said. "They aren't men otherwise."

"A girl can have her father's name," Amelia said.

"Until she is married. You know this," Charity said with a touch of exasperation. "You took your own husband's name. When you marry your husband you belong to him."

"Because I did not have a human name of my own,"

Amelia said. "Not because I became his property. Jack never thought I belonged to him."

"Then your husband was exceptional," Charity said, "and you were blessed. For I belong to my husband, who expects me to obey him in all things, and who feels free to disregard my wishes or to mock me in front of others. And I don't believe my husband is different from most men."

Amelia realized then that she had something Charity had never had—a choice. If Charity had not married P. T. Barnum, then she would have married some other man, or lived in the house of her father until she died. She would not have left her home the way Amelia had, or lived on her own, or traveled to a different city and put herself on display. She would have done exactly what was expected of her, always, as most women did.

"I am sorry for you," Amelia said. She knew this wasn't the correct thing to say, that one was not supposed to show pity and that Charity was particularly sensitive to it.

"Do not feel sorry for me," Charity snapped. Then, more calmly, "I have my girls. Taylor may not value them, but I do. It's more than some have."

This seemed like a pointed remark on Amelia's lack of fertility, and she was surprised that it hurt. Each time she thought Charity would open up or change her mind about Amelia, she'd been wrong.

"I will be moving to the hotel tomorrow," Amelia said,

stiff with politeness. This was the thing she must do—show gratitude to her hostess. Charity did not wish anything else from her. "Thank you for allowing me to stay in your home."

Amelia went into her room before Charity could respond. She didn't want to engage any further with her, and as she lay on her bed, she realized she'd only wanted something she'd never had before—a friend.

And because it hurt, because she hated the pried-open feeling of being vulnerable, she decided she would no longer try. What need had a mermaid of friends? Why become attached when her situation was only temporary?

After all, she knew very well she would leave New York City one day. And even if she didn't, she was going to live a very long time—longer than Barnum or Charity, longer than Levi Lyman, perhaps even longer than little Caroline or Helen or Frances.

She did not wish to weep, so she turned her head into the pillow and pretended she did not feel the tears.

The next day Barnum arranged to have a coach take Amelia (dressed in one of her new dresses and wearing a bonnet to hide her bound hair) and her trunk to the Park Hotel.

The hotel was visible from the American Museum, and Amelia thought it absurd that Barnum pay for a coach—a thing he was sure to complain of later—to take her there when the walk was less than a minute long.

"No one must know you've been staying here," Barnum said. "I've asked the coachman to drive north some way before turning about and coming back to the hotel."

Amelia failed to see how he would guarantee that the coachman didn't speak of this to the mobs of reporters that hovered outside the hotel, but then she saw the generous allowance he gave the man and realized he'd solved the problem the same way he did everything—with money.

Levi was to meet her in front of the hotel upon arrival. Barnum suggested that she not speak to or acknowledge the reporters at all.

"I think it's best if we pretend that you can't speak," Barnum said.

"Why?" Amelia asked. They were at the breakfast table with Charity, who seemed more restrained than usual, as if she were sorry to have spoken so freely to Amelia the night before.

For Barnum's part, he did not mention at all Amelia's angry leaving. He went about with his morning and his business as though she'd never left.

"If you don't talk, it increases the mystery," Barnum said. "It will also keep them directing their questions at Levi."

"And Levi is better at lying than I am," Amelia said.

"To be frank, yes," Barnum said. "It's safer if we tell them you can't communicate in any human language."

"What will happen if they ask Levi how he convinced me to come here, then?" Amelia asked. This seemed like a fairly large flaw, in her eyes.

Barnum waved that away. "He'll think of something. He'll tell them he drew pictures to show you or some such thing. Really, the boy can generate the most outlandish stories at a moment's notice."

So Amelia was bundled into the coach and taken for a ride around the city, and then returned to the hotel at the prearranged time to find Levi as Dr. Griffin waiting for her, patiently taking questions from the reporters who each jostled for supremacy, shouting over one another in an attempt to have their questions answered first.

She watched from the window as he smoothly detached himself and strode to the coach, snapping his fingers for the hotel porter to take her trunk. The mob followed him like they were attached to his coat by string.

"Lady Amelia," he said, offering his hand for her to take as she stepped out.

"Lady? How can a mermaid be titled?" one of the reporters asked.

"Thanks to a type of sign language I have worked out with the mermaid, she can communicate only with me. I have determined, during our conversations, that she is a kind of princess among her own people. Given this, I believe I should honor her heritage," Levi said.

Amelia wondered if Levi had thought of this fiction prior to her arrival or if he'd made it up on the spot.

She soon discovered that despite Levi's insistence that she could not speak nor understand them, the reporters persisted in shouting questions at her.

"Lady Amelia! What do you think of New York?"

"Lady Amelia! Why did you come here with Dr. Griffin?"

"Lady Amelia! What do mermaids eat?"

"Lady Amelia! How many more of you are there?"

And on, and on, and on. There seemed to be no question too trivial, and her refusal to make a noise or even turn her head did not deter them. The hotel staff had to be engaged to keep the reporters from following her and Levi up the stairs; she wondered how much money Barnum had paid to ensure their cooperation.

Their rooms were on the fifth floor of the six-story building with a view of St. Paul's across the street. Barnum had explained that the hotel had a strict policy of not allowing unaccompanied women to enter, but since she was there as a "guest" of Dr. Griffin, it was permitted. However, "for your own safety," a guard would be posted outside her door at night. Amelia doubted very much that her safety was Barnum's concern. Rather, it was a ham-handed attempt at keeping her from scarpering. She wasn't concerned. If and when she wanted to leave, she was confident she could do so and that Levi would aid her in that quarter if necessary. Let Barnum gnash his teeth about the expense of the guard in the meantime.

The hotel was not, she noted, significantly quieter than in the museum. For one thing the intersection below was always filled with people; for another, when the window was open, she could hear the terrible band that Barnum hired to play outside the museum. The office of the *New York Herald* was also nearby, and doubtless half of the reporters lurking in the hotel would rush across to file their dispatches shortly.

The room, she supposed, was luxurious, but to her luxury simply meant there was too much of everything. Too many folds, too many fabrics, too many objects on tables and shelves. The windows were large but covered in long curtains. At least the windows allowed in some light and air, a quality that had been lacking in the Barnums' guest room.

She was to leave the hotel almost as soon as she arrived there, for another "exhibition" was scheduled for the Concert Hall that day. Barnum had hired a contingent of twenty men to stand about the hall and at the doors. Though each was dressed respectably, they had a rough look about them, as if they'd been drafted from places where they regularly washed blood from beneath their fingernails.

The second performance went much as the first one did, with the exception that the audience seemed both prepared for the spectacle and wary of the looming guards.

Several people stood when she changed, craning their

necks and pointing, but no one tried to rush the stage again. She swam in a few loops inside the tank, unsure what else to do. The rehearsals had always been concerned with the timing of her entry onstage and affirming that the change could occur inside the tank; no one had discussed what she should do after that.

She broke the surface to look at the audience without the warping of the glass between them. When she did several people clapped and oohed, and she felt she had done what was expected of her.

Levi reemerged from the wings to take questions from the audience. Amelia dove back into the water then, swimming in various patterns and wondering how long she was supposed to do this.

Her days quickly became a tiresome repetition of that one. She would rise in the hotel, breakfast, walk the gauntlet of reporters and lookers-on with Levi, climb into a coach to the Concert Hall, change into a mermaid, and swim in circles until Levi declared the performance ended for the day. Most days she took her supper in her room, for if she did not, she would be bothered throughout her meal by men in the hotel who wanted to speak to a "real mermaid," and who would not be put off by any amount of glib replies from Levi.

After a weeklong engagement at the Concert Hall, Barnum took out an advertisement in the newspaper stating that he'd made an agreement with Dr. Griffin to bring the mermaid "at a most extraordinary expense" to the American Museum for the benefit of his "discerning public." Despite the extra cost to him, Barnum made sure that it was known that the mermaid would be exhibited "without extra charge."

Amelia was not permitted, despite this change of venue, to return to her small guest room in the Barnums' apartment.

"How can you advertise the program if you're not in the hotel?" Barnum said. "The museum show won't begin for at least two more weeks."

"I don't think it's necessary to advertise any longer, Mr. Barnum," she said. "As you have hoped, the whole city has mermaid fever."

"Maybe the whole country," Levi said. "There were reporters from plenty of out-of-state papers today."

They were meeting in Levi's room in the hotel, it being deemed easier for Barnum to come in than for Amelia and Levi to go out.

Barnum laughed in delight. "Soon all the monarchs of Europe will cross the ocean to see you."

Amelia did not particularly care who came to see her so long as the new tank that Barnum built inside the museum was larger than the one at the Concert Hall. If she must swim in circles endlessly, then she wished for those circles to be greater than the ones to which she was currently confined.

"Lady Amelia," "Dr. Griffin," and a select cohort of journalists were invited to tour the new exhibit in the museum prior to its opening to the public. A crowd of the curious gathered in two long rows between the hotel and the museum to watch Amelia and Levi and the reporters cross the street between the buildings.

Amelia had already spent many days with people gawking at her, but she never felt so foolish as during that promenade between the hotel and the museum. Her face was hidden by her bonnet and she abruptly felt the necessity of the parasol. When she opened it she had somewhere to put her hands, and the shade could be tilted to hide the size of the crowd if too much of it peeked through the brim of her hat.

Barnum waited at the entrance to the museum with his showman's smile and a wave. He kissed Amelia's hand like he was greeting true royalty. She was barely able to restrain herself from snatching her hand away from his dry lips.

The doors were securely locked once all the party had entered the museum, and two more of Barnum's toughs were set outside to glare at anyone with thoughts of trying to follow.

The sixth saloon had been designated the "mermaid room." This forced ticket holders to pass through many other exhibits first; Barnum didn't want folk coming to the museum only to see the mermaid and then rushing out again. After all, he needed to sell programs, and the programs were useless if people didn't enjoy the rest of the museum.

"Also," he'd told Amelia earlier, "one day you plan on leaving me, don't you? And I'll still have to sell tickets to the museum. If everyone who comes to see you loves the other exhibits, then they'll tell their friends that Barnum's American Museum is worth their Sunday afternoon and a quarter."

Once inside the mermaid room, they were immediately confronted with a large copy of the woodcut Barnum had used in the advertising pamphlets. This depicted three beautiful mermaids, one of which was seductively combing her hair. The copy had been printed on a long, billowing curtain that hung down from the ceiling.

This effectively blocked the rest of the room and, Amelia realized, created more anticipation. The effect was duplicated almost as soon as a visitor turned the corner. Before them was a large white sign with another picture of a mermaid; next to this was text describing Dr. Griffin's encounter with the mermaid in the waters of Fiji.

Below this, safely hidden under glass, was a small notebook with a leather cover open to a diary entry in which Dr. Griffin wrote of his marvelous discovery. On the next page was a small sketch of Amelia. Levi had done this himself, and Amelia was impressed with how well he'd captured her real likeness. She looked like what she was—a mermaid, an alien thing, not the lovely creature that Barnum used to sell tickets.

This notebook was entirely empty otherwise. Barnum had aged it by bending the leather and bindings and dripping salt water on the edges so they would curl up. It looked like a real naturalist's notebook, but it was just another of Barnum's humbugs.

Every turn of the exhibit had another display like this— one with a seashell necklace that was supposedly a gift from Amelia to Dr. Griffin, a copy of the letter Dr. Griffin had sent to the London Lyceum, and so on. The very last stop before visitors reached the tank (which was twice as large as the one at the Concert Hall) was the very dried-up mummy fish that Barnum's friend Kimball had used to propose the mermaid exhibit so many months ago.

The thing was horrible, but all the reporters stared at it in fascination before asking Amelia how it felt to see one of her very own dead ancestors there. Despite her continued silence they never ceased trying to see if she would answer.

The result of all this twisting and turning was something like a maze that would force visitors through the saloon slowly. They wouldn't be able to rush to the tank, for no one could even see the tank until they turned the last corner and reached the very end. And of course, there would be guards present to ensure no one got any untoward ideas, like trying to climb into the tank with her.

Amelia almost hated to praise Barnum, but he'd done an exceptional job of designing the mermaid room to maximize interest. Additionally, the constant press of people behind them would keep viewers moving through to the next room. No one would be able to stand indefinitely in front of the tank and block others from seeing her.

The result of that bit of genius would mean the museum could accommodate more people, and more people meant more ticket sales. Amelia should have been pleased about this; her contract stated that she took a portion of the sales, and Levi had assured her that he'd been keeping careful track of Barnum's accounting. But somehow she couldn't think of dollars and cents as Barnum did. She could think only of the eyes, the parade of eyes that would march past her all day.

"How about a demonstration from the mermaid?" one of the reporters asked Barnum.

Half of the men looked at Barnum and the other half at Amelia. She felt suddenly the discomfort of being the only woman in a room full of men, men who gazed at her with speculative eyes. Her body did not seem to be protected by her clothes, and she resisted the urge to turn away. They would not make her ashamed of herself. They would not make her a human woman.

She pretended not to know what the man had said and gazed at each one in turn until their eyes dropped away.

Barnum said, "I can't believe a demonstration would be necessary. Not when all of you lads have surely seen the lady at the Concert Hall this week."

"I've seen it, but I'm still not sure what actually happened," one man said. "How does she change? How can it even be possible?"

"The good Lord created many wonders before he rested," Barnum said.

Amelia marveled at the way a lie rolled off his tongue. He didn't even seem to think about it.

"Dr. Griffin, you're a naturalist. What do you think?"

Levi smiled easily, the smile that Amelia thought of as his showman's smile. It wasn't really Levi when he smiled like that.

"I'd have to agree with Mr. Barnum. Some wonders can't be explained," he said.

The man looked as though he wanted to continue that line of questioning, but then Barnum promised all of them a glass of whiskey to celebrate and they filed out.

Amelia lingered behind, staring at the tank, trying to remember why she was doing this. She tilted her head, walked around it. She thought of the long and tiresome days at the Concert Hall, and the more she looked at the tank, the more it looked like a cage.

CHAPTER 9

Barnum wanted Amelia to climb into the tank every morning before the crowds arrived and then swim in circles for the duration of the day. This meant hours and hours and hours of dull repetition while people stared at her.

"No," she said. "I won't do it from morning until night."

Amelia and Levi and Barnum were at Barnum's dining table, a place that had become an unofficial conference area for performance-related discussions. There were doors that could be latched shut on either end of the room, thereby keeping Caroline out (she always wanted to be near Amelia if the mermaid was in the building).

The reporters had been politely shooed from the museum, each one promising a sensational write-up of the new exhibit. Barnum had been unable to keep the glee off his face as he locked the museum doors behind them. The only thing Barnum loved more than ticket sales was the thought of free advertising.

"Young lady, may I remind you that the point and purpose of the exhibit is to see you. If you are not present, then who will buy tickets?"

"I will be present," Amelia said. "But I won't be present all day from the museum's opening until its close. Even you must agree that's an unreasonable request, Mr. Barnum."

"Even I?" Barnum spluttered. "And just what do you mean by that?"

"You've got to give her a rest, Barnum," Levi said, giving Amelia a warning look.

Amelia stared blandly back at him. She wasn't about to tiptoe around Barnum's feelings when he never did the same for her.

"If she's resting, she's not getting paid," Barnum said.

"You don't make your Mammoth Boys perform all day without stopping," Amelia said. "Why do I not get the same consideration?"

"The Mammoth Boys aren't the same draw you are," Barnum said. "It's a different situation. People are going to flood into the museum tomorrow with just one thing on their mind—to see the Feejee Mermaid. How can we disappoint them? If you're not in your tank when they arrive, they'll be angry and disappointed. They might even ask for their money back."

The horror of this thought could be clearly read on his face.

"Why?" Amelia said. "You've said many times that you aren't increasing the entry fee because of me. They can tour the rest of the museum if I am not there and obtain the same entertainment value that they always have."

"And then leave and tell their friends that old Barnum was at it again, that it was all just another humbug? I can hear it now—'I came all the way from Pennsylvania just to see the mermaid and there was no mermaid when I got there. Barnum's Museum is nothing but a lot of stuff and nonsense.' That would be terrible. *Terrible.* We need people to go home and tell their friends about how marvelous the museum is, how magnificent it was to see a real mermaid, how it is worth every penny to travel to New York City and take in the sights here."

Barnum stood, pointing his finger at Levi and Amelia. "I don't think either of you truly understand what's at stake. This is bigger than just the mermaid. This is about the reputation of this institution."

"I won't swim in circles all day without a chance to rest and eat," Amelia said, not deigning to acknowledge the reputation of the institution.

And get away from prying eyes, she thought. The tank in the museum would be much closer to the crowds than it was onstage. A rope had been strung around the glass to keep people from pressing up against it, but they would still be too close.

"What if we clearly posted the hours for mermaid viewings?" Levi said. "We could put them up where folks pay the entry fee. That way there would be no disappointment if they wanted to see Amelia. They would know that she was only on exhibit at certain times."

"What if people decide to leave and not pay the fee at all?" Barnum said. "We would be losing business. And that's your business, too, madam. Don't pretend that you're above such petty human concerns."

"What do you mean?" Amelia asked.

"You want to make money, the same as me, the same as everyone. There are things you want, and you can't get them without money. You're not so different from me at all," Barnum said, triumph in his voice.

Amelia stood. She wouldn't have him shouting down at her. "You don't know me, Mr. Barnum. You don't know why I am here or what I want. Don't think you can hold everyone to your same low standards."

"I am paying for you, and you will do what we agreed," Barnum said between his teeth.

"You are not paying *for* me," Amelia said. "You are paying me, and there's a difference."

"Barnum—" Levi began.

"And you," Barnum said, pointing at Levi. "Always taking

her side, always playing the knight-errant. If you want to get into the girl's skirts then do it, but stop getting in the way of my business."

"You seem to think that my skirts are available for lifting on demand," Amelia said. "I am not a whore, nor will I be one for you, Barnum, or you, Levi Lyman."

"Amelia, no, I would never—" Levi said. His cheeks were ruddy, and his expression was a cross between pleading and anger. The anger, she knew, was for Barnum, but she couldn't worry about Levi's feelings just then. She had to make things clear to Barnum.

There had always been the threat of his fist closing around her from the start. He wanted to control her, keep her in a bottle, make her a possession. Thus far she'd managed to squirm away from his grasp, but she was tired of it. He needed to understand that it was she who held the power now, not him. All the money that he wanted would not appear without her.

"I will dictate the terms of my performance, Mr. Barnum, not you. You've already expressed that the museum would suffer without my presence for an hour. I imagine it would suffer even more if there was no mermaid there at all."

"You signed a contract," Barnum said.

"You need a mermaid," Amelia said. "How will you ever recoup your expenses without me?"

She'd been careful not to smile or to express any

annoyance or anger in her face. Throughout the conversation she'd remained perfectly cool and blank, but it was difficult to suppress her glee at the trapped look in Barnum's eyes. She had him, at least for now.

Amelia didn't fool herself that Barnum was beaten. It was only a temporary setback to him, and he was too crafty to try such a straightforward assault again. There would never be a time when she would not have to be on her guard against him.

Barnum laughed then, a short, sharp bark with no mirth in it. "Lady Amelia wants rests and meals, and so she shall have them."

He gave an exaggerated bow in her direction. She nodded. Levi seemed to be struggling to keep up, which was unusual for him. Amelia thought he must still feel embarrassed about Barnum's crude statement. Later, when the two of them returned to the hotel, Levi asked if he might enter her room for a moment to speak to her.

Barnum had kept on a few of the toughs who'd guarded the stage at the Concert Hall to watch Levi's and Amelia's hotel rooms at night. They appeared in an irregular rotation so that Amelia was never certain if she saw the same man twice, particularly since they superficially resembled one another. They were all large and squinty-eyed and wore good coats, but they could not hide the scabs on their knuckles.

The necessity of their services had been increased from

night watch to all-day and all-night watch due to reporters. Several of the men who seemed to live in the hotel lobby had become more aggressive of late.

One morning Amelia had opened the curtains in her room to discover one of these newspapermen hanging from a rope outside her window. As soon as her curtains parted he began shouting questions through the glass. If he thought to startle her into speech he'd been badly mistaken. Amelia had calmly left her room, knocked on Levi's door, and told him (in a quiet undertone, just in case there were reporters outside his own window) what had occurred.

Levi called the hotel manager, and the man was removed with much fuss and bother, as he had lowered himself down in a kind of rope seat but apparently lacked the strength to pull himself up again. A crowd of onlookers gathered below, clogging up the already busy intersection. Several of the hotel staff were forced to help drag the man up to the roof in a kind of tug-of-war.

This man was later to be the butt of many of his colleagues' jokes when a drawing of him dangling like a spider appeared on the front page of his own newspaper. He'd been the biggest news story that day, and his own publication couldn't miss the chance he'd presented. While he hadn't gotten any quote from "Lady Amelia," he did tell the thrilling eyewitness tale of having seen her at her window in a white dressing gown.

The newspaper was able to make hay of this again when

a number of scandalized letters were written impugning the reporter for daring to look upon a lady in her private clothes, and worse for writing about it.

The scandal bumped the paper's numbers for several days, which had the unfortunate effect of encouraging the remaining pool of reporters to similar feats. It seemed they had nothing better to do during the lull between Amelia's Concert Hall appearances and her opening at the museum.

Thus the need for more guards, though Amelia did not fool herself that it was all for her benefit. Barnum didn't want his prize to fly away.

Levi seemed overconscious of the presence of the man at the door while asking if he could speak to her. Amelia thought it was likely the man didn't care in the least what Levi was about but that he would probably report the incident to Barnum.

Barnum at first had seemed amused by Levi's interest in her (Levi, of course, appeared unaware that anyone but he knew of his feelings), but Barnum now seemed to find it personally insulting. He relied on Levi much more than he would admit, and it clearly troubled him that Levi never seemed to see things his way any longer.

Amelia nodded and let Levi into her rooms. She did not invite him to sit, but she did remove her bonnet, breathing a small sigh of relief as she pushed it off her head.

She didn't know what she hated more, the bonnet or the

petticoat. Both of them scratched at her and kept her from moving about as she wished—the bonnet by restricting her sight and the petticoat by restricting her walk. One could not run in a petticoat (though Charity had informed her that women of good breeding did not run in any case).

She placed the bonnet on one of the many small tables and immediately began unbinding the braids that were tied in a bun at the back of her neck. She'd never bound her hair for Jack, and she despised the expectation that she should now.

Levi watched her in obvious fascination as she loosed each bit of hair. It was apparent he'd forgotten why he'd asked to come into her room in the first place.

"You wished to speak to me, Mr. Lyman?" she asked.

He shook his head, and when he looked at her again, the spell was broken.

"I wished to apologize for what Barnum said to you earlier. The implication that you were an, er, unclean woman," Levi said.

"He didn't imply I was unclean. He said I was a prostitute," Amelia said. "And I don't see why you should have to apologize for his behavior. Mr. Barnum should apologize for himself."

"Barnum doesn't know how to say he's sorry," Levi muttered.

"That's because he never is sorry," Amelia said.

"Still, he insulted you, and someone ought to apologize for that, even if it didn't seem to bother you," Levi said, looking at the ground.

He seemed very young in that moment, a little boy trying to make things right but not knowing how. She felt a sudden swell of affection for him—this man who had struggled to make things better for her, this man who wanted something from her that he would never ask for.

She went to him and took his hand. He glanced up in surprise, for Amelia was always careful to keep physical distance between them.

"It did bother me," she said. "I never saw a prostitute until I came to this city, but I know what it means now. I know Barnum meant to insult me, that he lashed out because he couldn't have his way. And I know that you feel that insult on my behalf. I haven't said this to you as much as I should have, Levi, but I thank you. Thank you for what you have done for me."

She saw the conflict in his eyes—the quiet pleasure at her words and then the impulse to press his advantage, to ask her for more.

She was surprised by the sudden spark she felt, the answering impulse to lean into him. That feeling had her loosening his hand, stepping back, running her hand over her hair in a nervous gesture that was entirely unlike her.

Levi cleared his throat. He had a habit of doing this when

he was uncomfortable. It had irritated her at first, but now she found it endearing. That was worrisome, too. She should not find his silly habits endearing.

He seemed to be casting about for something to say in response to her thanks. She could almost see the words on his tongue, considered, and then swallowed.

Finally he said, "I always wish to be of any possible assistance to you, Mrs. Douglas."

Mrs. Douglas. She was always Mrs. Douglas when he was most afraid of her being Amelia. He gave her a little bow and left the room.

Amelia blew out all the air in her lungs and plunked herself into one of the delicate chairs in the sitting room. For a moment she'd felt something like desire toward Levi, but she couldn't feel that, could she? Because if she did it meant that she was betraying Jack, and she couldn't do that. She was his wife even if the sea had taken him from her.

But he had been gone so long. So very, very long, and when she tried to remember his face and the touch of his hand, it was mixed up with Levi's, and she could not recall Jack's voice at all.

She felt the bitterness of her choice then; she'd chosen to leave Jack's home, and in doing so she'd left his memory behind. No matter what she did now, he would fade more and more, until all she had left of him was his name even if she never did love another.

Love another? Did she even want to? If she loved Levi, what would happen?

"He will die," she said aloud.

Yes, he would die. He would die and she would go on living, on and on and on alone, and then all she would have left of him, too, would be his name.

It might never come to that, she reflected. Amelia would leave New York when her contract with Barnum was over. She knew Barnum hoped she would change her mind, that he could convince her otherwise, but she would leave. There were only so many hours she intended to spend inside his tank.

She would leave and Levi would stay, for he was unlikely to trail around after her while she traveled the world— though traveling the world had lost some of its shine for her, too. If she went to any of the great cities of the world, places like London and Rome and Paris, there would be people just as there were in New York.

And Amelia was heartily sick of people—the smell and the sound of them, the heat and the noise of them, and most of all the way everyone around her wanted something from her. Would she truly be able to be anonymous in a new city, or would some curious newspaperman find her out?

They wouldn't even need to find her out, she realized. She was unable to go anywhere without a horde following her. On the day she left the hotel, they would all surely see her off at the dock, and all it would take was one word from someone on board and everyone in her new place would know her identity. Would she always be Barnum's Feejee Mermaid wherever she went?

She didn't know what she wanted anymore. Amelia stood and paced the room, a thing she hardly ever did; she felt restless and longed to swim in the ocean or to leave her room, even if it was only to walk the streets of the city. Either action would only invite harassment—from the reporters who frothed about her every time she appeared, from the general public who recognized her from her show at the Concert Hall. Barnum didn't need to lock her inside, she realized—she was already a prisoner.

She'd run from the cottage on the rocks, from being Mrs. Jack Douglas, and now she was Barnum's mermaid no matter how she turned the picture. Would she ever just be only herself again, be that girl who chased the ship and dreamed of unseen wonders?

It was nearing the dinner hour but she wasn't hungry. Amelia undressed and climbed into the too-soft bed with its smooth sheets. She missed the worn wool blanket that smelled of Jack.

She closed her eyes. It was a long, long while before she was able to fall asleep.

When she woke, she remembered dreaming not of Jack, or of the sea, but of Levi.

CHAPTER 10

Amelia left the hotel very early in the morning on opening day at the museum. Levi had knocked on her door before the sun was up, and the sky was pink and grey above the rooftops of the city when they crossed the intersection to Barnum's.

Despite the early hour, a crowd was already forming outside the doors. Barnum had sent four of his goons to form a kind of honor guard around Amelia so she could enter the building safely. Their presence did not deter many people, who shouted her name and tried to rip off pieces of her skirt.

One woman—middle-aged and dressed like a perfectly respectable matron—managed to dart between the men and snatch Amelia's parasol out of her hand. She disappeared back into the crowd before Amelia's guard had a chance to do anything about it.

Amelia wouldn't weep any tears for the loss of the parasol, but she was astonished at the audacity of the woman. She also didn't understand why the thief had wanted the parasol in the first place.

"She certainly looked as though she could afford to buy one herself," Amelia said to Levi once they were safely inside the museum.

"But a new parasol wouldn't have been touched by you," Levi said.

Amelia gave him a quizzical look.

"Either she'll hold it as a keepsake of the Feejee Mermaid or, more likely, she'll sell it for ten times its value."

"But why would anyone want to buy a parasol for that much?" Amelia asked as Levi led her to Barnum's apartment. They were supposed to have breakfast with Charity and Barnum and Caroline.

Levi shook his head. "It's more valuable because it was yours."

"I don't understand," Amelia said.

This was one of those human conundrums that she would never solve. Objects were more valuable depending on who owned them? Paintings were more valuable depending on who painted them?

Humans often valued what they should not, she reflected, and most often they did not value what was right before their eyes.

Barnum wasn't at the breakfast table when they arrived. Charity was there, holding little Frances in one arm.

"He's gone to examine the exhibit one last time," Charity said. "He wishes for everything to be perfect today. Cook will be bringing out breakfast shortly."

Amelia nodded and sat down. She'd never been as comfortable with Charity since the night they'd spoken, and she hadn't had a chance to begin again because she'd been forced to move to the hotel. She'd hoped that Charity would be friendly to her again once she forgot her initial discomfort, but Charity had returned to the brisk, distant personality she'd had upon their first meeting.

"Now," Charity continued. "Caroline wishes to see you change, or whatever it is you call it. I don't want her to go through the exhibit with the crowd outside. Taylor said it was becoming quite large, and I would rather not expose my daughter to a possibly dangerous situation."

"It won't be dangerous, Charity," Levi said.

"And how can you know that, Levi? The very first day this woman appeared onstage, another woman was trampled to death."

"Barnum's hired guards—" Levi began.

"Yes, I know all about these thugs of Taylor's. I don't like to think where he had to go to find them in the first place. They glare at me every time I leave the building, as if I were committing some crime."

Amelia was astonished by the idea that Charity might leave the building at all. She never seemed to go anywhere except to make the occasional afternoon call.

"But I don't think it will be dangerous for Caroline," Levi said. "There will be plenty of children throughout the day, I am sure. And Barnum's planned the exhibit very well, so that there is no chance of a mob rushing the tank like the first performance."

Amelia noticed that Levi used to refer to his friend as "Taylor," as Charity did, but lately he only called him "Barnum." It was a small thing, but it seemed Barnum was slowly losing Levi. Levi's words told her that even if nothing else did.

"Nevertheless," Charity said. "I wish to ask Mrs. Douglas if she will perform her trick for Caroline prior to the official opening of the show."

Amelia did not bristle when Charity called her change "a trick," but it was a close thing. She had to remind herself that Charity did not believe, despite what all the newspapers told her. Charity was the sort who needed to see the truth with her own eyes.

"Of course I will," Amelia said before Levi could intervene. "For Caroline."

Charity nodded her thanks, and the cook carried out their breakfast.

* * *

It was strange, Levi reflected, that he felt more nervous now than he had the first day at the Concert Hall.

Perhaps it was because he had less control of the situation. When he was Dr. Griffin, he was the one who opened the program, who took audience questions, who spoke to reporters. He could decide when Amelia had had enough and cut the program short.

He couldn't do any of those things once Amelia was inside the hall. In fact, after today, "Dr. Griffin" would no longer exist. Having left his mermaid in the care of P. T. Barnum, Dr. Griffin would shave off his beard and trim his hair and return to his sober brown suits and become plain Levi Lyman again.

And when he was plain Levi Lyman again, he wouldn't have the right to stay near her all day as he did now. Barnum wanted him to "duck out of sight for a while," so Levi would remain confined to his apartment for a week or two so people wouldn't associate him with Dr. Griffin.

When he told Amelia this, she'd said she was sorry that he had to stay inside for so long. She hadn't said a thing about missing him.

He must have dreamed that spark in her eyes the other night. If it had been there (and not the product of his too-hopeful imagination), then surely he would have seen it again. But her eyes remained the same—grey and serious and cool—and his heart persisted in wishing for a feeling she didn't share.

Caroline tugged his hand in excitement as they, Amelia, and Charity walked through the empty halls of the museum. Barnum was at the breakfast table enjoying his breakfast "in peace," as he put it.

"Levi, is Amelia so beautiful when she's a mermaid?" Caroline said.

"She doesn't look like those pictures," Levi said carefully, conscious of Amelia and Charity listening in. "But I do think she is beautiful, yes, in a different way."

"I'm sure she's the most beautiful creature in all the world." Caroline sighed.

Levi noticed a little spasm on Charity's face. Caroline's worship of Amelia had been hard on Charity. The girl was headstrong to begin with, and since Amelia's arrival, no one was as interesting, wonderful, or worthy of attention as the mermaid.

"I'm not beautiful," Amelia said.

Levi looked up at her, ready to contradict her, to declare just how lovely she was, but she wasn't talking to him. She was talking to Caroline.

The little girl released his hand and went to Amelia. "You're not?"

Amelia shook her head. "I don't resemble the pictures. Mr. Lyman told you that. When I am in the water, I'm not half human, half fish. It's a mistake to think that I am."

"What are you?" Caroline asked, her eyes wide.

"A creature of the sea," Amelia said. "Don't be afraid of

me, for though I may look very different, I am still the Amelia you know."

Caroline glanced back at Levi. "Is she scary?"

"A little," Levi admitted. "She has quite long claws. And sharp teeth."

Caroline gazed up at Amelia's somber face. "Is this true?"

Amelia nodded.

Caroline squared her shoulders and lifted her chin. "I can be brave. I'll know it's still you because you told me so. You're still Amelia inside."

Amelia held out her hand to the small girl. "Come and see me, then."

Charity watched all of this with the expression of slight bemusement that she always had around Amelia. Levi was worried what Charity would think when she saw Amelia change. Barnum's wife had been holding on hard to the idea that Amelia was nothing but a humbug. Levi had never seen a person so insistent that something real was actually a trick.

When they reached the sixth saloon, Caroline was inclined to ooh and ahh over the various pieces of the exhibit. She wanted to read all about how Dr. Griffin had met the mermaid in the waters of Fiji.

"You know all this is not true, don't you, Caroline?" Amelia said.

The little girl ignored her, peering into the glass case at the sketch of Amelia in the diary.

"Is this what you look like?" she asked. Her eyes were rounder than Levi had ever seen them.

"Yes," Amelia said. "Mr. Lyman did a very good job."

"You *are* scary," Caroline said. "But now I know what to expect, and so I won't be afraid."

They wound through the maze of the exhibit until they reached the tank. The guards were not present yet, nor were any of the museum attendants or other performers. It was still quite early. No one moved in the museum except the four of them.

Amelia went to the back of the tank where the ladder leaned against the glass. Because there was no way to block her naked body from view, it had been agreed that Amelia would enter the empty saloon in the morning and be in the water when the first visitors arrived.

At the time of her first break, the saloon would be cleared and then Amelia would climb out of the tank, change into her clothes, and rest behind a curtained area that Barnum had established a few feet behind the tank. Levi had put in a comfortable chaise and a tray with bread and cheese and cold meat for her to eat.

Amelia climbed out of her dress, which was much more complicated than it had been onstage. Then she always dressed simply, but now she had to struggle out of several layers of undergarments as well as her gown.

Charity gasped when she realized what Amelia was doing. "Turn around, Levi Lyman. And Caroline, you too."

Levi obligingly spun on his heel and the little girl copied him. He heard the quick ringing of Charity's heels as she went to Amelia and the rustling and murmuring as she helped Amelia out of her clothing.

He remembered Amelia on the beach under the moonlight, her skin glowing like a pearl. He remembered, too, her shining silver tail silhouetted against the horizon. Yes, he thought she was beautiful in all her forms and all her ways, but she would never believe him if he told her so.

Charity's steps approached them again, and the ladder squeaked as Amelia climbed it. Levi peeked over his shoulder and saw her at the top—her black hair flowing over the small pink buds of her breasts and down to her delicate waist. Then she dove into the water.

At the splash Caroline turned around and ran toward the tank. She ducked underneath the rope meant to keep guests out (*better tell Barnum that other children might do that,* Levi thought) and squashed her face against the glass.

Amelia floated there, her tail curled just under and back, her hair swirling all about her head. She watched them with her grave eyes, but Levi noticed that she wasn't really looking at Caroline or himself. She was watching Charity.

Charity stood frozen, both her hands clasped over her mouth. Silent tears poured from her eyes, dripping on her fingers and over them to the floor.

"Charity," Levi said, touching her arm.

She dropped her hands and spoke, but she could not tear her eyes away from Amelia.

"It's true," she said. "It's true. It's not a trick at all. She really is a mermaid. It's true. It's true."

"Of course it's true, Mama," Caroline said, waving at Amelia inside the tank. Amelia waved back, and Caroline gave an excited little gasp at the sight of Amelia's claws. "She told you it was, and Amelia doesn't lie."

"But your father does," Charity said, so low that Levi almost wasn't certain he'd heard her say it. "He lies like he breathes, so how could I possibly believe in a mermaid?"

Levi wanted to say, *But I told you it was true*, and then he realized it didn't matter. Charity had been raised to believe that her husband was the arbiter of all things, and it had been a bitter draught for her to discover that this authority was full of humbugs. Still, she wanted to believe him, to do what she thought was right, and that wanting always bumped up against who Barnum really was.

It couldn't have mattered to Charity if Levi had told her that Amelia truly was a mermaid, because Barnum had said it was true and therefore it must be false.

Now she was faced with the truth—that mermaids were real and one had been sitting in her parlor drinking her tea for several weeks. Levi felt sorrier for Charity than he ever had, and he felt sorry for her most of the time.

Caroline giggled, and Levi saw that Amelia was swimming

in circles so that her face passed closely where Caroline's pressed against the glass. Amelia turned upside down and flapped her tail against the surface of the water, and Caroline clapped her hands in delight.

Levi had never seen Amelia having fun in the water like this. In fact, he wasn't certain that he'd ever seen her so light and loose and easy as she was now, on land or otherwise.

Barnum strode into the hallway. "That's enough of that, now. We can't have Lady Amelia tiring herself out before she sees the public."

"But, Papa," Caroline said. "This is the first time I've ever seen a mermaid."

"It won't be the last," Barnum said. "She's under contract."

As soon as he arrived, Amelia's head broke the surface of the water. She stared at him with the bland look she seemed to reserve expressly for Barnum—a neutrality that concealed her dislike. Any joy she had felt was wiped clean by Barnum's presence.

"What's the matter with you?" he asked Charity brusquely. Then, without waiting for an answer, he said to Levi, "Take them back to the apartment, will you? I'd like to have a word with Mrs. Douglas."

There was another splash, and Levi looked up to see Amelia reaching into the jar of sand on the platform.

"Ooooooh," Caroline said as she watched the scales on Amelia's body disappear.

Levi looked at Charity, who was wiping the tears from her eyes with a handkerchief, and then at Amelia, who was climbing naked down the ladder as if no one could see her. He wished suddenly to sweep them up and take them away—Barnum's wife, his children, his mermaid—take them away to a place where they could be free of him. He'd been friends with Barnum for a long, long time, but he'd never realized just how careless and mercenary Barnum was until Amelia arrived.

Amelia pulled on her underclothing but not her dress and waited for Barnum to speak.

Barnum turned his face halfway to the ground and said, "Once you're dressed, Mrs. Douglas."

He didn't appear embarrassed or as if he cared about her modesty. Rather, it seemed to be a sop to Charity's sense of decency.

Charity said, "Taylor, you ought to get the girl a dressing gown for this. She can't possibly change into and out of her ordinary clothes several times a day."

"I bought her a dressing gown," Barnum said. "That damned reporter told half the city about it."

"She can't be expected to carry her dressing gown from the hotel to the exhibit and back again every day," Charity said.

"Charity, I did not come here to talk about dressing gowns," Barnum said. "Take Caroline back to the apartment, please."

"What *did* you come to talk about?" Amelia asked.

Barnum glanced around at Levi, Charity, and Caroline watching him. "I'd prefer to speak to you in private."

"I wouldn't," Amelia said. "Especially as I noticed this morning that there was no sign near the ticket-taking booth indicating the hours I would not be exhibited. I can't read very much, but even I can tell if a sign isn't present when it's supposed to be."

Levi started. He hadn't noticed that the sign wasn't up. He'd been too busy thinking about Amelia—about her ordeal in the crowds that morning, about what she might expect inside the museum. He'd assumed—rather foolishly, as he knew Barnum almost as well as Charity did—that the matter was settled.

Barnum scratched the back of his neck. "As it's the first day, and the crowd outside is so large, I thought—"

"No," Amelia said. "That is not what we agreed."

"We didn't agree to your spending half the day lounging behind a curtain," Barnum said.

"Taylor," Charity said, sounding scandalized. "You can't possibly think of leaving this woman in the tank all day without a rest or food. It's not human."

"She's not human," Barnum said. "You just saw that for yourself. What's the difference between her and a tiger in a cage?"

"I am not an animal," Amelia said. "And I won't stay in

the tank all day, even if it means climbing out naked in front of all your precious ticket holders."

"You can't climb out if someone takes your jar of sand away," Barnum said.

Levi started toward Barnum. He didn't know what he was going to do—hit him? Levi wasn't practiced in violence, but he'd never felt the impulse to it so strongly. Caroline's voice drew him up before he could do something he might regret.

"That's a terrible thing to say, Papa."

The little girl's eyes were enormous and so full of disappointment that Levi thought they must pierce the cash register Barnum had in place of a heart.

"Caroline, this is not business for you to hear," Barnum said. "Charity, I told you to take her away."

"No, Papa," Caroline said, and ran to Amelia's side. "Amelia is a mermaid. She's not an animal, and you can't treat her like one. If you do, she'll run away, and I will, too."

"Caroline, enough of this nonsense—"

"And so will I," Charity said. "I will take the children and I will leave you."

Barnum stared at Charity. "You can't divorce me. You have no grounds."

"I didn't say I would divorce you. I said I would leave you." Charity's voice trembled and so did her hands, but she would not drop her eyes.

"Over this?" Barnum said, pointing to Amelia. He seemed barely able to speak, choking on his astonishment. "Over a mermaid?"

"Can't you see she's something wonderful, Taylor?" Charity said. "Can't you see that she's not a thing to be bought and sold? I know you want this museum to be a success. I know how hard you have worked your whole life to this end. But Amelia is not yours. She came here for her own reasons, and she will leave for her own reasons. Until then, you need to respect her as a partner, as a being who has her own will. You can't put her in the tank and leave her there just because you want to sell more tickets."

"And you agreed to her terms, Barnum," Levi said. "I witnessed it."

Barnum looked from Charity to Amelia to Levi to Caroline. He threw his hands into the air. "Let the lady have what she wants then. She wants a sign, I'll make a sign."

He left the exhibit without another word.

Levi wondered when his friend had become a newspaper cartoon, when Barnum's love of money had overcome his humanity and his common sense. He'd always thought of Barnum's avarice as a small part of his personality, something to laugh about but not truly characteristic. But it had become apparent that the mermaid had made him mad.

Charity crossed to Amelia and put her arms around her.

Levi saw surprise, then joy, then a strange kind of sorrow on the mermaid's face. She returned Charity's embrace, her eyes closed, as Charity wept into her shoulder and said, "I'm sorry, I'm sorry" over and over and Amelia murmured, "It's all right, don't cry now."

Caroline wrapped her little arms around Charity's and Amelia's legs and pressed her face into her mother's skirt and the three of them seemed so far away, so enmeshed in one another, that Levi had to leave the room. They didn't notice him go.

They were all against him, Barnum thought. All of them! They all sided with the mermaid no matter what he did. He wished Moses were there. He could talk to Moses about his troubles, but Moses was back in Boston running his own museum.

He used to be able to talk to Levi, once upon a time. The boy had been his glad co-conspirator, full of mischief. He'd enjoyed pulling one over on the public with Joice Heth, at least at first.

Then the woman started saying she wanted peace, that she wanted to die. Levi hadn't ever really forgiven him for not letting the woman go, or for charging an entrance fee to see Joice's autopsy. He had extracted a promise from Barnum that it would never happen again.

And yet here they were, Barnum mused. He'd gone too far, just as he had with Joice Heth, and Levi was angry with him again.

He'd never seen Charity like that, either.

She would leave me—threaten to leave me—over a mermaid! When she never says boo to a goose most of the time. It had shocked him to see her like that, it truly had.

Couldn't she see that he was only trying to make a good life for her and the children?

Still, perhaps it was unreasonable to expect the mermaid to perform all day. As she herself had pointed out, he didn't expect it of his other performers.

But it was difficult, so difficult, to reconcile that thought with the money he imagined he would lose.

Do you want to lose your wife and children instead? The thought, unbidden, emerged from somewhere in the depths of his mind.

No, he didn't want to lose them. There was nothing more embarrassing than a man whose wife left him, and the newspapers would surely get wind of it.

He felt something tight in his stomach unclench then. He would have to let the mermaid have her way. He couldn't be at loggerheads with her and the others for the duration. He would just have to think of a way to make up the lost income while she was lounging about. Keepsakes, perhaps. Mermaid dolls? Or books about the mermaid?

Barnum felt a slow smile cross his face. Yes, he could still profit by her even if the mermaid wasn't swimming in the tank. And her contract didn't say anything about souvenirs. He wouldn't have to share a cent with her.

CHAPTER 11

THREE WEEKS LATER

The man had been watching her for too long.

Amelia usually avoided catching the eye of any one person in the crowd. The number of faces quickly became overwhelming, so she'd developed a technique of passing just over their heads with her gaze.

This gave the sense that she was looking at them, and perhaps even had looked directly at one person (she'd heard more than one delighted squeal of "She looked right at me!" even through the suppressing blanket of the water). The only exception was for children.

She made a special point of waving at them, doing tricks for them, and generally trying to convince them that she was not as frightening as she looked.

She didn't want the children to be afraid of her. She wanted them to wonder at her, like Caroline did.

The man who'd stared too long stood just to the left of the front of the tank and far enough back that he hadn't attracted the attention of the two guards. He was not very tall but he was extremely thin—his shoulders could hardly hold up the sleeves of his jacket. His face had the sharp angles of near-starvation.

Amelia could tell, even with her limited knowledge of such things, that the man's coat was of good quality, so it was not poverty that kept the food from his mouth. His face was expressionless, but his eyes burned—burned with a passion that she thought she'd seen before.

There was a traveling preacher who'd passed by her cottage one day, a long time ago, and had tried to tell her of the Lord and the sinfulness of women and repentance and other things that sounded like nonsense to her and she'd told him so. His eyes had burned the same way the staring man's did, lit by fire and righteousness.

The preacher wouldn't stop shouting at her, so she'd gone inside her cottage and locked the door and made tea until he'd gone away to find some other woman to shout at.

This man wasn't shouting, but he looked as though it might be a natural state for him. He looked as though he might share that traveling preacher's ideas on the sinfulness of women and the need to repent.

Amelia glared at him and showed her teeth. Several people gasped at the sight, but the man appeared unaffected. Amelia decided it was best to ignore him as she had done with that preacher.

The saloon will be cleared soon, in any event, she thought. *He'll be shooed out with the crowd and that will be the end of that.*

But when she returned to the tank after her rest and a much-needed pot of tea, she discovered the man had returned also. He took up his spot again, staring at her, letting the crowd eddy around him. A few people looked at him askance, but for the most part he was invisible. Everyone was looking at the mermaid, and so no one noticed or cared about one strange individual who seemed fixated on the very being they wanted to see.

It was the same after every break for the remainder of the day. The staring man would be removed; when the crowd returned, so did he. As the day dragged on, Amelia found it difficult to pretend she didn't see him there, and her eyes strayed more frequently to his corner.

I shall speak to Levi about him, she thought.

Levi had been released from his two-week isolation after "Dr. Griffin's" return to London. The removal of the beard and the return of Levi's American accent and plain dress seemed to be enough to convince everyone they were not the same person. Amelia understood now why people were so easily fooled by Barnum's humbugs. No one observed closely enough to see the truth.

Since his return to the museum, Levi had been certain to stop and see Amelia throughout the day. Sometimes it was just a wave from the back of the moving throngs; sometimes he came in to see that she had enough food or drink or blankets when she was resting. He always waited for her at the end of the day, whistling outside the curtain while she labored into her clothes, and then escorted her to Barnum's for dinner.

Since the day Charity had seen Amelia's true self, Charity couldn't do without her at the dinner table and for many hours after. Amelia was happy to be there with her, for now that the other woman had thawed, they spent many a happy evening side by side on the sofa in the parlor, playing games or whispering to each other like schoolgirls, with Caroline often their third conspirator.

Yes, she would tell Levi about the man. Levi could arrange to have the guards keep watch for him. There was little Amelia could do from inside the tank, especially since they were still maintaining the fiction that she could not speak.

Amelia was dressing at the end of the day when Levi called out to her.

"Nearly ready?" he asked.

Amelia hurriedly tucked her damp hair into a braid and emerged from behind the curtain.

Levi smiled when he saw her, but before he could ask about her day (a thing he liked to do, even though nearly every day was the same as the last and she said so) she told him about the staring man.

Levi frowned. "He was here all day? You're certain?"

"Of course I am," she said. "One could hardly miss him."

"Well, the guards obviously did," Levi said. "If he was standing there all day, then he must have kept circling around to the front and paying the entrance fee over and over. It's not easy to return to this saloon—the flow of people means you can't really double back, and surely it would have caused a noticeable fuss if he kept pushing against the crowd."

"Why would anyone want to pay to stare at me all day?" Amelia asked.

"I have some ideas," Levi said. "I've been half expecting something like this to happen. Although I thought there would be some editorials first, or demonstrating in the street while women wailed and men read from the Bible."

"I thought he reminded me of that preacher," Amelia murmured. "His eyes burned."

"When we first proposed the exhibit, I was worried about the church ladies," Levi said. "There's a fair bunch of folks always concerned about indecency. Even if you are clearly not human when in the water I thought they might object to . . ."

He trailed off, then gestured awkwardly in the direction of his own chest.

"You thought they might object to my bare breasts?" Amelia said, her lips curving at his discomfort. "That might be true, but I think most people who see me just don't think of me as human, or even half human. Especially the ones who have only seen me here at the museum. At the Concert Hall the audience saw me walk across the stage first. They were aware that part of me was human. Here they only see me as a—"

She stopped, because she hadn't really considered this before, and now that she had, it bothered her.

"As a what?" Levi asked.

"As an animal in a cage," Amelia said. She shook her head. "Barnum was right about that."

Levi looked shocked. "You're no animal, Amelia. Barnum was wrong."

"I know I'm not," she said. "It's not that my feelings are hurt over it. But he was correct in that people would—and do—view me that way. That's why you haven't seen those 'church ladies,' as you call them. They're not worried about the corruption of children. They just think I'm a clever fish who can do tricks."

He frowned, obviously unhappy with her characterization of herself, but he didn't pursue it. "I'm going to talk to Barnum about those guards of his. They're perfectly fine at thumping heads, but they clearly can't see trouble when it's right in front of them. Describe this man to me and I will stay all day tomorrow. When I see him, I'll have the guards remove him under some pretext."

"Perhaps he won't return tomorrow," Amelia said, though without conviction. The staring man didn't seem the type to go away without being told to do so.

Levi didn't bother to contradict her.

Amelia did her best to be cheerful at dinner, but Charity glanced at her several times with a little frown and Amelia knew she hadn't succeeded. Barnum's wife waited until Caroline had left the table—attendance at the museum had tripled since Amelia's arrival, which meant Charity was finally able to hire a nanny to help with the children—and then asked Amelia what was wrong.

"There was a man at the museum today. He was behaving in a very strange manner," Amelia said carefully. She didn't want Charity to worry, but she didn't want Barnum to dismiss her concerns.

"What do you mean by 'strange'?" Charity asked.

"He kept returning throughout the day, after every one of my resting periods," Amelia said.

Barnum, who'd been perusing the evening papers in search of mentions of the museum, looked up at that. "Was he coming back into the saloon from the egress? I put those signs in the museum so that wouldn't happen."

He referred to the large signs posted near the exit of the last few saloons that read *This way to the Egress*. Barnum knew most folk didn't know the meaning of the word and thought they were being led to a wonderful new exhibit. Instead they found themselves outside the museum with the new knowledge that *egress* meant *exit*.

Amelia shook her head. "No, he was following in with the first crowd every time the exhibit reopened. Then he would stand there for the duration until the doors closed."

"He must have been paying the entrance fee every time he reentered," Barnum said. He didn't seem remotely concerned about the man's behavior. If anything, he appeared pleased that one person would pay the ticket fee repeatedly.

"Barnum, why didn't your guards notice this fellow?" Levi asked. "I thought you wanted them there to keep Amelia safe."

Barnum appeared discomfited. "Of course. That is why I hired them. But it doesn't appear that her safety was in danger. He didn't approach the glass or threaten you in any way, correct?"

"No," Amelia said. "I don't think his behavior could be considered normal, though. His stare was quite uncomfortable."

Barnum waved that away. "I can't have a paying customer removed because he made you uncomfortable."

The unsaid phrase was *especially not one who is willing to pay for the privilege multiple times.*

"Taylor," Charity said with a glance at Amelia. "The man

might be disturbed. If you won't have him removed, then at least you might warn the guards about him."

"Warn them about what?" Barnum said. "That he's staring too long at the mermaid?"

Amelia had been afraid of this: that Barnum wouldn't take her seriously. He wouldn't understand unless he saw the man's eyes. His eyes were burning.

"I'm going to speak to the guards tomorrow," Levi said, and said it in a way that brooked no further discussion.

"Be careful," Barnum said. "I don't want you drawing the attention of any of the crowd. Someone might remember you as Dr. Griffin."

"There's no worry about that," Levi said. "We've said Dr. Griffin has returned to London, and anyway everyone is too busy looking at Amelia to care about me."

"Just be cautious," Barnum said. "Perhaps I should be the one to have a word with the guards. What did you say this man looked like?"

Amelia described the staring man (*the burning man*), though it was clear that Barnum was more concerned that someone might discover Levi was Dr. Griffin than about any danger the man might present to her.

"Taylor, perhaps Amelia should stay with us again," Charity said. "I don't like the idea of her alone at the hotel, especially now that Levi isn't there any longer."

"She's got to stay there!" Barnum said. "Every day the

reporters wait to see her, and then I have a chance to talk about the museum."

Barnum had taken to walking Amelia from the hotel to the museum every morning. There were many fewer reporters now than there were three weeks ago; perhaps the newspapers no longer saw the value of a Barnum quote.

In any case, while the mermaid was still popular among the public, her attraction was dwindling for the reporters. There were only so many times one could describe her clothes, Amelia reflected, and since she would not talk, they had nothing else to write about.

Every day one or two out-of-town reporters appeared, but their remits were not indefinite. They stayed for a day or two, observed the exhibit, talked with the determined few who stuck it out in the hotel, and then left for their hometowns.

Despite the increased attendance at the museum, Barnum clearly still felt there was some advertising value in her staying at the hotel. If it meant one more person would buy a ticket who wouldn't otherwise, then it would be worth it to him.

Levi walked Amelia back to the hotel that evening, as he always did. They didn't talk, for they couldn't risk anyone possibly seeing her speak in public, and Levi couldn't come up to her room as he had done when he played Dr. Griffin. One of Barnum's guards would meet her outside the hotel and escort her upstairs.

As Amelia walked, her arm tucked into Levi's, she felt like someone's gaze was scorching the back of her neck. She looked over her shoulder, expecting to see the staring (*burning*) man, or perhaps even her long-lost traveling preacher.

There were still folk about, but not as many as during the day, and they all seemed engaged in their own business. No one waited and watched.

Now you're being fanciful, Amelia thought. Why would the man wait for her outside the museum?

Why, though, would he return hour after hour to watch her swim around the tank? Was he a religious zealot, as Levi suspected, or was he just so fascinated with her mermaid self that he would pay any amount to see her again and again?

Neither one was a comfortable choice, Amelia thought. They each meant a kind of obsession, and obsessions could be dangerous.

She leaned closer to Levi. He was warm, and she felt so very, very cold.

That night she pulled the curtains of her room a little tighter, letting not a sliver of light in. It took her many hours before she was able to sleep, for she knew that when she slept, she would dream of him, dream of his staring burning eyes and his thin hands like claws grasping for her.

The next day, the burning man returned. Barnum had kept his promise to speak to the men who watched over her (Charity had insisted upon it), and Amelia saw the two guards confer briefly when the man entered the saloon for the first time. But they were under orders from Barnum not to approach him unless he physically threatened Amelia.

And he did not threaten her. He didn't walk near the glass, nor did he refuse to leave the saloon each time it closed. He did nothing overt, nothing that could justify the growing sense of disquiet in Amelia.

But he stayed. And he stared. And his eyes were lit by flames from within.

Levi also stayed. The former Dr. Griffin entered in the morning and took note of the man (he was easy to find if one was looking—he was the only person who did not move at all) but per Barnum's adamant instruction did not approach the burning man.

Later, when the museum was closed, Levi admitted to Amelia that the staring man disturbed him, too.

"He doesn't seem to blink," Levi said. "Like a reptile. And he never takes his eyes off you, not even for a moment."

"I don't want him to come into the exhibit anymore," Amelia said.

Two days of the man's intensity had her feeling simultaneously exhausted and restless. She didn't think she could take another day of it.

But Levi's attempt at persuading Barnum that the man might be dangerous fell on deaf ears.

"Barnum, it's not natural. It's not natural the way he

stands there and looks at her," Levi said.

"You just don't want anyone looking at her but you," Barnum said, stirring his sugar in his coffee.

It was a mark of how distressed Levi was that he didn't blush, or stammer, or do any of the other things that he usually did when Barnum implied that Levi was attracted to Amelia.

"You haven't seen him," Levi said. "There's something very, very wrong with that man. I think he may mean Amelia harm."

"What proof do you have of that?" Barnum asked.

"Taylor, if he's upsetting Amelia, isn't that enough?" Charity asked. "If she's upset, then she might not be able to go on with the show. You might have to post signs saying that the mermaid is ill and there will be no performances."

Ah, that was brilliant, Charity! Amelia thought.

As if she heard Amelia's thought, Charity gave her friend a very small wink when Barnum wasn't looking.

Barnum looked ill himself at the thought of it. "You're not that distressed, are you? Not so much that it would make you sick?"

"He makes it difficult to perform," Amelia admitted. "His presence is a distraction, and because I am uncomfortable it is sometimes impossible for me to eat. What if I faint under the water? What will happen then? I will have to be taken out of the tank and put to bed for the remainder of the day."

Amelia thought this privately absurd, but it was well

known that men of Barnum's type thought women were delicate and prone to vapors. The mermaid was not above using human trickery if it meant the burning man would be removed from the museum, if it meant she would no longer have to endure the continuous pressure of his gaze.

Barnum appeared appalled at the thought that Amelia might be bedridden for a full day. She could read the words in his eyes: *But the ticket sales! Who would come to the museum without the mermaid?*

"Very well," Barnum said. "Tomorrow I shall come into the saloon myself and have a look at this gentleman. If he appears to be as great a threat as you say, I will have him removed. For the sake of your health, of course."

"Of course," Amelia murmured.

"Of course," Charity said.

Levi muttered something rude under his breath, but they all pretended not to hear it.

Barnum hated to admit it, but the boy and the mermaid and Charity were right. There *was* something very wrong with that man, the one Amelia called "the burning man."

It wasn't just the staring—though that was disconcerting enough—or his profound stillness. It was the way he didn't seem to breathe, and how he seemed completely unaware of the press of people all around him.

Barnum thought if he climbed inside the man's skull he would see only one thing—the mermaid. The man didn't even appear to see the tank. Only Amelia.

Yes, Barnum could see how the man would make the mermaid uncomfortable. He made Barnum uncomfortable, and Barnum wasn't the one being gaped at.

"Now do you see?" Levi hissed in his ear.

Barnum scratched his nose. "I see. What I'm wondering is how to solve the problem without drawing attention to him."

"Send your goons out with him when the saloon closes," Levi said. "They can encourage him to go outside and make it clear he's not to return back in."

"Are you implying I should incite those men to violence, Levi?" Barnum asked.

"Yes, if it's necessary," Levi said. "There must be no uncertainty on his part. He can't think he's welcome here."

The boy really did want that staring fellow away from his mermaid, Barnum thought. Levi wasn't the sort to condone a beating for no reason. If anything, Levi had expressed several times that he was uncomfortable with the guards Barnum hired and the threat they represented.

"And what if he does return?" Barnum asked. "What then?"

"I can sketch a likeness of him," Levi said. "We can give it to the ticket takers and the guards at the front door and tell them he's not to be allowed in."

"It's a solution," Barnum said. "You go and get something to sketch with and make his portrait. Bring it right to the admission booth when you have it, and make one for each of those simpletons at the front door as well. They'll need to keep it in their pocket to check against the folks coming in."

"You'll tell the guards here to follow the man out of the building?" Levi said, hovering instead of getting on with the task Barnum gave him.

"I'll make sure your mermaid is safe," Barnum said. "You used to trust me, Levi."

Levi hesitated, then nodded and left.

It wasn't an easy thing, getting over to the guards to speak to them. Barnum was a celebrity in his own museum. Once Levi left, many people felt free to talk to him, to compliment him for managing to get hold of the mermaid, to ask him questions, or just to shake his hand.

He fell into what he did best—performing. He told stories about the Feejee Mermaid that he claimed to have heard from Dr. Griffin. He promised all and sundry that the mermaid would be at the museum for five more months, and that they certainly should write to their relatives in North Carolina or Pennsylvania or Tennessee to come and see her. He agreed many times that the mermaid was an eighth wonder of the world.

Then the clock struck the hour, and everyone was chivvied

out of the saloon. By the time Barnum managed to extricate himself from the last person, the saloon was empty. The staring man was gone.

It will be all right, Barnum told himself, though he felt a slither of unease. Levi would have his drawing, and the man wouldn't be allowed back in the museum.

Even if he did somehow manage to pay his admission fee and enter again . . . well, Barnum would just tell the guards now what they ought to do when the next performance ended. They were to follow the staring man out and explain that he wasn't to return. Barnum would make it clear that this explanation could be made using their fists.

Amelia climbed out of the tank and looked expectantly at him.

"Don't worry, I'm making an arrangement," Barnum said, turning his head away from her. The girl had no shame about her nakedness at all.

He lingered in the saloon after the performance started again, but he did not see the staring man.

There, he thought. *Levi's drawing will do the trick.*

But when he went to speak to the clerks at the end of the day, none of them had seen the staring man since that morning.

"I recognized him, though, when Mr. Lyman showed me the picture," Jeremiah Steward told him. "He pays a fee about twelve times a day. I always wondered why. But today he only entered one time. Is he a criminal?"

"He might be," Barnum said evasively. It was too much to explain to this wet-eared boy that the man stared overlong at the mermaid and made her feel sick to her stomach. "If you see him, you be sure to tell one of the guards, make sure they remove him."

"I will, sir," Jeremiah said.

Amelia did not feel comforted by the staring man's abrupt disappearance. Rather, it somehow made her more uneasy, and she kept watching for him to reappear for the remainder of the day.

"He probably was warned off by Barnum's presence in the hall. Whatever he wanted from you, he wasn't about to try it under the owner's nose," Levi said. "Barnum can be good for some things, occasionally."

But Amelia could not lose the feeling that the man had not given up. He had only shifted to the shadows instead of the light, and every moving shadow made her heart stop.

That night she told Charity, in private, that she no longer wanted to stay at the hotel.

"I know Barnum thinks it's a benefit to the exhibit," Amelia said. "It's only that I don't feel safe there, even with the guards."

"I'll speak to Taylor about it," Charity said.

She had been different since the day she told Barnum she would leave him—more confident, more certain of her own power.

"Levi and I will have you out of that room and back here before tomorrow evening," Charity said. "Tonight will be the last night, I promise you."

Amelia rested her head on Charity's shoulder. "Thank you."

Caroline, seeing the two of them sitting close together, ran to put her own head on Amelia's shoulder. Charity laughed.

"Can't anyone have the mermaid except you?" she asked.

"No," Caroline said, and put her arms possessively around Amelia's waist.

Amelia stroked the girl's hair and wished she could stay right there, safe in the embrace of her sisters.

"It's only one more evening," Charity said. "Taylor will take some persuading. You know how he enjoys holding forth for the reporters every morning."

"Yes," Amelia said.

But when the time came for Levi to escort her back across the square, Amelia did not want to leave. She hugged Charity at the door with an urgency she couldn't explain, and when they parted, Charity had tears in her eyes.

"Amelia," she said.

"Let the girl go. She'll be back soon enough in the morning," Barnum said.

"Taylor, let her stay here tonight," Charity said. "It's not safe with that man out there. We don't know what happened to him."

"He had his fill of the mermaid, or he ran out of pocket money," Barnum said. "If he tries to enter the museum again, he'll be turned away. There's no need to fuss, Charity."

Amelia could see that for Barnum, the incident was already fading, that his memory was telling him the man wasn't as much of a threat as he had seemed, that the whole thing had been nothing but a woman's imagination run wild and now his own wife had caught the disease.

"I'll watch out for her, Charity," Levi assured her. "I promise."

Charity gave him a fierce look. "You had just better, Levi Lyman, or I shall never forgive you."

She embraced Amelia again and kissed her cheek. "I will see you in the morning."

Amelia thought Charity meant it to sound like a promise, but it seemed more like a wish, a prayer against harm. Amelia did not know who heard such wishes and prayers, but she hoped they were listening.

Barnum and Charity closed the door behind them as Levi and Amelia walked through the short hallway to the outer door. Amelia paused before they went out into the night.

"Levi," she said.

She had so many things inside her, so many feelings rising up, filling her throat and her nose and her eyes. There was so much she couldn't speak, couldn't tell him about the thing that had been slowly building every time he took her arm or tried to make her smile or arrived with an extra bowl of sugar cubes for her tea.

She didn't know how to tell him that she relied on seeing him each day, waving from the back of the crowd, that the knowledge that he was somewhere about and would appear was her greatest comfort. She didn't know how to tell him that she knew what he felt and that he was straight and true and she wanted him, wanted him as she never thought she would want another man after Jack died.

It seemed a strange time for her to finally face these feelings, these things that she'd been pushing down inside and pretending weren't there ever since the night he stood in her hotel room and apologized for something he hadn't even done.

Levi looked at her, misinterpreted her expression, and patted her shoulder. "Don't be troubled by him, Amelia. I promised Charity I would keep you safe, and I will."

"It's not that," she said, and she kissed him.

She tasted surprise on his tongue, and wonder, and delight. And inside her was an answering delight that rose up to mingle with his.

Then she pulled away and looked at him.

"Why now?" he asked.

"Because I wanted you to know," she said.

He accepted that, the way he accepted all things about her. He offered her his arm again and she took it, and she walked a little closer to him than was strictly polite.

The burning man waited for them.

CHAPTER 12

He rose out of the darkness, and Amelia saw the muzzle of the gun only for a moment before it flashed fire.

Her nose filled with the stink of gunpowder. Levi cried out, but all she heard was *his* voice, the burning man's voice. It was slender and reedy and had no power except that of belief.

"*This* I say then, walk in the Spirit, and ye shall not fulfill the lust of the flesh. For the flesh lusteth against the Spirit, and the Spirit against the flesh: and these are contrary the one to the other: so that ye cannot do the things that ye would."

There was blood on her dress, and pain in her body, and she fell to the ground and she was so surprised, surprised and amazed because she thought she couldn't bleed like this. She had thought she couldn't die.

The ball was in her stomach, she felt it scorching through her like the burning man's words, and she didn't want to discover that she really was mortal after all, not when she'd found Levi and she wasn't alone anymore.

Levi's boots were beside her head and then they weren't. She heard a huffing sound and the impact of a fist on bone, but the burning man didn't stop talking; he didn't even slow down because he was on fire inside and Amelia could hear it; she could hear the crackling of the flames and she was sorry for him, sorry because inside him was all this heat and smoke, and if you're on fire you don't know what to do with that except light someone else so that they catch fire, too.

"Now the works of the flesh are manifest, which are these: adultery, fornication, uncleanness, lasciviousness, idolatry, witchcraft . . . of which I tell you before, as I have also told you in time past, that they which do such things shall not inherit the kingdom of God."

"Levi," Amelia said, or thought she said.

Levi, don't. Levi, help me. Help me. It hurts.

Her voice seemed so quiet and so small. She wasn't sure her words made it out of her mouth. They seemed stuck behind her teeth.

There was more thudding, the persistent wet sound of Levi's fist hitting the other man's face and making it bleed.

"Levi," she said.

Help me I'm on fire.

But he couldn't hear her, because her insides were blazing and her voice was trapped in the smoke and the door to the Barnums' apartment opened behind her and then Charity was screaming, screaming, screaming.

She's not getting better," Levi said.

Dr. Graham had exited Amelia's sickroom with such a sober expression that Levi didn't need to hear what the man had to say. Charity stood beside Levi, her fingers twisting in a handkerchief. She hadn't stopped crying in the three days since Amelia was shot.

Caroline had taken to her room, where she did nothing except lie on her bed and stare at the ceiling. She refused to eat more than a few bites of toast and would not speak to her father at all.

This, Levi thought, was because Caroline had come upon Charity shouting at Barnum that this was his doing, and that if he'd only taken Charity's concerns seriously, Amelia would never have been out at that hour so that a madman could shoot her.

Barnum had stuttered and stammered and tried to tell her that he'd done everything he could, but Charity felt the shooter would never have had his opportunity if only

Barnum had listened to someone besides himself.

Caroline, who always sided with her mother, had given Barnum such an unforgiving glare that he'd subsided into silence and not attempted to defend himself since.

The doctor shook his head. "Her fever is still too high. I'm afraid to bleed her. I don't know what it would do to a mermaid's body."

Dr. Graham had removed the lead ball from Amelia's stomach, but he'd been reluctant to do much more than that. Levi didn't know if this was because he was genuinely worried about the effect of human medicine on Amelia or if he was genuinely worried that Barnum would blame him for any negative outcome. The doctor seemed to think that Barnum might become litigious if Graham were somehow responsible for Amelia's death.

He was also under the misapprehension that Amelia "belonged" to Barnum. Neither Levi nor Charity bothered to correct him on the subject. Levi, for one, didn't care at all what the man thought as long as he made Amelia better.

But he didn't make her better.

"I changed the poultice, and I left a bottle of laudanum if she wakes and has any pain," Graham said, putting on his hat and coat.

"Do you think that's likely? That she'll wake?" Levi asked.

Dr. Graham looked at Charity, who was watching him with a hopeful expression, then shook his head.

"I think you should prepare yourself," he said. "I don't know what can be done for her."

Charity sobbed into her handkerchief and left the hall. Levi saw Dr. Graham to the door. He managed to remain polite to the man, but Levi felt unreasonably angry with the doctor. He thought Graham could do more, try harder . . . what did it matter that he wasn't a specialist in mermaid biology? There was no one on land who had such a specialty. Was it better to let Amelia die because he was afraid?

Levi went into the bedroom where Amelia lay with her eyes closed. The room smelled of sick, sickness and death, that sour-sweet decay that made Levi think of rotting leaves.

He lifted the bandage and poultice the doctor had applied so he could check her wound. A foul-smelling greenish ooze emitted from the hole in her stomach. Dark lines radiated away from the wound, covering her skin. They were spreading like tree branches, growing longer and longer each day.

Her skin was covered in sweat, soaking her hair, but her lips were dry. Amelia's whole face was sunken, the bones of her face sharp like the man who had shot her.

His name was Elijah Hunt, and the newspaper reporters who'd waited night after night in the Park Hotel for a story had been rewarded when they heard Charity screaming. The reporters were there before the constables, before the doctor, even before Levi had finished beating Hunt senseless. They saw Amelia on the ground, covered in blood, and the "eyewitness reports of the mermaid's condition" resulted in several gruesome and tasteless drawings on the front pages the next day.

The night watch arrived after Barnum lifted Amelia and took her into the apartment, firmly closing the door on the crowd of reporters outside.

In lieu of Barnum or a bleeding mermaid, they had crowded around Levi and the unconscious Hunt, but Levi wouldn't tell them anything. He only hung on grimly to Hunt's arm until a watchman arrived, and then the watchman sent a runner for a constable.

In the meantime, Hunt regained consciousness enough to start talking again. Levi heard a lot of nonsense about the wages of sin being death and the temptations of women's flesh, so he shook the man hard and told him to shut up.

The reporters all complained and told him to let the man speak, that he had a right to tell his story, and they asked Hunt, "Why did you do it?" but the man only repeated that the wages of sin were death and that the mermaid had been sent by the devil to tempt man to unnatural lust.

"Unnatural to want to fornicate with a sea creature, an animal with half a woman's form," Elijah Hunt said. It made Levi sick to be near him, this madman with spittle on his lips and the light of righteousness in his eyes.

Elijah Hunt had been taken to the Tombs, where he was to be held until his trial for attempted murder. In the meantime, a few enterprising writers paid off the guards to have a chance to talk to the man who'd shot the mermaid. The reporters were practically slavering for the trial—a murder trial (even if it was only an attempted murder trial) was worth thousands of newspaper sales.

It didn't matter if all the papers put the same information on the front page. Readers loved tales of blood and scandal and madness, and this case had all of that plus a mermaid and P. T. Barnum.

Levi didn't care about Elijah Hunt or his reasons. He didn't care about the man's trial, either, and he hoped like hell it wouldn't be for murder. If Elijah Hunt was tried for murder, that would mean Amelia was dead, and he couldn't bear the thought of it.

And Levi was sick to death of the reporters. As Dr. Griffin he'd performed for them, manipulated them. As Levi Lyman he was tired of the way the newspapermen hovered and buzzed and pressed, the way they refused to leave even if you refused to speak.

Barnum cared about Hunt, though. He cared because the man's zealotry had brought, as he put it, "all the other Bible-readers out of the woodwork."

Every day now there was a demonstration of good Christian men and women outside the museum, reading scripture passages and holding signs condemning the museum for propagating sin. Letter writers wrote passionate invectives excoriating Barnum for showing what amounted to a naked woman in his museum.

A fair number of letter writers also wrote in defense of the mermaid, citing the wonder they'd felt at seeing one of God's truly magical creatures. Barnum liked these letters, but the tally pile for them was a great deal smaller than the angry ones.

The museum had been closed indefinitely, because it was impossible to keep out the chanting righteous crowd of Christians. They kept pushing into the front doors and dispersing without paying the fee. They would run about the museum and disrupt the enjoyment of the customers. Barnum decreed it all past bearing and shut the museum down entirely.

The next day there was a headline in the *Herald* that read, *GRIEVING BARNUM CLOSES MUSEUM IN HONOR OF MERMAID FRIEND.*

Barnum had snorted at this but reflected that at least it put him in a good light. Everyone else seemed determined to paint him as some kind of purveyor of sin.

Levi reached for Amelia's hand. It lay limp in his own, no spark to be found. Her breathing was so quiet that he had to check several times that she was still alive, leaning close to her face and listening for the faint whistle of air.

She was so thin and small and still. This wasn't his mermaid. This wasn't his Amelia.

And it might never be again, for the doctor would not help her as he should. Levi should have studied medicine instead of law; he might have been able to do something useful for Amelia now if he had.

The door opened, and Levi hastily wiped his face with his sleeve, expecting it to be Charity. Instead, Caroline stood in the doorway, her small face so serious it broke his heart.

"Mama is crying again," Caroline said. "She won't stop. Is it because Amelia is going to die?"

Levi never lied to Caroline. Something about the little girl demanded the truth. Amelia said she'd felt it, too, the first time the mermaid met Barnum's eldest child. Caroline had demanded to know if she was a mermaid, and Amelia had to tell her yes.

"The doctor doesn't think Amelia will live," Levi said.

Caroline approached the bed, taking Amelia's other hand. "Why?"

"He can't fix what's wrong with her. He doesn't know how."

"If Amelia was with her own people I bet they would know how," Caroline said. "Mermaids have to have doctors, don't they? Maybe we should just put her back in the ocean and they will come and find her."

Levi smiled a little at this, the thought of a whole parade of mermaids appearing out of the depths of the ocean, perhaps with a stretcher to carry their lost daughter back home. Then he stilled.

Put her back in the ocean.
Put her back in the ocean.
Put her back in the ocean.

Of course! He was a goddamned fool. He'd seen for himself that when Amelia changed from woman to mermaid, her skin seemed to fold itself inside-out, like there was a completely different creature inside her body. And Amelia had told him that she thought the change from her mermaid form to her human form kept her from aging.

If they returned her to the ocean, she would change back into a mermaid. And if she changed back into a mermaid, her sickness might heal. It might be as if the shooting had never happened at all.

Caroline was watching him, and he realized she'd solved this problem before he had. It was the reason she'd gotten out of her bed in the first place—to explain to the foolish adult that to mend a sea creature you needed to return her to the sea.

"We can't tell Papa," Caroline said. "He'll make objections."

Yes, he likely would make objections. Levi was too tired to think of what those objections might be, but Barnum was sure to invent something. Barnum always objected if the idea wasn't his in the first place.

"We can trust your mother, though," Levi said.

"Of course. We can't do it without her in any case. She'll

need to hide the fact that we're gone," Caroline said.

She appeared very grown-up to Levi all of a sudden, not at all the little girl who'd thrown a tantrum when Amelia first arrived.

"Someone will have to pay for a carriage," Caroline said.

"Don't worry," Levi said. "Your father is not the only one who makes money around here."

When the time came it was the easiest thing in the world to get Amelia out of the apartment right under Barnum's nose. Barnum had taken to spending most of his days at his desk inside the museum, and that particular day he did not return for supper. They did not have to worry about hiding their plans from him if he wasn't present.

Charity arranged with their cook to go out and hire a carriage that would meet them after midnight three blocks away. Though they would be leaving the museum very late at night, there was always the chance some reporter might be lurking about. The good Christians all went home to pray after dark; Levi had yet to see one who lingered much past the dinner hour.

Charity and Caroline dressed in their darkest clothing and covered their hair. Levi wrapped Amelia in a blanket and pulled it up over her face so that her pale skin would not gleam in the moonlight and give them away. The wound in her stomach stank, and once they were inside the closed coach, the smell was unbearable.

Levi kept Amelia in his lap, holding her tight so she didn't roll away from him as they clattered over the cobblestones. She had not stirred at all or made a single sound when he moved her. He was afraid their cure would come too late, and when he saw Charity's worried expression, he knew she had the same fear.

The coachman stopped a short distance from the dock. It was the same one where Levi had found Amelia after the first performance at the Concert Hall. He had a strange and superstitious idea that the place held more magic because of this, that it was *their* place and that Amelia would know and wake up from her deathly sleep.

Levi paid the man and then asked him to stay.

"Whatcha got there? Dead body?" the man asked, indicating the too-still Amelia inside the blanket.

"No, a sick woman," Levi said.

The driver raised his eyebrow, as if to say he didn't believe Levi but it wasn't any of his business. Then he shrugged and pulled a bottle out of his jacket. Levi hoped this meant that he would stay. He didn't fancy walking through the streets of New York this late with Charity and Caroline in tow. He didn't know how he would explain such a thing to Barnum, especially if their attempt to cure Amelia did not work.

He carried her to the edge of the dock, Charity and

Caroline trailing silently behind him. When he reached the end, he unwrapped Amelia. They had removed her nightgown before taking her out of the apartment, for Caroline had been insistent that any clothing would only be in Amelia's way when she changed back into a mermaid.

Levi looked at Caroline, who nodded. He lifted Amelia up, kissed her damp forehead, and threw her into the sea.

He took two steps back then, and Charity and Caroline each grasped one of his hands.

"How will we know?" Charity said. "How long might it take?"

Levi shook his head. "I don't know. The change . . . you saw it. It happens as soon as she's in the water."

"And if she's in the water and she's turned into a mermaid then she'll get better," Caroline said. "She won't leave us here to worry about her, so she will come back up right away."

"How can you know, Caroline?" Charity asked. She sounded desperate.

"Because I know, Mama," Caroline said.

They all three stared at the dark water, shifting in the half moon's light, and waited.

Then something broke the surface a few feet from them, something long-haired and sinuous and beautiful, something gleaming silver as it splashed out of the water and arced up in the air.

For a moment her whole body was visible from tail to

head, and Levi saw that her eyes were closed, her whole expression one of absolute bliss.

It had been a long time since she'd swum in the ocean, he remembered. A very long time.

Amelia splashed down into the water and disappeared again.

Charity ran to the edge and called out her name. "Amelia! Amelia!"

Levi put his hand on Charity's shoulder. Her body was taut, as if she might break apart at any moment. There was no relief that Amelia was alive, only the distress of a mother bird whose chick has not returned to the nest.

"She'll come back to us, Mama," Caroline said. "You don't have to worry anymore."

"But how do you know?" Charity asked, the desperation not yet gone from her voice.

"I told you, Mama—because I know," Caroline said. In contrast with her mother, Caroline seemed supremely assured.

"She'll want to swim for a few hours," Levi said. "Let's get you back to the apartment before Barnum finds you missing."

"He won't notice," Charity said. "All he can see are his dreams crashing down around him with the museum closed."

Levi handed Charity and Caroline up into the coach.

"Left your sick woman in the water, eh?" the coachman slurred. "Costs a lot less than a funeral."

Levi didn't bother answering. The less he spoke to the man, the better. If they were fortunate, he would forget he'd ever seen them when he woke with a headache the next morning.

"Well, now that Amelia is well, Barnum will be able to open the museum again. That ought to make him happy," Levi said.

Charity shook her head. "He won't be able to open the museum again as long as those dour-faced scripture readers are outside telling all and sundry that Barnum's is a den of sin."

"That damned Hunt," Levi swore.

"You watch your language around my daughter, Levi," Charity said.

"I apologize," Levi said.

"Although I am inclined to agree with you. The man has caused more trouble than we could have imagined."

"Barnum can't afford to keep the museum closed indefinitely," Levi said.

"No, he cannot," Charity said. "He feels very strongly about the responsibility of the loan he took out to buy it in the first place. I know it seems sometimes he's only interested in profit for profit's sake, but he doesn't want the loan to go into arrears."

"I know," Levi said.

He did know. Barnum talked about the loan often, especially in the early days of the museum. And Levi also knew that the tripled attendance had gold coins dancing in Barnum's eyes, as he dreamed not only of the end of his loan but the luxuries to come after so many years of thrift.

"He's not going to be able to open the museum with Amelia in there again, at least not right away," Levi said. "As long as there is a mermaid, there will be someone to protest her presence."

Elijah Hunt had drawn all the creeping things out of the dark and into the light, Levi thought. Without his spark to light the flame, there might have been some grumblings or the occasional editorial, but his shooting of Amelia had made it impossible for the mermaid exhibit to go on.

"Will Amelia have to leave if there's no exhibit?" Caroline said. "I don't want her to leave."

"Someday she will have to," Charity said. "She belongs to the ocean, not to us."

"I want her to belong to us a little while longer," Caroline said.

"So do I, my love," Charity said, stroking Caroline's hair.

So do I, Levi thought.

After seeing Charity and Caroline safely back home, Levi collected some clothing for Amelia and returned to the dock. It wasn't so very far to walk, really, especially when he was alone.

He knew she was there before he even stepped onto the dock. She was splashing about near the pilings, and when he reached the edge, she looked up at him.

Her face was glittering silver and her teeth were sharp, but her eyes were still Amelia's and they were shining, shining out of the darkness at him, and he felt punched by a lust so strong he could hardly stand.

"Amelia," he said.

She climbed out of the water, her body changing from silver to pearl, and there was no sign that the bullet had ever touched her. Her skin was as smooth and perfect as it always was when she changed, like she'd been born anew.

She kissed him, kissed him while she stood there naked and gleaming and his hands went everywhere they could reach, though he knew he shouldn't, not there, not where someone might be watching.

Amelia pulled her face away and smiled, a smile so full of mischief and temptation that he almost forgot himself again.

He picked up the clothing he had dropped and handed it to her wordlessly. Her smile widened, and she kept her gaze on his as she slowly (so very slowly) put on all her layers, all the armor that women wore to keep their flesh safe from the eyes of men.

Then she let him offer his arm, and she took it, and they walked home in the silent hour before dawn.

CHAPTER 13

I've been thinking on our problem, Miss Amelia," Barnum said after dinner one evening a few days later.

"And what problem is that, Mr. Barnum?" she asked.

Barnum didn't quail away from her gaze or the curious glances of Levi and Charity as he usually might. That meant he was determined to have something, and Amelia hoped that whatever he was determined to have did not mean more grief for her.

"The problem of having a mermaid exhibit without a mermaid," Barnum said. "Now we do have Moses's mummy, and that's at least enough to keep the public interested for now. But I can't have you back in that tank with all those Bible-loving folks outside talking about Barnum's American Museum like it's some kind of whorehouse. Sorry, Charity."

Amelia noticed he didn't bother to apologize to her.

"But you did sign a contract, and I know you want to make a salary. And you can't make a salary while you're sitting in my parlor."

Unsaid but fervently implied was *sitting in my parlor, eating my food and drinking my wine and taking up space instead of tripling the attendance numbers as you ought to be doing.*

"And what is your proposed solution to this dilemma, Mr. Barnum?" Amelia asked.

"We'll send you on a tour," Barnum said triumphantly.

"A tour?"

A tour, Amelia thought. A chance to see more places, more things, more of the country. She would have a start, at least, on the old dream of seeing all the world and all its wonders—although she didn't know anymore that it was a worthy dream. Still, she felt her life was on hold again, like it had been after Jack's death, and leaving for a tour would be a chance to begin again.

Charity looked startled. "But, Taylor, how can she go on a tour? You've complained all along about how difficult it was to build the tanks for her. How can you send a tank from town to town?"

"Well, Charity, I've been thinking on that," Barnum said.

He looked so pleased with himself that Amelia nearly laughed out loud. He'd obviously spent a lot of time formulating his plan and was prepared for their questions and objections.

"We can build a wagon, a regular sort of wagon with wood on three sides and make it watertight, like a whiskey barrel or a ship. And then on the fourth side we can have a piece of glass and folks can view Amelia through the window."

"That sounds like it would be very small, Barnum," Levi said. "How can Amelia swim around in something like that?"

"We won't have her swimming all day like she does in the museum," Barnum said. "We can go back to the old way—a performance before an audience. You can put a ladder up behind the wagon with a curtain around it. She can take off her clothes and jump in the water before anyone can properly see her, just like at the Concert Hall."

"I don't know, Mr. Barnum," Amelia said. "It won't be easy for me to dive into something as small as a wagon. And where will we have these performances? Outside?"

"We'll have to have them outside if we want to use the wagon," Barnum said. "But there will have to be a tent or some such thing to cover the wagon, because otherwise no one will pay."

"And what about the water?" Amelia asked. "How will we get the seawater to the tank every day?"

"I've already thought of that," Barnum said. "We'll confine your tour to cities and towns along the coast. A second wagon will go with you filled with whiskey barrels.

When you reach the next stop on the tour, the second wagon will be sent to the ocean to fill them up with water, and then they will be dumped into the viewing wagon. When you leave town, the wagon can be drained to make it easier to travel, and then it can be filled up again when you arrive in a new place."

"How many people will we need for such an enterprise?" Levi asked. "You'll need men to set up the tent, to arrange for seats inside it, to fetch the water and prepare the tank every day. All that will cost money."

Amelia thought Levi was trying to dissuade Barnum with the thought of the cost.

She could understand, though, that Barnum wanted to get the most use out of her. And she did sign a contract to perform.

But she was no longer Jack's wife, no longer the mermaid on the cliff by the sea. And if she wasn't the Feejee Mermaid, then who was she? If she went on tour, perhaps she would find out.

"If I leave and go on tour, you'll be able to reopen the museum," Amelia said. "And you'll be able to make money from that as well as the tour."

"But your contract only states that you make a percentage of the tickets for *your* exhibit," Barnum started, but Amelia held up a hand to stop him.

"I'm not asking for more pay, Mr. Barnum. I am only

thinking that it is a fairly elegant solution. The exhibition can continue, the museum can reopen, and without my presence here, the disruptive forces will lose interest."

Barnum appeared astounded to discover that she agreed with him. He was accustomed by now to Amelia contradicting him at every turn.

"Is this really what you want, Amelia?" Charity asked. Her brow wrinkled in concern. "It's not Taylor who will have to submit to the rigors of the tour, but you."

Amelia nodded. "It does seem like the best thing to do. Mr. Barnum is right. I can't stay here in the parlor forever."

Charity reached out for Amelia's hand. "But Caroline and I will miss you so."

"I will miss you, too, but I'm not leaving tomorrow." Amelia laughed. "At least, I don't believe I am."

Barnum smiled his showman's smile. "You're leaving as soon as I can make the arrangements. I've already contacted a shipwright to help build the watertight wagon."

"You seemed very certain of my cooperation, Mr. Barnum," Amelia said, though this was no more than she'd expected. Barnum liked to feel he had something up his sleeve always.

"You're a smart girl. I knew, sooner or later, you'd see things my way."

* * *

Levi and Amelia stood just outside the apartment door, the only place where Charity would permit them to be alone for more than a few moments.

Once she realized that Levi and Amelia were "courting," as she put it, she seemed more determined than ever to chaperone every moment they were together.

"But I'm a *widow*, Charity," Amelia said. "And you know Levi's a decent man."

"All the more reason for you not to lead him into temptation," Charity said tartly, but she smiled when she said it. "And I keep explaining to you, Amelia—you just don't look like a widow. You look like a young girl just out of the schoolroom."

Now Levi took Amelia's hand. She leaned in to kiss him—it was her favorite part of the day, finding all the secrets he concealed on his tongue—but he pulled back. She looked at him in surprise.

"What's the matter?" she asked.

His fingers were shaking a little. "Amelia, I know you can never love me as much as you loved Jack."

"I've never said—"

"Wait," he said. "Wait. I have to get it all out."

He inhaled deeply, coming to some internal decision.

"I think you know that I love you, and that I have for some time," he said. "I know nobody can replace your husband, and I don't ever want to. But I hope that you would consider . . . that you would do me the honor of becoming my wife."

It was strange, Amelia thought, that his stumbling words moved her so much. It was strange that his trembling hand meant more than the fist he'd used in her defense.

Jack had never asked her to marry him. It had just happened. She wanted to live with him, and in order to live with him they had to marry. There were no declarations of love like this. Jack had made his declaration the day he loosed her from the net and let her leave him.

It was not better or worse, she reflected, only valuable in a different way. And it was unfair to this man who stood before her, every part of him straining in hope toward her, to think of Jack at a time like this.

"Of course I will," she said. "Of course I'll be your wife."

He didn't kiss her then, but he took her in his arms and buried his face in her hair and she thought a very odd thing then—that she ought to thank the burning man, for if he had not done what he did, then she might never have realized how much she still wanted to live and that she loved Levi Lyman.

They were married as soon as the arrangements could be made. Levi told Barnum of their plans with some trepidation, but Barnum was thrilled.

"It makes everything easier, you see?" Barnum said. "Now

you can travel with her on the tour and share one room because she's your wife, and we won't have to worry about hotels that don't allow unaccompanied women or men making advances on her because she's unmarried."

Barnum paused, then added, "Congratulations."

The preacher came to Barnum and Charity's apartment to say the necessary words over Levi and Amelia. Barnum had pushed for a public wedding, attended by reporters. He had an idea that a wedding would wash away any taint of sin from Amelia—she would be a married mermaid, and therefore the objections of the Elijah Hunt supporters would be invalid.

Amelia had nipped that idea before it was able to fully flower. "I'm not marrying Levi in front of everyone in New York. That, Mr. Barnum, is not in my contract."

And when Charity chimed in that a wedding was between a man and a woman and if they didn't want it witnessed by every newspaper in Christendom then it was their affair, and not Barnum's, the showman had to subside.

Levi brought Amelia home to his little apartment under the same cover of night that he'd used to sneak her out to the ocean to save her.

He unbuttoned all her buttons and unlaced all her laces, and when he put his hands on her, he shuddered and so did she.

"I've dreamed of you for so long," he said.

They stayed inside that little apartment for three days, and on the fourth day Barnum came to the door holding an advertising bill.

"The tour is all arranged," he said. "You leave tomorrow."

That night Amelia felt something different when Levi arched above her, something quicken in her belly.

Later, when he was sleeping, she lay awake and put her hands over her stomach and whispered.

"My daughter," she said, and she wept. "I've waited for you for so long."

PART III

THE TOUR

CHAPTER 14

When Barnum had proposed the tour to Amelia, she'd gained the impression that it would be an exhibition of the "Feejee Mermaid" alone. In her mind, she'd imagined a traveling coach for herself and Levi and the two other wagons that carried the tank and barrels and tent, as well as a few men to fetch the water and perform other labor.

She soon discovered that she was wrong, and she realized she'd been a fool to even consider such a notion. Barnum didn't know how to do a thing by halves, and of course in his eyes the more pomp and pageantry, the better.

Thus she and Levi found themselves in a parade of vehicles that carried not only the necessary accessories for the mermaid but also an artist who blew beautiful glass ornaments; a magician who performed ventriloquism and other tricks; Signor Veronia's mechanical figures, which were said to "represent human life"; and a wide variety of birds and beasts, including a duck-billed platypus from a place called Australia and an orange orangutan with such sad eyes that Amelia could hardly bear the sight of her in the cage.

"She ought to be set free, Levi," she told her husband after the evening of their first performance.

Amelia was the final act of the show, and so she had gone out to watch Mr. Wyman perform his magic tricks until it was time for her to get ready. The orangutan had been made to dance by her handler, and though the audience laughed at the miserable-looking creature, Amelia had left the tent with tears in her eyes.

"We can't do that, Amelia," Levi said. "She belongs to Barnum."

"She's a wild thing, Levi," Amelia said. "Wild things ought to be free. They can't belong to anybody, not really."

It was hard not to think of Jack then, of how easily he'd loosed her once he looked into her eyes. The orangutan had eyes like a human's, she thought. She might not speak their language, but she could see into the orangutan's heart just as Jack had seen into hers.

"I don't disagree with you," Levi said soothingly, rubbing her shoulders. "But Barnum thinks a little differently about such things. And besides, the poor creature isn't from this country. She's from someplace hot and far away, and if we let her go, then she'll only die here, or be taken by someone else."

"Hot and far away," Amelia said. "Like Fiji?"

Levi frowned. "You don't belong to Barnum. And you're not a performing animal."

"Am I not?" she asked, and sat on the edge of the bed. She rubbed her forehead. "Sometimes I'm not so certain."

"You chose this," Levi said, but in a way that told her he wasn't accusing her, just stating the facts. "You told me that so many times, that it was your choice. And if it's your choice to stay, then it's your choice to leave. If you don't want to do this anymore, then we'll go to Barnum, you and I, and tell him the traveling mermaid show is over."

The only other occasion when she'd wanted so strongly to leave the show was the first night at the Concert Hall. Somehow seeing that ape turning in circles (*just like you in the tank, swimming in circles for the waving crowd*) had set off the urge to flee, to run until she found the ocean and disappeared into the sea.

But she couldn't do that to Levi. And she couldn't leave him for her own sake.

"No," she said. "I made an agreement with Barnum, and I'll keep it. But I wish we could help that orangutan. I wonder if we can find the place where she belongs—the place where she really comes from, I mean."

"And what will you do then?" Levi asked. "Travel across the ocean with her in a rowboat?"

"Perhaps I shall," Amelia said. "And make you do the rowing."

"I wonder if there's a library or a bookshop where we could find out more about orangutans," Levi said.

Amelia frowned at him. "What good will that do?"

Levi shrugged. "If we know about her home, or what she likes to eat, or—I don't know, Amelia, I thought we might be able to make her happier, even if she did have to dance in circles at the end of a rope."

"A bird in a cage still knows it's in a cage, even if the bars are made of gold," Amelia said softly.

But it was a kind thought that he had. Levi was always kind. It was one of the reasons she loved him.

He sat down beside her. "Is that how you felt today? Like you were in a cage?"

"It's not like the tank," Amelia said. "In the tank there was glass on all sides. I could see everything around me and feel that I was a part of it. And there was room to move, much more room to move. In the wagon . . ."

She trailed off. She didn't want Levi to worry about her.

"I'll worry if you tell me or not," he said.

Amelia leaned close to him and peered into his eyes. His eyes were very dark brown, so dark that the color blended into the pupil.

"What are you doing?" he said, laughing.

"I am trying to see if you can read my mind like one of

Barnum's fortune-tellers," Amelia said. "I think that you can."

"No, but I can read your face," he said. "I've been studying it."

He ran his fingers around the bone that circled her eye, down her cheek, under her chin, back up the other side. "I used to think you unreadable. As mysterious as the sea."

"The sea is not as mysterious as you think," Amelia said. "You only have to swim under the surface."

"Yes, I've learned that," he said, and kissed her, but in a gentle way that didn't ask for more. "Tell me about the wagon."

"It's like being in a box," she said, and sighed. "A very small and tight box. I am taller, longer, when I'm a mermaid, and my tail fin is very wide. I don't think Barnum took that into account. I can't swim, only float, and it's nearly impossible to turn. So I'm stuck there, in whatever direction I've fallen in. And, Levi, the audience here is . . . different."

"Yes," Levi said.

She could tell by his grim tone that they were thinking of the same incident. When Amelia fell into the tank (and it was falling, really, there was hardly enough room to dive) a man in the audience had started hooting and shouting about the "naked lady." He'd continued even after Amelia changed into her sea form, making ribald remarks about her fish tail and her bare chest. Several people had hushed him, and plenty were so mesmerized by Amelia's appearance that they hadn't noticed him at all.

But Amelia couldn't help noticing him, and the wagon was so small and there was much less water in it, which meant it was easier to hear what he said. His words were so crude that she wanted to hide away, but there was no room to do so.

When the man wouldn't cease, Levi had spoken to two of the traveling show laborers and they'd happily escorted the man out of the tent. Amelia didn't know what happened to him after that, but the man had not returned.

"That never happened in New York," she said. "Not once. Yes, there were the people who claimed I was immoral, but that's not the same."

"It is, er, much more rural here," Levi said.

"I spent many years of my life in a rural place," Amelia said. "I've heard Barnum refer to it as Middle of Nowhere, Maine, when he thought I wasn't listening. But I promise you that no matter how countrified we were, no one would ever have had the bad manners to behave in such a way."

"The man had too much whiskey," Levi said. "I don't believe you'll need to worry about that happening at every performance."

"And everyone else—the way they stared at me. It was different, Levi, different from how it was in New York," Amelia said.

"I don't think it was as different as you do," Levi said.

"The trouble is that in the wagon you don't have any way to turn away from the way they stare."

"And in the museum the crowd was constantly moving," Amelia said. "They didn't stay in place and point."

"They did at the Concert Hall," Levi pointed out.

"But I was on the stage then. I was above the crowd, not at their eye level," Amelia said. She felt that she wasn't explaining properly. He didn't understand how much more exposed she felt in the wagon.

"I suppose if it makes you that uncomfortable we can find a way to raise the wagon. Put it on a little stage. We would have to build it at each stop on the tour, though," Levi said.

She saw him calculating the cost, the trouble, and the need for explaining both of those things to Barnum.

"I can become accustomed to it," she said. She didn't really care about Barnum's expenses or grievances, but she didn't like Levi bearing the brunt of them. "It's only that it's new, I suppose."

He took her in his arms then, and it was a long time before either of them thought of anything but each other.

"Let's find a bookshop tomorrow, or a library," Amelia said, her cheek pressed into Levi's chest. She liked listening to his heart beat and hearing the deep rumble of his voice rising out of his lungs. "I want to know all about the orangutan and where it comes from. And all about Fiji, too."

"Fiji?" Levi asked. "Why, after so many months?"

"I'd like to know more about where I am supposed to be from," Amelia said. "But you'll need to read it to me. I still can only read a little."

Amelia had been trying to learn more, simply because there were words everywhere, and most folk relied on the newspaper. She felt she was at a disadvantage when everyone talked about things they read in the news.

"I can teach you anything you don't know. Then you'll be able to read it yourself," Levi said.

They were not able to find a book that contained any information about orangutans, but Levi discovered a missionary's journal from the South Pacific. This contained descriptions not only of Fiji but of many other islands where the missionary had traveled in hopes of spreading the word of God.

Amelia scowled at this bit when Levi read it aloud.

"What's the matter?" he asked.

"Why does he want to go about interfering with other people?" Amelia said. "I'm sure the people on those islands were perfectly happy without missionaries."

Levi shifted uncomfortably at this. Like almost every American he'd been raised with the Bible, and while he wasn't as fervent as some, he still believed in the basic rightness of the Christian word. Amelia, having been raised in no such manner, did not think it good or right that Christians plowed over everyone who did not think as they did.

"Well, Amelia, they are savages," Levi said.

"What's a savage?" Amelia said. "Someone who doesn't live as you do? Someone who doesn't have gaslight and shoes and cobblestoned streets?"

Levi took a breath and tried again. "These are simple people who haven't been exposed to—"

"And why is simple something that needs to be fixed? Why must all people everywhere be cast in the same mold?" Amelia said.

She felt unreasonably angry with Levi for not understanding the basic wrongness of this idea. These people had their own lives, their own gods, their own ways. A missionary traveled across the ocean and told them that everything they believed and lived by was incorrect. It was the same as if a human came to her people under the ocean and told them that they could no longer be merpeople.

Amelia was surprised, too, for Levi was always kind and it seemed out of character for him to think of himself as above anyone, especially an island dweller who lived thousands of miles away.

"Perhaps we shouldn't read this book right now," Levi said, closing it and putting it aside.

"No," Amelia said, snatching it from his hand. "You're not to do that. You're not to treat me like a child because you don't want to have a disagreement."

"This is just something you don't understand, Amelia,"

Levi said, the first sparks of anger in his eyes. "Missionaries have a duty to save others from damnation."

"That's what Elijah Hunt thought he was doing when he shot me," Amelia said. "I can't believe you would think the same as someone like that."

"It's not the same thing," Levi said, his face showing his exasperation. "Elijah Hunt had an extreme view."

"A view that was shared with all those people who wrote to Barnum about me, and the crowds that demonstrated day after day outside the museum," Amelia said. "How is Elijah Hunt different from a missionary? Their intention is salvation at any cost. Maybe it's you who doesn't understand."

Levi didn't say anything else. He quietly put on his coat and left their hotel room. This infuriated Amelia, who felt it deeply unfair that he was able to leave if he was angry and she was not (it being unsafe for her to walk about on her own—this was truer now than it had been in New York, since the crowds they'd encountered were more unpredictable). She was also angry that he would rather leave than listen to her.

She threw the stupid missionary book across the room. It was the first time they'd ever really disagreed, and since he wouldn't stay and let her convince him she was right, she didn't know what to do with herself except pace and argue with him in her head instead of in person.

She paced until she was exhausted, and then she lay on

the bed and cried, because she had all this energy and nowhere to put it.

A while after that he returned bearing dinner on a tray and said he was sorry he'd left her. But he didn't apologize for believing he was right, and Amelia didn't apologize either, and they were very careful with each other for several days after.

And in the meantime, they went from town to town, moving ever farther south. It was terribly hot no matter where they went, and Amelia grew resentful of the humidity that sapped her energy and the mosquitoes that plagued them constantly and the eternal press of the sunlight.

She'd come from a cold clime, where the air was crisp nearly year-round and the ocean was even colder. The poor orangutan suffered, too, particularly since her handler didn't see fit to give her water frequently enough.

One afternoon they stopped in a small town in North Carolina. As the men began to raise the large white tent Amelia caught sight of the orangutan's handler, whose name was Stephen White, whipping the ape for moving too slowly out of her cage in the wagon to the ground.

She didn't think. She left Levi, who'd been saying something about finding suitable lodging for the night, and crossed the grounds to White.

As White raised the whip to hit the cowering animal again, Amelia tore it from his hand. She nearly dropped it, for it was an ugly thing and it felt ugly and mean in her hand, but she was so very angry.

"What the—" he said.

As he turned toward her, Amelia lashed him across the face with the whip. White screamed, both hands coming up to cover his left cheek. A large welt raised there almost instantly, and it ran from his mouth to his ear.

"You goddamned bitch," White snarled, stepping toward her.

Amelia raised the whip again. White paused, looking not at her but at the weapon in her hand. She felt that ugliness against her palm, the hate that White bore for anything he thought lesser than him, and how it had seeped into the whip. It made her want to throw it away and wash her hands until they were pink and clean and she was certain that none of his meanness had seeped inside and infected her.

"You are not to use this on that creature again," Amelia said, holding on to the whip. She had to hold on so he would know she was a threat. He was the kind of man who only understood violence. "You are not to hit her, or pull her on a rope, or let her go hours without water or food. If you do any of those things I will see to it that you are not paid for your services here."

"Mr. Barnum hired me, not you," White said. "You don't get to tell me what to do. You're not even human."

"And I am grateful for that, if you're an example of

humanity," Amelia said. "I'd rather be a mermaid, or even an orangutan, than one of your tribe."

"I'll do what I please," White spat. "It's nothing but a dumb animal, and so are you."

"You'll do what you please elsewhere," Amelia said. She was not surprised to discover that White thought this way. She imagined that many of the other laborers did as well. Barnum had said there was no difference between her and a tiger in a cage, and Amelia knew that most people thought the same. They didn't think of her as one of them. "Take your things and leave."

"I signed an agreement with Mr. Barnum," White said. "I told you, you don't get to tell me what to do or where to go or end that agreement."

"But I do. I am the executor of that agreement," Levi said from behind Amelia. "Mr. Barnum invested his authority in me, and I say you are no longer employed by this institution."

White looked astonished. He had expected, Amelia thought, that Levi would support him if it came down to it—perhaps because Levi was also a man and Amelia only a woman with no power. "Because I only treated a dumb beast as it deserved to be treated?"

Levi looked at the man steadily. "You insulted my wife."

"Your wife," White spat. "Does she wrap you in her tail at night? Does she sleep in a tank? What kind of babies are you going to have with a fish, Levi Lyman? Your wife is an abomination. I can't insult an abomination. They're supposed to be destroyed."

"If you don't leave now I'll call the local police and have you jailed," Levi said. He didn't physically threaten White, or tighten his hands into fists, or do anything besides let the other man see in his eyes that he meant it.

"What about my pay?" White said. "I earned money on this venture, and I want it."

Levi crossed his arms and stared at the animal handler.

White swore and stormed off. Amelia lowered the whip to the ground, dropping it. She rubbed her palm with her other hand, trying to take off the taint of the weapon.

The other workers had gathered around to watch the exchange. When White left the spell was broken, and they all hastily rushed to their tasks before they, too, were summarily dismissed without pay.

Amelia walked slowly to the orangutan's side. Her legs were shaking, but she thought nobody had noticed and if she moved carefully they wouldn't.

There were stripes across the creature's neck and shoulders, and she lay on one side with her eyes closed. Levi called two of the other workers to carry her inside the tent and give her food and water.

Amelia started after them, but Levi put his hand on her shoulder. "Let them be," he said. "I'll make certain that the animal isn't mistreated."

"What you mean," Amelia said bitterly, "is that they won't listen if I tell them what to do. Just as Mr. White wouldn't leave until you said so."

"Men generally don't recognize the authority of women," Levi said very gently. "It's the way of the world, Amelia. I'm sorry it distresses you."

"The world," Amelia said, "is wrong about so many things."

She couldn't miss the sideways glances many of the workers gave her for the rest of the day, and for many days after. White had only said aloud something many of them thought—that she was unnatural, that she should not be.

That was the look that was in the eyes of many of the people in the audience as well, the elusive thing she hadn't been able to pin down. Some of them thought she was a miracle, but a great many of them seemed horrified by her existence.

It is not a comforting thing to realize that many people think the world a better place without you in it, Amelia thought.

With each passing day she felt more restless, and more angry. She couldn't explain exactly what had put her in that state. There were so many slights and discontents that added up to more than the sum of the whole.

Maybe it was the feeling that there was a wall between her and Levi, that there were more subjects on which they disagreed rather than agreed. He still loved her, and she him, but they turned away from each other in frustration as often as they fell into each other's arms.

She hadn't forgotten the way he'd walked away from their first disagreement about the island people he called savages, and they returned to the subject time and again to the benefit of neither. They could not agree, but Amelia continued to try to convince him.

He would not be convinced. Amelia finally realized it was because he himself did not understand what it meant to be different and to have people expect you to change for their sake. She realized that no man could understand this, really, though they expected their wives to do so every day.

After that she stopped pressing him on the subject, but the kernel of her disappointment lay inside her and festered until it was an eternal ache at the bottom of her stomach.

Perhaps her anger and restlessness was because of the exhaustion of touring or the horrible wagon she was supposed to confine herself in night after night. Perhaps it was because she was tired of being a creature with no voice, who was supposed to pretend to be unable to speak, and thus was not able to defend herself from the men who leered at her through the glass.

Perhaps it was because the more she saw of humanity, the less she liked it. She realized that even though the people of her village hadn't always been the kindest or most welcoming, they did at least leave well enough alone. She rarely saw outright cruelty, and once you belonged to them, they would defend you as if you were their own child. She'd felt this, especially after Jack's death.

Everywhere she traveled in the south she saw what the evil men did, an evil that had simply not been present in her hometown. They passed field after field of black men and women in chains, toiling for white men in shaded hats who sat on horses and bore whips like the one Amelia had used on Stephen White.

She could feel the hate that radiated from these men, the contempt, the smug superiority, and she never passed by one without wishing to knock him from the back of the horse and hope the animal kicked him to death.

When they went by these places she felt, very profoundly, her helplessness, her inability to free the people from their pain, the need to *fix* this and knowing she could not. She had not even been able to fire an animal handler who abused his animal without the authority of her husband. None of these men on horses would listen to her. They'd probably tell Levi to take her back inside where she belonged. That was what that sort of man did.

And maybe it was because inside her there was a little mermaid growing (Amelia could feel her daughter swimming in her belly, like little bubbles swirling under her skin) and she wanted, very badly, to return to the sea where her child belonged. She wanted her daughter to know the ocean, to know its dangers and its beauties.

The ocean was a violent place, yes, but it was violence without malice. When a shark ate a sea lion, it did not hate the sea lion. It only wanted to live.

The human world was not so marvelous as it had seemed from the water. And her reasons for staying in New York, for going on this tour, for being a part of Barnum's performance machine, now seemed both shallow and foolish. Money? She'd wanted money to travel and see all the wonders of man? What was there to see besides the misery people inflicted on one another?

The castles of Europe and the mountains of the west were nothing to her now. She wanted only the comfort of the ocean, to feel its embrace all around her and know that was her place. That was where she belonged. She did not belong in a tank with dead water around her, humans treating her like something that did tricks only for their amusement.

But she could not simply run to the water and leave as she might have months before. She couldn't because she loved Levi, even with the space between them, and because she bore his child.

She had not told him of the child. Her belly did not yet indicate her daughter's existence, and she wanted to keep the baby to herself for a while longer. It was selfish, but Amelia did not want to share her little mermaid with Levi just yet. Not when she'd dreamed so many secret dreams for so many years only to wake up barren.

And, too, Amelia was afraid of what might happen if anyone else found out she was pregnant. The people who paid fifty cents to see her change from human to mermaid and then gaped at her in horror—what would they think if they knew the horror was breeding? Would they call for her extermination? Would they try to take her from Levi?

No, it was safer for the time being to keep her child a secret, even from the child's father.

Whatever the reason for her anger and her restlessness and her general feeling of discontent, by the time they entered Charleston, Amelia was at the end of her endurance.

Barnum had arranged for a man to go ahead of the wagon train and leave handbills advertising the program in every town and city. Charleston was large enough to justify an extended stay, and so Barnum booked several dates at the Masonic Hall. He wrote to Levi that he expected the crowds there to be numerous and regular, and that he was sending an indoor tank for Amelia ("at great expense," Amelia noted) so they could duplicate their Concert Hall performance.

The advertisement in the *Charleston Courier* showed a full-figured mermaid of the sort Barnum had told Amelia the public wanted. Amelia had been unable to convince Barnum that he should make the mermaids in his woodcuts more accurate—they still looked too human and not very much how she actually appeared.

"The public isn't interested in reality," Barnum had said.

"That's not what we're trying to sell them. If we were, you wouldn't be the Feejee Mermaid."

Underneath the drawing was a paragraph that read,

This grand, interesting and very cheap Exhibition, at Masonic Hall, embracing the most wonderful curiosity in the world, the MERMAID, and the ORNITHORYNOUS, OURANG OUTANG, & c., with FANCY GLASS BLOWING, by a most excellent ARTIST; together with a unique and astonishing entertainment on the stage, at 7 ½ clock P.M., consisting of Signor Veronia's inimitable MECHANICAL FIGURES, representing human life; and VENTRILOQUISM and MAGIC by Mr. Wyman, who has scarce an equal in the world in his line. Admission to the whole, only 50 cents, children under 12 half-price.

"Barnum has classified me with the animals again," Amelia said after Levi read the advertisement aloud. It was no more than she expected. "It's no wonder the audiences here treat me as they do."

She paced around the hotel room—another anonymous room, just like all the rooms she had been in all the other places—and felt like the tiger Barnum had once said she was. There was not enough space in a hotel for a wild thing.

There was nothing like home anywhere. Levi's apartment in New York, and their few days of happiness there, seemed so very far away.

Levi put down the newspaper. She saw him gathering up his patience, the little lines of strain around his eyes. He'd felt the distance between them, too, and seemed just as incapable of bridging it. "Amelia. You are a performer. Frankly, performers aren't accorded the same respect as ordinary women."

"And this means that I deserve their jeers and their derision?"

"There are just as many folks who think you are a marvel," he said. "It's not all terrible, is it? Why would you do it otherwise?"

"I hate it here," she said, her misery bursting the dam of her silence. "I've had enough of traveling, enough of people reminding me that I am not the same as them. I'm tired of the way some of them treat me like the orangutan, too stupid to understand what they are saying. I'm tired of pretending I don't have a voice. I want to go back to the sea, where I belong."

Levi stilled. "And what does that mean for me? What am I to do while my wife returns to the ocean?"

Amelia stopped. She saw the hurt in his eyes, and she was sorry for that. She was sorry that there was so much distance between them that he thought she would leave him without a care. She was sorry that she wasn't human enough to mend this.

"I—" she began. She didn't know what she would say, but she wanted to say something. She wanted them to be happy again. That happiness had been so fleeting.

"I always knew this might happen," Levi said quietly. "Your eyes . . . your eyes told me from the beginning that you could never belong to me. Always a part of you belonged only to yourself, and to the sea, and no matter what I said or did or wanted I could never touch that bit of you. I thought I could make you happy, like Jack did, make you want to stay here on the shore with me."

"Jack never had that part of me, either. He didn't try to. He knew that was for me and me alone," Amelia said. "But he loved the ocean, the same as I did, and we made our home halfway between sea and shore. This life . . . I can't be happy with this. I thought I could, for your sake, for the dream that I used to have. But I can't go on with this."

"And yet you told me that it was your choice," Levi said, and she was sure she had never seen him so sad.

"And yet you told me I could make another choice," Amelia said, and she was equally sure his sadness would weigh on her heart forever.

She went to him then, and took his hands, and forced him to look at her. "I don't believe that we can be happy with Barnum's shadow over us. Even when he's not here, it's as if he is looming, telling us what to do and how to do it."

"He's not a monster," Levi said, pulling his hands away from her.

"Isn't he?" she asked. "He wants to own and profit by everyone and everything around him."

"And we can profit by it, too," Levi said, his sadness shifting to that impatient way his anger manifested itself. "We already have. That's why you made this choice, isn't it? Because you wanted money?"

He said it so scathingly, as if he thought less of her for wanting, even briefly, the thing that so many humans seemed to crave.

"I dreamed not of money but of a future," Amelia said. "I thought I could live with humans, be a part of them. That's why I came to New York. And you're not to pretend that money has no meaning for you, else you would have returned to Pennsylvania to practice law a long time ago."

"You agreed to be Barnum's mermaid," Levi said. He clung to this idea, his face set. "For a period of six months, and your agreement is not expired yet."

"And a woman died," Amelia said. "I nearly did, too. I should have left him then, after Elijah Hunt shot me for his God, and told Barnum that his contract didn't mean anything to me."

"Don't human contracts mean something to you?" Levi asked.

He wasn't asking about her agreement with Barnum. Of

course he wasn't. He wanted to know if their marriage certificate was waterproof.

"I love you, Levi," she said. "I am happy to be your wife. But I can't stay Barnum's mermaid and your wife, too. I need for this tour, these performances, to be over. Whatever we were both looking for—it wasn't really money. It was magic, the promise of a life washed clean of our past. Barnum can't give us that, but maybe we can give it to each other."

"I don't think you are happy with me," he said. "I've watched you, you know. I've seen your face, that face I once thought as deep and dark and unfathomable as the ocean. You can't hide the way you feel anymore, not from me. I'm not the man you wanted me to be."

"Levi, it's only all this that's making me unhappy," Amelia cried. "It's not you. It's not."

"I'll write to Barnum," Levi said, as if he hadn't heard her. His eyes had gone someplace cold and far away. "I'll tell him that after Charleston you will leave the tour. Barnum will make such a fuss over the cost of the hall and the tank otherwise. If he wants to continue with a mermaid exhibition he can always send Moses's mummy out. That was the idea in the first place. We never thought we'd come upon a real mermaid."

"And then?" Amelia asked.

"And then you will be free—from Barnum, from me, from life as a human. You can be free to go to the ocean, where you will be happy," he said. "I only ever wanted you to be happy."

Amelia couldn't believe she was hearing this. Had he heard nothing she said? She didn't want to leave him, only Barnum.

"It will make me happy to stay with you," she said, trying to show him with her eyes what was in her heart. "I have loved so many things about you—your kindness, the way you try so hard to make me laugh, the way I feel when you hold me. I love you and I have never lied to you. I've never lied to anyone, not even when I was the Feejee Mermaid, for I've never had to tell the lies Barnum spun. Why will you not listen to me when I speak? Why will you not understand?"

"I understand better than you think," Levi said.

"No, your pride is hurt," Amelia said. "And because your pride is hurt you've decided what's best, and what's best is for me to leave so that *you* stop hurting."

"I'll write to Barnum," he said, and left the room.

She followed him out. He heard her footsteps in the hall behind him and turned back.

"Go back inside," he said.

"No," she said.

"Shhh. Someone might hear you," he said, taking her by the wrist.

She wrenched away from him. "I don't care. This fiction of my being unable to speak is ridiculous. If you leave I will follow you. I will shout and scream and cause a scene until you come back inside this room and understand what you mean to me."

His face reddened as he realized she was in earnest. He was imagining the fuss, the scene, the people staring at him. "I'll come back inside, and we will speak quietly about this."

"If I want to speak loudly I will," Amelia said. "You can't stop me."

"No," he said, his façade of calm breaking. He slammed the door shut behind them. "I can't stop you from doing anything you don't want to. Barnum always said it, and I thought it was funny when it was him you had twisting."

"I don't belong to you," Amelia said. "You thought if I married you that I would, but I don't. I don't belong to any man—not to Jack, not to Barnum, not to you. I only belong to myself. But belonging to myself doesn't mean I don't love you or that I don't want to stand beside you."

"You don't understand human marriages," Levi said. "A woman is supposed to cleave to her husband, to trust him to make the best decisions for her."

Amelia took a deep breath. "You're right. If that's the way you want us to live then I should leave. But if you don't—if you can see things my way—then I want to stay with you. I want to be your partner, not your possession."

His face contracted, and she saw so many emotions pass there for an instant and then disappear—anger, and pride, and confusion, and longing. Finally it settled into a deep, deep sadness.

"I don't want to live without you," he said.

It cost him something to admit it, she could tell. He was giving up some wrongheaded notion he'd had of her, some human idea of a woman that had lodged in his brain.

"I was dazzled by you the first time I saw you on that cliff, dazzled by your difference, the way you were unlike anyone I'd ever seen. I have loved everything in you, everything that made you not human—the way you never back away from an argument, the way you look so clearly into my eyes and expect me to meet you there. I didn't marry a human woman. I forgot that, for a little while."

"Then isn't our love more important than your pride?" she asked, and she felt something in her pleading for him to say yes. "Isn't it? We can be happy. I know we can."

"I don't know if we can," Levi said. "But I want to try."

She went to him then, and the space between them dissolved, and though there wasn't any joy yet, she thought there could be. They had only to seek it together.

"I'll write to Barnum," Levi said. "After Charleston it will all be over."

CHAPTER 15

The first sign of trouble was the editorial in the *Charleston Courier*. It didn't seem a portent at the time, Levi thought later, for the review of the exhibit was primarily positive.

"'The natural curiosities too are well worth a visit from the curious and scientific—and most curious among them is the Fee-jee beauty—the mermaid, hitherto believed to be of fabulous existence,'" Levi read aloud. "He called you a beauty."

Amelia shrugged. "I'm sure his opinion isn't widely shared, but Barnum will be happy if it brings more people to the exhibit."

Levi continued. "'We, of course, cannot undertake to say whether this seeming wonder of nature be real or not, it not being in our power to apply to it any scientific test of truth;

but this we deem it but just to say, that we were permitted to handle and examine it as closely as could be effected by touch and sight, and that if there be any deception, it is beyond the discovery of both those senses.'"

Amelia frowned. "He's lying. He never touched me, nor would he be allowed to. No one is even permitted to approach the tank."

"I believe he's trying to convince anyone who doubts you exist to come and see the exhibit," Levi said. "And he's trying to establish at least some degree of scientific credibility, and perhaps an impression that as the editor of this newspaper he is afforded special privileges."

"Are there still people who don't believe I'm a real mermaid?" Amelia asked, her voice full of surprise. "Anyone who has seen the exhibit has to believe at least that much. I can't believe anyone thinks I'm a hoax."

"I'm not certain," Levi said, frowning. "I didn't think that doubt would be a concern at this late date. But perhaps the people of Charleston are more skeptical than their northern neighbors."

"I suppose I would rather have them doubt me than cast me as a woman of sin," Amelia said. She sighed and took his hand. "I will be relieved when this fiction is over."

Levi had written to Barnum of their decision to leave the tour. Amelia had written—or rather, dictated to Levi what she wished to say—to Charity separately, for she felt that if Barnum made difficulties, Charity would smooth them over. There had been no reply from either; Levi had assured her that this was not unusual and that occasionally it did take quite a long time to receive mail and even longer to get some back.

Privately he worried that Barnum would take the first available conveyance to Charleston and attempt to force Amelia to stay on the tour. This couldn't have a good outcome for anyone, and Levi didn't need Barnum wading into his marriage with Amelia and disrupting their fragile peace. They were both, he thought, trying so hard to mend what had been broken—to make an effort to meet each other halfway, to be patient even when they didn't want to be, to show each other that they loved each other instead of just saying it.

They spoke often of where they might go to live—a quiet place near the ocean, away from reporters and crowds and any pressure Barnum might be tempted to use to convince Amelia to come back.

"What about Fiji?" Amelia asked.

"That doesn't seem wise," Levi said. "If you disappear from Barnum's show, the first place anyone will think to inquire of you is the place where you are supposed to be from."

"But I thought you said it's far away," Amelia said. "Very far away, and that it would take many, many months to get there by ship."

"It is," Levi acknowledged. "That would make the trip difficult for me, if not for you. I don't like boats."

"You don't?" She looked startled.

He laughed. "I never told you how awful it was for me to travel by boat to see you in Maine. The rocking of the ocean made me sick nearly the whole time."

Amelia frowned. "I've never known anyone made sick by the ocean."

"You lived near a village of fishermen, love," he said. "Anyone made ill by the sea would be unlikely to stay there."

"What about one of the other islands on the map near Fiji?" Amelia asked.

"Why this sudden desire to go to an island?" Levi asked. "I thought perhaps we could live somewhere along the coast, in some place where I could be a country lawyer and you could visit the ocean as you did in Maine."

"I'm afraid to stay here," Amelia said. "I'm afraid that a reporter will find me, or another madman like Elijah Hunt. If we live on an island far away it won't matter that they all think I'm from Fiji. No one is likely to travel so far simply to find me again. Even madness has its limits."

Levi wasn't so certain, but he had to acknowledge it was unlikely. Still, the idea of a months-long journey to an island in the Pacific did not appeal. Just the thought of that much time on a ship made him feel queasy. But he wasn't inclined to argue with Amelia again, so he helped her look up the names of different islands and they read about them together and discussed their various merits.

"Ra-ro-ton-ga," Amelia pronounced carefully, as they studied a map of the Cook Islands. "I like the sound of that place. It sounds like music."

"It's nearly as far away as Fiji," Levi said.

"No it's not; it's a whole thumb closer," Amelia said, placing her digit between Fiji and Rarotonga. "Particularly if you go around South America."

Levi hoped that if they went so far they *would* go around South America rather than around Africa. He couldn't imagine anything more terrible than having to cross the entirety of the Atlantic first, and then the Pacific, too.

Secretly he still hoped to convince Amelia to stay somewhere in the United States, but he thought he would wait to mention this until after they had left the tour. She still seemed fragile, like she might bolt away at any moment.

That evening there was another performance at the Masonic Hall, and the next day another review of the show appeared. This time it was in the *Charleston Mercury*.

It was written by a man who called himself "the Rev. John Blackman" and it stated, in no uncertain terms, that the mermaid was a fraud perpetuated "by our Yankee neighbors." The Reverend Blackman claimed to be an amateur naturalist and thus spoke with greater authority than the editor of the *Courier*.

"Did this man actually attend a performance?" Amelia asked.

Levi scanned the article. "He claims to have done so."

"But it's absurd," she said. "If he saw me then he must *know* that I'm real."

"He says that your very presence in the company of such tricks as ventriloquism prove that the mermaid is nothing more than a clever illusion," Levi said. "I wouldn't let it trouble you, Amelia. I don't think that very many people will agree with his opinion, especially if they have attended the exhibition themselves."

But in that Levi was wrong. Almost immediately letters began appearing in each publication both for and against the veracity of the mermaid. The *Courier*'s editor, Richard Yeadon, wrote daily pieces dismissing the claims of Reverend Blackman, and Blackman took up the opposite cause in the *Mercury*.

The crowds that attended each performance swelled. It seemed every person in Charleston wanted to see Amelia for himself and take a side in this very public disagreement.

"Barnum will be pleased, at least," Levi said. "We are selling so many tickets that people have to be turned away each day."

There was still no response from Barnum or Charity, a fact that Levi found ominous. He didn't share his worries with Amelia, however. He still hoped to complete their run in Charleston without the sudden arrival of the showman.

The next night the exhibit went on as usual, at least at first. Levi watched Amelia from the wings of the stage as she climbed the ladder and dove into the tank that Barnum had sent especially for this exhibit.

It was larger than the small wagon that had served as performance space since they left New York, but Levi could tell that Amelia wished for the unfettered freedom of the ocean. There was nothing in her performance any more besides dull obligation.

Not that it mattered, Levi thought. People's reactions were always the same whether Amelia swam in circles, waved to them, or simply floated in the tank with a blank expression on her face. First surprise, then disbelief, then dawning realization that what they saw was true.

A scuffle broke out at the back of the hall. Levi, fearing a repeat of the first night at the Concert Hall when the crowd rushed the stage, ran out of the wings to see what was happening.

There was a thud, the sound of flesh on flesh, and several people gasped. A small circle of people had gathered around two men who apparently had decided to disagree with their fists.

Levi gestured to two of the men stationed near the front of the stage to break up the fight. The laborers who worked in their wagon train were not as large or as intimidating as the guards Barnum hired in New York, but they were plenty able to disrupt a fight between two gentlemen.

The workers were nearly to the crowd when another fight broke out. This time Levi heard what they were saying.

"Use your eyes, man! How can she possibly be a fraud?" one man screamed at another, his eyes bulging.

"I for one am not about to be fooled by a pack of damn Yanks here to steal our money," the second man said, shoving the first.

Several men shouted down the second man, while another chorus joined in favor of his argument. Women stumbled away from the suddenly jostling and dangerous group, several of them fleeing out the doors of the hall into the night.

Levi realized the crowd had turned ugly. He bent to another one of the workers and said, "Better go and get the local constable before this becomes dangerous."

The man nodded and climbed the stage to stand next to Levi. "Best if I go out the back exit. Else I might get caught up in that mob."

Levi nodded as the man disappeared backstage. Then he ran to the rope that controlled the curtains and pulled them shut. The noise seemed to grow louder once the crowd was out of sight.

It's only your imagination, Levi told himself. Terrible things always seemed more terrible when you could not see them.

Amelia was already climbing out of the tank, her hand in

the jar of sand on the platform. He scooped up her dress and carried it to her as she stepped quickly down the ladder.

"We have to leave," Levi said.

"Of course we do," Amelia said. "Even I can tell that lot will kill each other over their sense of injured honor, and if we're still here they might decide to kill us, too, for fooling them in the first place."

He took her hand, and they hurried to the backstage area. Just as they slipped out into the night they heard an angry cry.

"The mermaid's gone!"

"They must have sneaked out the back!"

Levi pulled Amelia along, thinking only of getting her back to the hotel. They would be safe there, he thought. Once they were in their room and out of sight, the crowd would calm down. The constable might arrive soon, in any case, and disrupt the proceedings before they could go any further.

Amelia struggled along beside him, and Levi realized her feet were bare. He hadn't thought of her shoes, only of covering her body and getting her away before someone tried to hurt her.

I'm not having another Elijah Hunt, he thought. It would kill him to see her hurt like that again, even if he did know the cure.

"I'm sorry," he said, panting from the effort of hurrying. "Can you walk?"

"A rock cut my foot," Amelia said. "It's bleeding."

Levi glanced behind them and saw, in the dim light, the dark track that Amelia left behind her. He also saw—and heard—three men searching for any sign of them behind the hall. Soon enough they would notice the blood trail and they would follow it.

He scooped up Amelia in his arms.

"You can't walk very fast like this," she said.

"Your foot is leaving a trail," Levi said. "If those men notice it, they'll follow us. And you can't walk very fast with your injury in any case."

They hurried along in the dark as fast as Levi could manage. Amelia weighed practically nothing, but it still wasn't easy to carry her this way for very long, and soon he was sweating and breathless from the effort.

"You'd better put me down," Amelia said.

"We're almost to the hotel," he said between his teeth.

But they rounded the corner of their building and Levi pulled up short. A surly crowd of twenty or so men had gathered outside on the porch, and the manager of the hotel stood in the doorway holding up placating hands to a red-faced man who pressed his nose very close to the manager's.

"Oh, no," Amelia said.

Levi disappeared back into the notch between the hotel and the building next door. He placed Amelia carefully on her feet and bent over his legs, panting.

"What should we do now?" Amelia asked.

It was strange, he thought, that the one time she seemed inclined to defer to him was the one time he had no answers.

"The wagon train is on the outskirts," he said. "If we can get there we can take one of the wagons and leave."

Amelia shook her head. "That will be the next place they go if they can't find us at the hotel. Besides, what about everyone else—the workmen, Mr. Wyman, Mr. Veronia? The mob might go after them instead."

"I don't think they will," Levi said. "They just want you. They want to prove you're not real, or that you are, whichever it is that they believe more."

"I think the ones in front of the hotel want to prove I'm only human," Amelia said grimly. "They want a lynching."

"The only way to keep you from them is for you to leave," Levi said slowly. There was only one possible solution—the one that he wanted the least, the one that he'd known somehow would always be the only answer. Where did a sea creature belong except the sea? "They won't care about the others once you're gone. Amelia, you have to go to the ocean."

She stared at him. "You mean leave you? Leave forever?"

"Yes," he said, and grabbed her hand. Charleston was flush up against the sea. They only had to reach it in time. "It's the only way."

"Levi, I'm not going to leave you here," she said. "You're

my husband, and I love you."

"And I love you, more than I can say, and I won't watch you be hanged by that lot," he said.

He didn't think that throwing her in the ocean would fix a hanging the way it had undone her bullet wound. Everything inside him was breaking apart at the thought of her leaving, and all their arguments seemed foolish beyond reason. Did any disagreement matter more than the one you loved? But he would give her up to the ocean, and gladly, if it meant she would live. If it meant that one day he might see her again.

"Please, Amelia, if you love me you'll go. The only possible way for you to be safe is if you are in the ocean."

Amelia put her hand over her belly, "Levi. I'm going to have your child."

He felt as though he'd been sideswiped. He stumbled, his breath hitched, and then he stopped to look at her. "Truly?"

"Yes," she said, and kissed him. "Truly."

His child. His child inside the body of his wife, and an angry mob wanted to tear her body apart.

"If they kill you, they'll kill the baby, too," Levi said. *A baby. His baby.*

It was then he saw the realization in her eyes, and the resolution. "I'll go," Amelia said. "I'll go to Rarotonga, far away, and I will raise our daughter there. But, Levi, you have to come to us. You must."

"I will," he promised. "No matter how long it takes, I will find you there."

They went on in silence then, staying to the shadows, avoiding anyone who strayed near them in the night.

Levi remembered that night for many months after—the only sound their breath and their soft footfalls as they made for the salvation of the sea.

He remembered her kiss, and the way her hands clung to his arms, and the way his own arms didn't want to let her go. He remembered how she tore her dress away and ran toward the breaking waves as if she were afraid he might try to change her mind.

He remembered how he scooped up her dress and breathed in the smell of her, and for a long time afterward he slept with it curled around his pillow so that he would not forget, and sometimes he could almost imagine she was there.

He remembered the silhouette of her tail against the horizon, and how it disappeared under the water, and how it did not reappear no matter how long he watched or hoped for it.

Amelia swam, swam away from Levi standing alone on the shore, and she felt like she did on that day long, long ago when Jack caught her in his net and then let her go. She'd felt tethered to him then, tethered by his loneliness, and it had made a long cord that bound them and brought her back to him.

The cord between her and Levi was less perfect, less idealized, but it was no less strong. She loved him, and she loved the baby he had given her, and that love would remain sure and strong and true. She had seen into his heart, the way that women do, and she knew his love would be the same. She would wait for him on a sandy shore on a faraway island, her eyes always watching the sea for some sign of him. She would wait.

Until then, she was swimming fast and free in the ocean, and the ocean welcomed her home.

Well, Barnum reflected, the mermaid show was good while it lasted. He'd had an idea that he might be able to change the girl's mind and make her stay longer, but after the debacle in Charleston, it probably couldn't have been salvaged even if she hadn't disappeared into the sea.

Poor Levi had been mooning around the museum since he got back. Barnum had given the boy the notebook with Amelia's sketch in it and Barnum had been genuinely afraid Levi would burst into tears when he saw it. The boy had managed to restrain himself, though.

Barnum was on his way back from a business trip to Albany that hadn't borne the fruit he'd hoped. Because the river was frozen, he'd been forced to take the train; the only consolation was that it stopped in Bridgeport. His half brother Philo had a hotel there, and so Barnum thought it right to spend the night.

Yes, he thought again as he ate his dinner in the hotel restaurant. He'd made a good dollar off the mermaid. It was really too bad it hadn't lasted longer.

"Taylor," Philo said, shaking Barnum out of his reverie. "There's someone I'd like you to meet."

Standing next to his brother was a little boy, so little that he was practically doll-sized. "This is Charles Stratton. Charles, this is my brother, Mr. P. T. Barnum."

Barnum looked at the boy, who politely said, "How do you do."

A doll-sized boy! Barnum thought. Barnum could put the little fellow up onstage, dress him in costumes, give him a name. *Tom Thumb. He's just like Tom Thumb from the stories.*

A boy like this could make his fortune, Barnum thought. And there would be no disappearing into the ocean this time.

He smiled, a wide showman's smile that showed all of his teeth.

"I am very pleased to meet you, Charles."

* * *

FOUR YEARS LATER

Amelia watched over her daughter as she splashed in the shallow pool. They were in a little cove, protected by the shade of wide-leafed trees, and the water was not very deep. Despite this, Amelia had to keep a very sharp eye on Charity—the girl was likely to dart off into the deep water if Amelia looked away for a moment. Charity, like her mother once had, was always looking over the horizon for an adventure.

Amelia was grateful for the shade. While the waters of the South Pacific were blue and clear and beautiful, the island was far too warm for one long accustomed to the cold of the North Atlantic coast. Still, they were protected here— protected by the native people who kept them hidden from European colonists, so that word would not spread back to the mainland of a mermaid and her daughter.

Savages, the white men called them. But there was less savagery in them than ever she saw in a civilized country. They accepted Amelia and Charity, accepted what they were without judgment. The people here did not see the mermaids as a wonder, or a horror, or as animals, or as humans. The people saw them as mermaids and accepted them as part of the order of the world.

"Charity," Amelia said warningly.

The little mermaid had seen a hermit crab carrying its shell across the shallow pool, and followed it closely. When

Charity reached the edge of the shallow, the place where the sand dropped off into the deeper water, she glanced over her shoulder to see if her mother was watching.

Amelia shook her head. Charity's small mouth twisted when she realized she could not explore past the edge of the pool.

Charity's tail was red-gold and flapped in the water as she swam back to her mother. Amelia's daughter looked more like Barnum's woodcuts of a mermaid—her skin was still human above her fin and only changed to scales at her waist. She would, when she grew older, look exactly as so many sailors had dreamed—half human, half fish, a man's dream of a mermaid.

The tiny mermaid touched the sand and turned completely into a human toddler, dark-haired and dark-eyed like her father and nut-brown from the sun.

"It's time for dinner," Amelia said, and took Charity's plump little hand.

They strolled along the beach away from the cove. There was a little hut where they slept and ate a short distance from the shallow pool. Amelia had caught some fish earlier in the day, and they would roast these over a fire. Charity had very human tastes, preferring her food cooked instead of raw. Her teeth, even when she was a mermaid, were not sharp like Amelia's but flat like a human's.

She squeezed the hand of her daughter, the little miracle

that she had wished for, for so long. Her daughter would grow up here, safe from eyes that stared and claimed and tried to make something of her that she was not. When she was older she would make her own choice—to stay here, or to return to Amelia's people in the sea, or to live as a human in a land far away.

It was the fate of parents to have to let their children go, so they could make their own triumphs and their own mistakes. When Amelia thought of those days, she would, as now, pick up Charity and hold her tight and wish her daughter could stay in her arms forever.

Charity allowed the hug only briefly before squirming out of Amelia's embrace. She ran a little ahead of her mother, then stopped and pointed.

"Mama," she said, "who's that?"

There was a man standing near their hut, a white man in a suit entirely impractical for the island. His hand shaded his eyes, and he stared out at the ocean, looking for someone.

Amelia's heart leapt. She'd hardly allowed herself to think of him, to wonder if he would ever come, but she'd felt that cord that bound them always, and sometimes she would roll over in the night and reach for him and find he wasn't there.

"Mama?" Charity asked as Amelia began to run.

"It's your father," Amelia said, picking up their daughter and running with her over the sand. "Charity, it's your father."

AFTERWORD

When writing a book that includes a historical figure, there is always the temptation to cleave closely to the historical reality of that person—in this case, P. T. Barnum. Much has been written about Barnum (especially by himself—he wrote several books and modified his own autobiography numerous times), and so there was plenty of material for me to explore in writing this book.

However, I found that ultimately it did not serve the story if I presented the precise Barnum in all his complicated glory. My Barnum is a character who shares some characteristics with the real Barnum, but he is not meant to be a true, historically accurate rendition of Barnum.

He is the Barnum who suits my story, and if it's not exactly reality—well, the Feejee Mermaid didn't really exist, either.

I did use much of the existing historical record about the Feejee Mermaid hoax, including the performance by Levi Lyman as Dr. Griffin and the southern tour, and modified it to suit my mermaid.

As for Levi Lyman, he is often presented only as one of Barnum's co-conspirators for the two most famous Barnum hoaxes—Joice Heth and the Feejee Mermaid. I wanted to know more about Levi Lyman but found information on him after the hoaxes to be very sparse. Like all fiction writers, I made up his story when I couldn't find the one I wanted to read.

ABOUT THE AUTHOR

Christina Henry is the author of national bestselling Black Wings series featuring Agent of Death Madeline Black and her popcorn-loving gargoyle Beezle. Her dark fantasy novel *Alice* was one of Amazon's Best Books of 2015 in Science Fiction and Fantasy, and came second in the Goodreads Choice awards for Best Horror. Christina enjoys running long distances, reading anything she can get her hands on and watching movies with samurai, zombies and/or subtitles in her spare time. She lives in Chicago with her husband and son.

For more fantastic fiction, author events, competitions,
limited editions and more

VISIT OUR WEBSITE
titanbooks.com

LIKE US ON FACEBOOK
facebook.com/titanbooks

FOLLOW US ON TWITTER
@TitanBooks

EMAIL US
readerfeedback@titanemail.com